GREEN CANVAS

A LISE NORWOOD MYSTERY

ANDREW NANCE

Green Canvas
Red Adept Publishing, LLC
104 Bugenfield Court
Garner, NC 27529
https://RedAdeptPublishing.com/

Copyright © 2023 by Andrew Nance. All rights reserved.

Cover Art by Streetlight Graphics[1]

No part of this book may be reproduced, scanned, or distributed in any printed or electronic form without permission. Please do not participate in or encourage piracy of copyrighted materials in violation of the author's rights. Thank you for respecting the hard work of this author.

This is a work of fiction. Names, characters, places, and incidents either are the product of the author's imagination or are used fictitiously, and any resemblance to locales, events, business establishments, or actual persons—living or dead—is entirely coincidental.

---

1.   http://StreetlightGraphics.com

Chapter 1

Monday Night

The small young girl was in an alley on a night the sky opened its floodgates to release a ferocious downpour. In the darkness behind a rundown strip mall, she put down a filthy packing blanket under the overhang of the roof and out of the rain. She folded it lengthwise to serve as a bedroll. There was a three-foot pile of flattened cardboard boxes just outside one of the shop doors. She laid half of them over the blanket, not for warmth but so she would look more like a pile of trash than a person. She didn't want to be found. She knew that people could be cruel and abusive.

She'd been sleeping behind the big movie theater since running away. The dumpster had lots of leftover popcorn and candy, and a homeless camp was in the woods near there. She'd tried going into the camp once, hoping someone would be nice and take care of her.

A big man with a shaved head and red beard had chased her off. "Get outta here! We don't want no colored girl here!"

After that, she didn't go into the camp but would lie down close enough to hear people talk. It made her feel safer that someone was nearby, even if they didn't want her around.

The weather, when she had slept behind the theater, had been nice. She'd looked up through the tree limbs to see the stars. But because of the bad storm, she had to find somewhere dry to sleep and had ended up in the alley.

She felt eyes on her—had since she'd first gotten there—but she didn't see anyone else. Lightning flared and made the world appear black and white. She looked down to the other end of the alley, where a mound of old clothes was piled next to a shopping cart filled with what appeared to be more old clothes, cans, bottles, and plastic bags stuffed full. The things had been there when she'd set up for the night, and there hadn't been any movement, but she felt something radiate from them that wasn't good, so she made her bed as far away as she could.

Not quite ready for sleep, she sat with her back against the building and opened the ratty spiral notebook that she carried everywhere. With the stub of a pencil, she wrote.

> *I wonder if it's hard to end,*
> *and does it hurt to die,*

It was too dark to see the words, but with the frequent lightning strikes, she could see that her lines were straight and her words fell where they should. She gazed down the alley to the pile of old clothes and then turned her attention back to her writing.

> *I don't think that I'd mind it,*
> *I know I wouldn't cry.*

> *I wonder if it's hard to die,*
> *and does it hurt to end,*
> *I'm not too scared to find that out,*
> *Death might be a friend.*

She started to write more, but her gaze returned to the end of the alley, her uneasiness growing. It was like focusing on her bedroom door when she knew the smelly man was coming to visit. She decided to try for sleep and left the notebook leaning against the wall, as far from the rain as possible. She slid under the flattened boxes and between the folds of the packing blanket.

She was miserable, but it was still better than being back in her mother's apartment. Her mother lived to party, which meant a lot of drinking, drugs, and sex for money. When her mother was drunk or high, she liked to tease the girl and call her stupid and dumb. That was bad enough, but the reason she had run away was because her mother had started to make the girl party too. The smelly man had paid her mother to let him into the girl's room. He locked the door when he came in and told her he'd come to play with her. He made her touch his thing and wanted her to kiss it, but she wouldn't. She just held it while he rocked his hips and then made a mess.

Later, the girl said that she didn't want to do that anymore.

Her mother replied, "You're eight, kiddo, old enough to bring in some cash." She gave the girl a fake smile and patted her head, saying, "You'll learn to like it."

When her mother told her the smelly man was coming to see her again, she ran away.

She jumped when lightning struck so close that thunder boomed at the same time. She crawled out from the blanket and boxes to look down the alley when another blast lit up the sky. It seemed like the pile of old clothes was nearer. For long minutes, she stared in that direction. When another lightning strike came, she gasped and sat up, her eyes wide. A half dozen bolts of lightning flashed, one after the other, accompanied by thunder, and she screamed. The mound of old clothes was no longer at a distance. Now it was a man with scraggly gray hair and a beard tangled with leaves and twigs. In the strobe effect of the lightning flashes, he moved spasmodically as he crawled closer to her on his hands and knees. He reached for her, and she closed her eyes.

Somebody shouted, and she opened her eyes as the area lit up with another electrical blast. The man was no longer there. Just over the pounding of the rain, she heard grunts and movement. The next lightning strike lit up a man fighting with another out in the storm. With each celestial discharge, she saw dark clothes, hands rising and falling, and legs dancing as the brawling men sought secure footing. Between flashes, there was a meaty smack beside her. A moment later, she heard a scratch, and a match flared underneath the roof overhang. In the flimsy, flickering glow, she saw the crawling man lying next to her. His eyes were closed, and blood flowed from his nose and mouth.

She turned to the other man as he stood next to her and lit a candle inside a soot-stained lantern. He put the lantern down, and she looked up at a man with a long, wispy beard and hair that fell to his shoulders. A dark frayed overcoat hung to his ankles. He picked up a wide-brimmed black flannel hat and placed it on his head.

He held out a hand and said the strangest thing. "I hope to have the privilege of your intimate kinship."

Without taking her eyes from him, she scooched several feet away. She stared at his outstretched hand and noticed that he wore fingerless leather gloves.

"Come, my dear. There's no need to be frightened." He smiled, and his blue eyes reflected the lantern light. He talked funny, with an accent, like he was from England. "There are other boys and girls dying to meet you. Boys and girls just like you." He winked. "My name is Mr. Teacher." His voice was low, gentle, and warm.

He took a step, closing the distance, his hand still extended. Slowly, she reached out and took it. They shook once. He gestured into the storm, turned, and walked away while whistling a tune. Part of her wanted to climb back under the boxes and into her makeshift bedroll, while another part wanted to follow the person who had fought for her and saved her from the crawling man. He'd gotten a few steps away when she jumped to her feet and started after him.

Without turning, he held up a hand. "Don't forget your notebook, my dear."

She ran back and grabbed it, pausing to look down at the crawling man, who was either unconscious or dead.

Chapter 2

Courtney Myerson studied the black-and-white eight-by-ten glossy photo. "Hmm. I don't think I've ever seen it. Don't you have a color photograph?" The owner of the Sea Breeze Gallery in Daytona Beach placed the picture on the counter next to the cash register.

I waited until a ground-shaking eruption of thunder passed. A severe thunderstorm, a rarity in northeast Florida that close to Christmas, was passing through and would probably last the night. "It was taken back in the 1930s, and I'm afraid that's the only photograph of the painting that could be found."

"Mm-hmm," Courtney hummed, sounding skeptical. "So, Lise, you say this is a long-lost Frieseke, huh?"

"Yes."

"Sounds like an old wives' tale to me."

I didn't want to get into a debate on the reality of the painting, so I said, "Thanks for hanging around until I could get here."

Courtney opened her mouth, but a loud pounding interrupted her, followed by the shrill scream of a circular saw from the recently expanded entry to the space next door.

When the noise ended, Courtney rubbed at her temples. "My poor head. I've had to put up with that racket all week. After several delays, they promised to finish the remodel tonight, so I'd have to be here regardless of you coming or not." From an earlier phone call and the few comments we'd traded this evening, it was obvious Courtney was well heeled in the art of passive-aggressive conversation. Almost everything she said had me wondering if she'd just insulted me. Courtney was in her late fifties, with meticulously coiffed brunette hair, and she wore a white button-down blouse with carefully rolled sleeves, along with a gray business-style skirt.

Not sure how to respond, I said, "Congratulations on the expansion."

She gave me an insincere smile and nodded, as if saying *of course.* "They are already two days past deadline. And the grand opening of the new space is only five days away." The saw shrieked again, and as it died down, Courtney said, "I swear it's intentional that every time I complain, they slow down even more."

I figured she was probably right. "Well, as you say, they're winding it up tonight."

"I'm not holding my breath. Shall I give you a tour of the expansion?" She sighed as if it was a terrible burden.

The last thing I wanted to do was check out a construction project. "No thanks, Courtney. I want to wait until it's done before I lay eyes on it."

What I really wanted to do was cross Sea Breeze Gallery off my list and head back to San Marco. With the heavy rain, it would take me longer to get home, and I was already frustrated with the lack of progress. For the past two months, I'd been banging my head against the wall, working what I now had to admit was a hopeless case. Time was almost up, the exhibition opened in less than a week, and I had yet to locate the painting I'd been hired to find. Every possible lead had proven to be bogus. I wasn't looking forward to calling my client.

It had been almost a year ago that I helped the San Marco PD close the case on a serial killer who left his victims posed to replicate famous works of art. That story was in the news for weeks, along with my role in it. Around that same time, I also made the news with the discovery and recovery of an unknown sketch of a dancing ballerina that was the result of a casual collaboration between Picasso and Dali. That one created quite the hubbub within the art world, and I loved my name attached to that. I never dreamed that my degree in art history would come into play with me as a private investigator, much less with two such highly publicized cases. But that was how Marjorie Katherine Hamilton came to call on me at the offices of Annalise Norwood Investigation.

Mrs. Hamilton sat on the board of directors for the Garrido Museum, which was putting on an exhibition called *Florida, Masters in Passing*. The gist of the show was famous masters who had spent time in Florida and created paintings inspired by their time here. Homer Winslow vacationed in the sunshine state for twenty years and had plenty of Florida-themed work including *The Shell Heap*. John Singer Sargent only visited Florida once, but it was enough to inspire his 1917 masterpiece *Basin with Sailor*. As a child, Frederick Carl Frieseke lived in northeast Florida. The Garrido Museum was showing his works, *Alligator Hunting Pink Sea* and *Fishing Jacksonville*. There was another he had painted entitled *Cold Green Spring*, and that painting had disappeared back in the 1930s. Depicting a group of boys swimming in a Florida freshwater spring, it was the painting that Mrs. Hamilton had hired me to find. Its last known location was in south Florida. I'd spent weeks utilizing social media in my search, contacting art experts, galleries, and museums and chasing after a whole lot of rumor. All for naught.

As I prepared to bow out and get on the road, one of the carpenters came from the construction area carrying a toolbox in one hand with an orange extension cord coiled and hanging from a shoulder. His long hair was brown, streaked with gray, and braided down his back. He sported a bushy beard and was dressed in a sweat-stained T-shirt and worn jeans. He clomped up to us in heavy black leather boots.

"All done, Mrs. Myerson."

"About time," she said. Even though he was a foot taller than her, she still managed to look down her nose at him.

He didn't react to her snarkiness and added, "We'll clean up and get out of your hair."

When she didn't say anything, he shrugged and started to go but stopped when he glanced down at the photo of *Cold Green Spring*.

Courtney sighed. "What now, Pete?"

He kept his gaze on the picture. "My wife, she has this same picture." He turned his gaze up to me and added, "Only it's in color."

Chapter 3

Rather than bask in the glow of Courtney Myerson's personality, I sat in my car and waited, the downpour drumming on the roof. The carpenter named Pete had to help load his partner's work van, and then he and I were going to go look at his wife's picture. My heart was racing at the prospect of her owning the actual *Cold Green Spring*. My mind, however, was telling me not to get my hopes up. What were the odds that I'd be visiting that gallery at the exact time that a carpenter married to the woman who owned the painting happened to walk by and glance down at the photo? More miracle than chance, that was for sure. But then again, it wouldn't be the first time a carpenter was involved in miracles.

The passenger door opened, and Pete quickly sat and shut the door. "Sorry, gonna get your car wet."

He was soaked, but I told him, "Minnie can handle it."

"Minnie?"

"My car," I said.

"That way." He pointed to the left. "Minnie because she's a Mini Cooper?"

I started driving. "Yeah, sort of. A while back, my boyfriend and I spent the weekend at Disney World." I didn't tell him that we only hit the theme park once because we found that we preferred to spend our time in the hotel's lazy river or in our room, engaged in hotel sex, which in our mutual opinion, was always great sex. "When we checked out, we forgot where we'd parked. My boyfriend started doing a lousy Mickey Mouse impersonation." I did an even lousier impersonation of Nick doing his impersonation. "'Where oh where is Minnie?' The name stuck." I looked at Pete to see if I was boring him. When I saw he was attentive, I added, "I've never had a car with a name before."

"I call my pickup truck Ruby because she's red. I call my motorcycle Gladys. Turn right on Main."

"What kind of bike is it?" From his appearance, I assumed a Harley or an Indian.

"A 1949 Harley Hydra-Glide."

"Wow."

"She's a beast, usually starts on the first kick. Make a left here."

We continued a couple more blocks before he directed me to a partially paved road that ran behind some businesses. It was dark and unpopulated, and paranoia started to set in. I was alone in what was little more than an alley with a man I didn't really know.

Finally, he pointed at a place that had a neon sign that said Hole in the Roof. "Pull in here."

"A bar?"

"My wife's bar."

I pulled into a parking spot in front of what could be defined as a dive bar. Not that I was being snooty, as there are a couple of dives I like to visit on occasion. To me, it resembled an old mountain shack with two front-facing, dirty windows. The sign with the bar's name hung in one window. In the other was another neon design, this one the familiar silhouette of a sitting nude woman that was often seen on the mud flaps of eighteen-wheelers.

"My guess is that if it wasn't raining, there'd be a bunch of motorcycles out front," I said.

"Yep, including Gladys."

We got out and ran up the three steps to the single wood door and pushed our way in. Not as dark as the stormy night, the Hole in the Roof was still dim inside. Along with Steppenwolf playing at a surprisingly mild volume on the jukebox, a rhythmic ping of rainwater leaked through a hole in the roof and dripped into a bronze bowl on the bar.

The name of the place was a great example of truth in advertising. The air was thick with cigarette smoke. Smoking in a bar in Florida was legal if less than ten percent of the bar's revenue came from food sales, and I was pretty sure ninety-nine percent of the Hole in the Roof's profit was booze related.

I could almost feel the fifteen eyes staring in my direction. An odd number because one of the seven bikers in the bar had an eye patch. The last pair of eyes that bored holes into me belonged to the woman behind the bar. One look at her and I knew that she had been a real looker in her day. Now in her mid-to-late fifties, she was more handsome than pretty. At some point in the past year or two, she'd opted to stop dyeing her hair so that it was white from the crown of her head to just below her ears. Below that, the remaining six inches were as black as her T-shirt.

"I thought your philandering days were through," the woman said to Pete.

"Aw, put a sock in it, Wendy. If I'm gonna cheat, I wouldn't be stupid enough to bring her here."

Before she could answer, Pete grabbed my arm and pulled me along the bar, bypassing the taps and bottles of whiskey and vodka. He stopped at a collection of tequila. There on the wall above the bottles, enclosed in a dusty frame, was the painting *Cold Green Spring*.

Well aware that my jaw had dropped, I reached for the nearest barstool without taking my eyes from the painting and sat. Gesturing toward the painting, I said, "What were you thinking? Hanging that there." The moment the words left my mouth, I knew it was the wrong thing to say, confirmed by the anger that flashed in Wendy's eyes.

Before she could respond, Pete said, "Well? Is that it?"

I attempted to respond, but instead, I made a raspy noise.

"What?"

I needed something to calm me down. "Whiskey."

"Get her a shot of Jack," Pete told his wife.

"Get it yourself."

Pete shook his head and went around the bar to pour me a shot. As I downed it, he got the painting off the wall and placed it on the bar in front of me.

"What are you doing, Pete?" Wendy asked.

"Believe it or not, Wendy, this lady is a private eye. She's been looking for your painting."

"Why? It's not stolen. I paid good money for it."

I laughed out loud because that was the furthest thought from my mind. I think it was also because I was in a giddy state of shock that I'd just stumbled upon *Cold Green Spring.* However, the angry look on Wendy's face told me she thought I was laughing at her. I quickly turned serious. "No, I'm not saying it's stolen. Here's my card."

I handed her a business card that she let drop to the bar without glancing at it.

I cleared my throat. "Do you mind if I ask where you got the painting?"

By now, a couple of the other bikers ambled over to see what was going on.

Wendy pushed some beer glasses into a sink, put them on a drainer, and wiped her hands with a bar towel before answering. "Picked it up at an estate sale a long time ago. Was at one of those beachfront mansions in Ormond Beach."

"Wendy's into yard sales, estate sales, that kind of thing," Pete explained. "She picks up a lot of décor for the bar at them."

It didn't sound natural for the word "décor" to come from Pete's mouth, but I looked around at various paintings, photos, metal cutouts of fish on the walls, a few statues, some 1940 and 1950 vintage pinup-girl photos, and a whole lot of motorcycle memorabilia.

Looking back at the Frieseke, I asked, "Do you remember what you paid for it?"

"Sure. Thirty-two dollars and fifty cents."

I made an involuntary noise in my throat and gazed down on the masterwork. Not a huge piece, it was three feet wide and two feet high. And it was beautiful. A classic example of his impressionist work. Frieseke's use of vibrant colors, mostly in the cool palette, was incredible. The shifting light and color almost seemed to move. Frieseke had painted three boys swimming in the spring waters. One stood at the shore, stripping off his shirt, and I could feel his haste to join his friends. The fifth boy had launched himself in the air, curled up tight, preparing to splash the others with a cannonball. It was that boy's nakedness that told they were engaged in a good old-fashioned skinny-dip. Frieseke's spare use of warm colors—reds, oranges, and yellows in the boys' discarded clothing and a few blooms among the flora—seemed to pop off the canvas. And there in the bottom right-hand corner was his signature, FC Frieseke.

I was suddenly aware that a hand had moved in front of my face, fingers snapping. I looked up to Wendy. "Huh?"

"Hello. Earth to stranger. Do you hear me?"

"I'm sorry," I said. "I've been looking for this for weeks. I'd just resigned myself to the fact I'd never find it."

"Well, now that you found it, I'm not interested in selling it."

"No, we don't want to buy it. We're just going to borrow it," I explained.

"What?" She said it like I'd just announced I was going to sleep with her husband.

"But first, I'd like to take it and have it appraised," I said. "Well, I'm convinced it's authentic, but we still need an official certification. I can have my boyfriend do it."

"What the fuck are you talking about?" Wendy said.

I wasn't sure how I'd gotten on this woman's wrong side so quickly. "I'm sorry. I'm not presenting myself well. What I mean is that—"

Wendy leaned over the bar to get close to my face. "Look, I can promise you that I would never come into your place of business and start taking things out of it, so I'd appreciate it if you did the same for me."

"I think we got off on the wrong foot."

"No, my feet are fine. It's your feet that stepped across the line." Her face darkened, and I was happy a bar was between us.

One of the guys next to us whooped and shouted, "Catfight!"

"Shut up, Hubie," Wendy shouted. "Bowser, escort the lady out. She's no longer welcome at the Hole in the Roof."

A man the size of a Humvee gestured toward the door while someone behind me grabbed my ass. Without thinking, I spun and slapped Hubie hard across the cheek. Talk about your timing. The last song on the jukebox had stopped playing a second before, so the sound of the slap reverberated through the bar. Everyone froze and stared, except for Hubie, who put a hand to his cheek.

It was Wendy who broke the silence. "Kudos to you"—she picked up my business card from the bar—"Annalise Norwood, private eye. I've wanted to do that for years, but you still gotta go." She gestured for the door.

"Come on, Lise," Pete said and walked me out.

We stood on the steps under the little overhang, out of the rain.

"What just happened, Pete?"

"Oh, she's just in one of her moods. Now you know why people used to call her Wicked Wendy."

"She can't just leave that painting on the wall behind the bar."

"Oh, Wendy can do anything she wants."

"What I mean is that it's too valuable. If some lowlife knew how much that painting is worth, it'd be stolen in a heartbeat." I quickly added, "Not that I'm saying the people that come here are lowlifes."

"Oh, quite a few of them are. So, what do you think it's worth?"

"It's hard to put an exact figure on it, Pete. Let's just say you take what she paid for it and multiply it by three or four thousand."

I watched him silently do the math. The surprise in his eyes signaled when he got the answer. "Holeee shit."

"Look, I was hired by a woman representing an art museum in San Marco to find that painting. The museum wants to borrow it for an exhibition. If Wendy agrees, you'll learn a lot more about the painting, including its potential value."

"Tell you what. Let's give Wendy time to calm down. I'll talk to her, and why don't you come back tomorrow?"

"Yeah, okay. And I'll bring my brass knuckles."

"Don't joke about that. Wendy has some under the register." Pete went back inside, and I ran through the storm to Minnie.

Chapter 4

"Take my hand, little one," Mr. Teacher said. "It's treacherous in the dark."

She walked with him up an alley as the rain poured, and then Mr. Teacher led her into a cross alley that opened onto the parking lot of a closed supermarket. In a dark corner was an old car. A round, rusted chrome logo was attached to the front of the car that had a V and a W on it. Mr. Teacher opened the passenger door for her, and she got in. He shut the door, went around the car, took his place behind the wheel, and turned the key. The car made a whinnying sound for long seconds before it finally backfired and caught.

While the storm raged, he drove them through neighborhoods and finally to where there were fewer homes and businesses. The car slowed, and Mr. Teacher pulled into a narrow, broken driveway that was almost invisible from the street. The view was of darkness, rain, and trees, and then the headlights illuminated a ramshackle brick building with dim light flickering from one of the windows. When they got out of the car, she heard talking and laughter coming from inside. Mr. Teacher led her to a door, and they stepped in from the rain.

"Welcome, my dear, to what will be your new home." He held out his arms. "We call it Thieves Kitchen."

They entered an old building where much of the drywall had been ripped away or simply worn down to old red brick. A portion of the wall had collapsed, allowing smoke from a small campfire next to it to escape. A few lanterns were also scattered about, much like the one Mr. Teacher had lit after saving her from the crawling man. A freshly cut tree stood on an X of two-by-fours that had been nailed to the stump as a stand. Empty cans, shoes, shards of colored broken glass, paper cutouts of stars, and more served as Christmas tree ornaments.

At least a dozen other kids were there. A few were close to her age, maybe even younger, and the rest were older. She doubted the oldest, who was playing a guitar, was more than sixteen. Across the room, an older girl with fairy wings attached to her back was juggling three balls of different sizes. A young shirtless boy in front of her held another, and when the girl said, "Now," he tossed the ball toward her so that she juggled four. One black-haired girl was showing card tricks to a couple of others.

Mr. Teacher called out, "Everyone! Please come and greet our new friend."

The kids rushed over and encircled her. She spun to look at them all. Normally, she would have been nervous, but they were so oddly dressed that she focused on that. One of the older boys with long dark hair had a wide red headband, an open buckskin vest, and pants tucked into knee-high moccasins. The cowboy to his Indian was the youngest, a girl in a white cowboy hat, boots, and an Annie Oakley–style dress with two toy six guns belted high on her waist. There was also a pirate, a kid wearing an astronaut helmet, and the girl with fairy wings. The oldest boy, who'd been playing guitar, was barefoot and naked except for a loincloth. Some kids were White, some were Black, some were Latino, and one girl with shining black hair was Asian.

Mr. Teacher walked around behind the kids, throwing out names. "This is Dag, our ginger-haired surfer. Florence is who you see if you need a bandage or aren't feeling well. Nancy has a lovely singing voice. Dodge is imminently suited for our line of work. Say hello to Jimmy Mac, Carroway, and our comedian, Charly. Tarzan is everybody's big brother and plays a mean guitar. And finally, this is Borgia, Tink, Mackie, Clyde, Geronimo, Bet, Quint, and Mudge."

"What's your name, kid?" Dodge asked. He wore an old-fashioned green tuxedo jacket, goggles, and a top hat, under which his hair swept every way imaginable.

Suddenly, she felt anxious. Her mouth opened and closed several times.

Mr. Teacher pushed through the circle of children and knelt in front of her. "You can be whoever you want here. If you want to be your old self, that's fine. Or you can be someone new, and if that's the case, then you can pick your own name."

"I picked my own," said the Asian girl Mr. Teacher had introduced as Bet.

"Me too," Geronimo added, and then several others nodded as if they had as well.

She'd never thought about being someone other than her mother's stupid daughter. Did she want a new name? She did. But what? And then she knew. Her favorite TV show was about a pig in first grade who showed kids how to use their imagination and how to be good people. The pig's name, she always thought, sounded royal.

She cleared her throat. "I want to be called Olivia."

All the kids gathered around her, welcoming her, shaking her hand, patting her on the back and shoulders. She felt good, really good, and grinned.

Mr. Teacher turned to a boy wearing a derby. "Charly, is the washtub filled?"

Charly motioned over his shoulder with his thumb. "It's warming by the fire."

Mr. Teacher grinned. "Well then, Nancy, help Olivia with a quick washup and find her dry clothes."

A young boy, maybe a year her junior, stepped toward Olivia. He was the one who had tossed the ball to the juggler named Tink. Olivia could tell he was shy by how he looked everywhere else but right at her.

He had been shirtless but now wore a gray wool jacket. "Hi, I'm Mackie. A special tweat tonight, we got hot dogs foh dinnah."

Tuesday

It was the first time in a long while that she slept all the way through the night. Olivia woke an hour or so before noon and saw that someone had put her between the folds of a sleeping bag. She sat up, stretched, and looked around, seeing that Mackie slept near her. Olivia stood, rolled up the bedroll, and put it in a corner where it would be out of the way. She looked down at Mackie's sleeping form. Though she'd just met him the night before, they were friends, and she smiled, thinking that he may very well be her first best friend. She sang "Twinkle Twinkle Little Star," first in a whisper then gradually louder until Mackie woke. He rolled over, looked up at her, and grinned.

"Rise and shine," she said and then laughed because Mackie was so dirty that nothing about him could shine through the dirt.

"Wise and shine." He giggled back and sat up. "Dodge wikes to say, 'Wakey, wakey, eggs and bakey.'"

Mackie wasn't wearing anything from the waist up, and Olivia pointed at numerous round scars on his arms. "What are those?"

Mackie flushed and grabbed his gray jacket. As he put it on, he mumbled, "Nothing."

Olivia could tell she'd embarrassed him and changed the topic. "Wakey, wakey, eggs and bakey. Wish we had eggs and bacon."

Mackie's smile returned, and he led her to the campfire, where a huge plate rested next to it on carefully stacked bricks. He got a couple burnt weenies and passed her one. "Weftovahs."

In the full light of day, Olivia asked Mackie to show her around. He offered her another weenie, but she shook her head.

He nodded to the sleeping forms of the other kids and whispered, "You gotta be quiet if you get up befo' evewyone else. Some get cwanky if you wake them up, especiawy Tahzan."

They stepped past the sleepers to the Christmas tree, and he pointed to a small glass Santa ornament. "Mistah Teachah wet me hang this one."

Mackie nodded to a doorless entry, and they stepped through. Though they were surrounded by thick trees, the sun was almost overhead, and she and Mackie stood in the warmth, absorbing it like lizards.

"We got a bus. You wanna see?" Mackie asked.

"Sure."

He led her to an outbuilding that had once served as a garage or maintenance shed. A big opening was where the garage door used to be. They went in and walked up one side of the bus, Olivia running her hand along the metal.

"We call it the Bwue Goose," Mackie said.

Olivia could tell it was old and that someone had painted it dark blue. Hand-painted white letters on the side spelled out Grace United Baptist Church.

"Mistah Teachah says that if the police see a chu'ch bus, they won't pull it ovah."

Mackie yanked open the doors, and they got on.

He sat in the driver's seat. "Mistah Teachah dwives and tows his cah."

They took turns pretending they were driving until Mackie said, "Wet's go see if anyone is awake."

They approached the building where the kids slept. Mr. Teacher was on a nearby tree stump, smoking out of a white clay pipe. He took it from his mouth and pointed at the building and a few others that could be seen through the foliage. "Used to be a college."

"Mornin', Mistah Teachah," Mackie called out.

"Morning to you too." He wore an off-white linen shirt with puffy sleeves and big wooden buttons. His wool pants were old and patched, and he had on worn lace-up boots. "Looking around our little home, my dear?"

"A little."

"We just got back fwom the bus," Mackie said.

Mr. Teacher stood, keeping his eyes on her. "Let's show Olivia some more, shall we, Mackie? And step lightly. Last night's rain has left plenty of mud."

He turned and walked away from the building, Mackie in tow. She followed. They went a short while before stopping at a huge, square concrete hole in the ground. One end of the hole was three feet deep, but it progressively got deeper until it was a ten-foot drop at the other end. That end contained foul water that was almost black and was filled with tree limbs and leaves.

"This was the college's swimming pool." Mr. Teacher pointed at the buildings surrounding it. Each was like the building that housed Thieves Kitchen. Brick, three stories, most windows broken, abandoned, and rundown. "This used to be D.W. Roberts College, a college for African Americans. They opened their doors in the 1920s and closed in the early 1970s."

Mackie whooped and jumped into the shallow side and ran down to the deep end. He squatted at the stagnant water and poked at it with a stick.

"You like Mackie, don't you?" Mr. Teacher asked.

Olivia nodded.

"Good. He can use a friend." Then he held up a finger as if a thought had just come to him. "Even better, he needs a sister. You'd make a fine sister, wouldn't you?"

Olivia turned down her face to hide her grin, but she nodded.

"Do you like Thieves Kitchen, my dear?"

Again, she nodded.

Mr. Teacher stared at her a moment. "Did they not like you speaking where you came from?"

She didn't want to answer, but he had been so kind, had even fought the crawling man for her. She whispered, "They wanted me to be quiet."

"They?"

"My mother. Her friends."

"Why did they want you to be quiet?"

"Because I'm stupid and say stupid things."

A look of anger flashed on Mr. Teacher's face, which then shifted to a gentle smile. "I don't agree." He sat at the edge of the pool, and she sat next to him. "And you don't have to be quiet here, my dear. Be as loud as you want. Can you be a lion? Like this?" Mr. Teacher sat up straight and released a loud roar.

Olivia shook her head.

"Come, Olivia. Give it a try. Be a lion." He repeated his roar.

Olivia took in a deep breath and gave a roar that could barely be heard.

"Respectable, but really, that was more of a lion's purr." He pointed at the most-distant building. "Make it so loud that anyone in there could hear it."

Olivia nodded, took a deeper breath, and unleashed a screaming roar.

Mr. Teacher nodded at her with a grin. A second later, Mackie roared from down in the swimming pool, and Olivia and Mr. Teacher laughed.

She looked up at him, and the smile left her face. She asked, "What are those marks on Mackie's arms?"

Mr. Teacher leaned toward her so that they were eye level and explained, "Our Mackie used to live with a monster."

Olivia's eyes widened in horror. "A real monster."

Mr. Teacher nodded. "This monster liked to burn Mackie with cigarettes." He picked at the dirt before looking back at her. "Let me give you a quick lesson about adults. They can, generally speaking, be put into two categories: meddlesome or monsters. Meddlesome adults always want to know what you're doing, why are you there, where are you from. If they think you're an orphan or homeless, then they'll want to put you in a foster home. Worse than them are the monsters. They like to hurt children and do things to them that I don't care to speak of. And sometimes, when the meddlesome adults put a child in foster care, they do so without realizing that the foster parent is a monster as well. That's why it's best that you don't trust adults and stay away from them. Present company excluded, of course."

"Was Mackie in a foster home?"

"No, his monster was a cruel uncle with whom he lived. Can I have a look at your notebook?"

Her eyes sprang wide, and she scooted a few inches from him.

"I promise that I'll give it back. I promise not to call whatever's in there—or you, for that matter—stupid."

She had stuffed the tattered notebook into the waistband of the shorts they had given her the night before. A too-large green T-shirt with a cereal mascot hung loosely from her shoulders and covered the notebook. She pulled it out, stared at the torn cover for almost a minute, and then held it out to him while keeping her eyes downcast.

Mr. Teacher flipped through the notebook, stopping now and then to read, and finally studied the next-to-last written page.

He looked at her, his face serious. "You're a poet. And your mother was wrong. You are not stupid, my dear."

"Really?"

"Oh yes." He read more of her writing. "You are quite clever. This poem, about ending and dying and if it's hard and does it hurt, when did you write it?"

"Last night."

He nodded. "It's not hard to die. It can be painless, or it can hurt very much. It's something that comes to everyone, but it's nothing you should seek out. Do you understand?"

Olivia twisted her face in thought. "I think so."

"I want you to imagine what would have happened if you had died last night. You wouldn't have met us, your new family. You wouldn't have a friend named Mackie nor a home called Thieves Kitchen."

Olivia nodded at this insight.

"I once fought beside heroic men and women during a terrible war. And one time, when we'd been fighting for days with no sleep, I wondered aloud if it was hard to die and if it hurt. One soldier asked me if this was the lowest point of my life. I told him it was. He smiled at me. 'That's good news because things can only get better.' When you've reached the bottom, Olivia, what's the only direction you can go?"

She tentatively pointed her finger toward the sky.

"That's right. Up. See, you really are a clever girl." He stood and reached down a hand to help her up. He dug into his pocket, retrieving a palm full of coins. He selected one, closed his eyes for a moment, and then tossed it into the water. He held out his hand. "Make a wish."

She took a penny from his palm, closed her eyes, and thought *I wish that I can live in Thieves Kitchen forever.* She held the coin over the deep end and dropped it. It hit the water, making a *splorp* sound.

"Hey! You spwashed me," Mackie called, wiping at his face and giggling.

They went back to Thieves Kitchen, and Mr. Teacher brought them to an area that he called his private space. Opening a trunk, he looked through it and brought out a brown leather book with a long leather strap wrapped around it. A gold pen was tucked into the strap. He passed these items to Olivia.

Olivia took out the pen and unwrapped the strap, opening the book to blank vanilla pages made of coarse paper.

Mr. Teacher smiled broadly and held out a hand, indicating Olivia. "Do you know who this is, Mackie, my dear?"

"It's Owivia, Mistah Teachah."

"Not just Olivia." He moved behind her, placing his hands on her shoulders. "Olivia, our chronicler."

Both children looked at him blankly.

Mr. Teacher tapped the leather-bound book. "This is your journal, Olivia. In which, my dear, you shall record the history of Thieves Kitchen."

Chapter 5

"This is the place that has a Frieseke?" Nick asked as we stood outside Hole in the Roof.

"Over the liquor bottles," I said.

"That'd be appropriate for a Jackson Pollock. I don't think Frieseke was much of a drinker."

"Come on," I said and led the way in.

I looked to the bar, expecting Wendy to be there glaring at me, but the big guy who had started to escort me from the bar before I slapped Hubie was working it. He looked up, saw me, and smiled like we were buds. Apparently, the only person who cared if I slapped Hubie was Hubie.

"Wendy and Pete are in the office. She said to send you back." The big guy pointed to a short hallway.

I cast a glance to the wall above the tequila. The Frieseke wasn't there. I took Nick's hand and went to the hallway, bypassed a door that had the sign His 'n' Hers Head, and stopped at the one with Office written on it in block letters. I tapped with my knuckles.

"Come in," a voice I recognized as Wendy's called.

Girding my loins, I opened the door just enough to stick my head in. "Hi?"

"Hey, Lise," Pete said, standing.

Wendy sat on the other side of a wooden desk, looking at me without expression. "Come on in."

I grabbed Nick and pushed him in ahead of me.

We stood there a moment, and then I said, "This is Professor Nick Weldon, dean of the Department of Art and Art History at San Marco

University. I thought that maybe, if you wanted, he could look at the painting and answer any questions you have."

Wendy put her elbows on the desk, clasped her hands, and rested her chin on them. She looked me in the eyes. I'd played this game with Detective Baker of the San Marco PD in the past, so I just held her gaze.

Finally, she said, "Pete, you and the professor go get everyone a beer."

Pete shrugged and told Nick, "Let's get some beer."

Nick looked at me. I gave him a small nod, and he followed Pete out the door. I hoped they would leave the door open. They didn't.

Wendy stood, slowly walked around her desk, and perched on its edge, all without taking her eyes off me. "Pete says I need to apologize about how I acted last night." A second later, she gave me a shrug and a sheepish expression to go with it. "I agree. I'd had a bad day, some bad news confirmed, and was itching to take it out on someone. I was out of sorts, thought you were being pushy about how you were going to take it—"

"Borrow it... but only with your permission."

"Well, we'll see about that. Have a seat."

I took one of the chairs. "Thanks."

"So, Pete told me what you said. That a museum wants to show my painting."

"Right."

"And that it's valuable."

"Certainly worth a lot more than what you paid for it. Nick can help you with that better than I can." I paused for a moment. "I saw that you hadn't put the painting back on the wall."

"Nope. Once word gets out that it's worth something, it'll disappear quicker than a line of coke in a strip joint dressing room."

A second later, the door opened, and Pete peeked cautiously in. He saw we were being civil, came in, and handed me a cold bottle of Yuengling. Nick followed after him and passed one to Wendy.

She held up her bottle. "To valuable paintings."

We clinked and sipped. Wendy put her bottle on the desktop and went to a closet that she opened with a key. "I Googled the artist." Wendy reached to a shelf and came out with *Cold Green Spring*. She passed it to Nick. "Well, Professor, is it the real deal?"

Nick studied the painting for a minute. He tried sounding calm, but I could sense his excitement. "Do you mind if I take it out of the frame?"

Wendy said, "Go ahead." She watched him with amusement as he reverentially freed the painting from the cheap plastic frame.

Nick carefully took in every inch, angling the painting to catch it in different lighting. Halfway through, he smiled widely. Every now and then, he shook his head as if he couldn't believe it.

He put the picture on the desktop, picked up his beer, and took a deep pull. "Congratulations, you own a Frederick Carl Frieseke."

Pete gave a whoop.

"So what does that mean, owning a painting like that?" Wendy asked.

"Well, you have some decisions to make."

"Like what?" Wendy asked.

"Like where are you going to keep it. Here's not a good idea. You could keep it at your house, depending on how secure you think it would be. Keep it in a safe if you're worried. My suggestion is to allow the Garrido Museum to display it as part of its new exhibition while you figure all that out."

"What's it worth?" Pete asked.

"That's hard to say. At auction, Frieseke's pieces have sold for anywhere from tens of thousands to one that went for over two million dollars."

Pete whistled, and though Wendy kept a stoic expression, she paled.

"If you choose to sell it, your best bet is at auction, and there's really no way to tell what it will sell for. It's all about demand. I'd recommend that you insure it. I have little doubt an insurance company would put a valuation on it of a hundred to a hundred and fifty thousand dollars, maybe higher."

"If I agree to let the museum show it, what do we have to do?"

I took out my phone, punched Marjorie Katherine Hamilton's contact, and put the phone on speaker.

Marjorie answered, "Hi, Lise, how's the hunt?"

"The hunt is officially over."

I could hear the anticipation in her voice. "You found it?"

"Marjorie, you're on speakerphone with Nick and me, as well as Wendy and Pete Steadman, the owners of *Cold Green Spring.*"

Marjorie screamed with delight. "Mr. and Mrs. Steadman. I am so delighted to meet you, even if it is over the phone."

I asked Marjorie what the Steadmans would need to do if they chose to loan the piece to the museum, and she informed them it was a simple case of paperwork. When Marjorie asked about how Wendy and Pete had come into possession of the painting, I went into great detail about the discovery and how, for the past several years, it had been occupying wall space at their bar above the bottles of tequila.

Ten seconds of silence passed before Marjorie exploded with laughter.

Chapter 6

Friday Night

Olivia wandered around Thieves Kitchen, writing in her journal.
I have a home and have friends now,
I have a family.
My haves outnumber my have-nots,
I really have no needs.

She passed Tarzan, who sat against the wall, playing a recorder. He took the instrument from his mouth. "How do you do that?"

Olivia looked up. "Do what?"

"Write and walk at the same time."

Charly had been cutting up with a small group, throwing out joke after joke off the top of his head, and he picked up on what Tarzan said. "Ladies and gentlemen, there is the young lady known as Olivia. She walks, she talks, and she writes all at the same time. Tarzan tried that once and face-planted in three steps." The kids around him laughed. "Which answered the question of what he wears under that loincloth. I'll give you a hint. We all saw a full moon." More rowdy laughter erupted, and Tarzan threw a stick at Charly, knocking off his derby.

Olivia giggled, and Tarzan ruffled her hair.

"Oh, Olivia, my dear. Please come," Mr. Teacher called.

"Good luck tonight, Olive," Tarzan said. Not only did she have a new name, but some of the kids called her by a nickname.

"Good luck with what?"

"You'll see."

Curious, she crossed the room to where Mr. Teacher sat in a chair someone had made from bricks. It resembled a throne. He removed a pocket watch and glanced at it. "A little after eleven. A good time for your first lesson, my dear." He winked. "I want you to go out with Dodge and Mackie. Learn from them, especially Dodge. He's a regular little magician when it comes to it."

Dodge took off his top hat and bowed.

Mr. Teacher added, "I know that you will be anxious, my dear, but I'm never far when there's work to be done."

Dodge placed his top hat on the blankets he used for a bed and lifted his goggles so they perched high on his forehead. Mackie put on the old gray military jacket over his shirtless torso. Advised to wear dark clothing, Olivia selected a pair of black jeans with a tear in one knee and a dark-blue T-shirt.

Mr. Teacher donned his overcoat and hat. "Everyone! Wish Olivia good luck."

She was surrounded by her new friends, who all offered her something she'd never had before—words of encouragement. Tink, Bet, and Borgia waited until everyone was done and approached Olivia.

Tink took off her fairy wings and helped Olivia put them on. "They're not only good luck, but in case something goes wrong, they'll make you run so fast you'll think you're flying."

"Thank you. I'll bring them back to you."

"You can keep them. I have another pair."

Bet, who was always practicing magic tricks, said, "You need a good-luck charm. I happen to have a lucky coin." She showed Olivia an empty hand, and in the next second, she gripped a large silver coin between her thumb and index finger.

Olivia gasped.

"Go on, take it," Bet said.

Olivia reached for it, but Bet's hand twitched, and the coin vanished.

"Hmm, that's strange," Bet said. "I know. Check your pockets."

Olivia reached into one and pulled out the coin. "Wow."

"Enough of the hocus-pocus," Borgia said and helped Olivia put on a long pair of black gloves made of soft material. They extended high up her arms to her biceps. Borgia then went to the unlit campfire and grabbed a handful of ash, rubbed her hands together, and applied it to both of Olivia's cheeks. "Tonight, you don't want to be seen. Stick to the shadows, and you'll be invisible."

They left Thieves Kitchen and made their way to Mr. Teacher's old VW Bug. Olivia climbed into the back seat, leaning forward so as not to damage the fairy wings. Mackie sat next to her. Dodge took the passenger seat, while Mr. Teacher took his place behind the wheel, and with a blast of smoke from the exhaust, started the car.

Mr. Teacher turned to look at Olivia, a wild glint in his eyes. "Are you ready, Olive, my dear?"

She was oddly unafraid and grinned at him. "I really am."

Laughing, Mr. Teacher grinded the gears into first and took off.

"Nicking fwom cars tonight, Mistah Teachah?" Mackie asked.

"You are a bright boy, my dear. A good way to break in our little Olive, don't you think?"

Dodge didn't look back, but with his arm over the seat, said, "Me and Mr. Teacher thought we'd head over to the neighborhood past the college. There're houses and apartments galore."

Mackie leaned into Olivia and explained. "Mistah Teacher wets us out. We walk awound the neighbahood and check out the cahs."

Dodge picked it up. "We open car doors and see if there's anything of value inside. If there's a trunk release, we'll look in there. If we peek into a window and see something good but the car is locked..." Dodge finished his sentence by pulling a hammer out of his jacket.

"Won't someone hear the glass break?" Olivia asked.

"A clever girl," Mr. Teacher said.

Replacing the hammer to an inside pocket, Dodge said, "This is for what we call a smash and grab. If we see something good in a locked car, we smash the window, grab it, and go. We save those for last, since there's a chance someone will hear us and call the cops."

After a fifteen-minute drive, Mr. Teacher parked in a Walgreens parking lot, far from the store and away from the streetlights. All the kids got out and gathered around the driver's-side window.

Mr. Teacher sat low in the seat, his arm resting on the window frame. "Are you nervous, my dear?"

Olivia took a moment to take stock of what she did feel. "A little, maybe."

"That's fine. It's to be expected. Stick with the others, and do what they do. If they hide, you hide. If they run, you run. I'll follow along behind you. Far enough back that you won't see me but close enough that I can help if there's a problem." Mr. Teacher smiled and waved them away. "Now off with you lot." He locked eyes with Olivia. "Good luck on your first job, my dear."

They didn't do much at first, other than walking around the neighborhood.

"We're getting the lay of the land," Dodge said.

Mackie nodded knowingly. "Way of the wand."

At first, Olivia turned to looked behind them every few minutes.

"Don't bother looking for Mr. Teacher," Dodge said. "You won't see him, but he's always near, always has our six."

"Our six?" Olivia said.

"It's a military term. Mr. Teacher was in the army or marines or something."

"But he don't wike to tawk about it much," Mackie added.

"Think of us as a clock. We're facing twelve o'clock, so six o'clock is behind us," Dodge explained.

"Ohhh," Olivia said. "He's watching our back."

After a late-night tour of the neighborhood, Olivia realized they'd returned to where they started.

"Now we start nicking," Dodge told her.

Dodge and Mackie took turns approaching cars parked on the street and in driveways. If they looked promising, one would search it while the other hid next to nearby trees or bushes with Olivia, keeping lookout.

A lot of cars had change in their consoles, and Mackie grabbed the coins at first, but Dodge told him not to bother with them. "You'll jingle like Santa's reindeers if we have to run."

Plenty of car owners stashed paper money in their dashboard cubbies and consoles. Glove compartments offered up another hiding place, and Dodge found a brand-new iPhone in one. Mackie found a pistol, but Dodge made him put it back because Mr. Teacher didn't like guns.

As the night progressed, they added a wristwatch, two wallets with credit cards as well as cash, and a few pieces of jewelry with value yet to be determined. Mackie also helped himself to a fishing rod that he found in the back of a pickup truck.

"About time to wrap it up," Dodge said after they'd been at it for what Olivia thought was half the night.

"Cah's coming," Mackie said.

They crouched behind a hedge in the front yard of a small ranch house. Peering around the bushes, they saw a long black car so shiny that it reflected streetlights. The engine hummed low and strong as it swept past, and it turned into the parking lot of a construction site just up and across the street. The car approached a black SUV that sat deep in the lot, next to a white sedan with logos on the side and a light bar on the roof.

While Olivia and Dodge watched, Mackie stood behind them and whipped the fishing rod back and forth, taking delight in the whistling sound it made.

Dodge said, "Get down, Mackie. That's a damn cop car."

Mackie threw the rod into some bushes and knelt next to Dodge and Olivia.

The black car parked between the SUV and police car. A moment later, the driver got out and then someone from the passenger seat. The driver's-side door of the police car opened, and a uniformed officer emerged. Two people stepped from the SUV, and the person who'd been in the car's passenger seat approached them while carrying a briefcase. They all shook hands, and the briefcase was passed to one of the people from the SUV. The recipient opened the rear door of the SUV and put the briefcase inside.

"I wonder what's in it," Dodge said.

Mackie said, "I bet it's tweasuh."

"What kind of treasure?" Olivia asked.

"Diamonds!"

"Probably boring business stuff," Dodge said.

The figures stood by the open door talking, and then one closed it and pointed at the SUV. The headlights blinked as it locked. The police officer shook hands with one of the people, got in his car, and drove out of the parking lot and turned right as the other four started walking toward a single-wide trailer on the far side of the lot.

"What is that pwace, anyway?" Mackie asked.

Olivia read the sign out front, "Fu-Future Site of San Marco Center for the Per-Per-forming Arts."

They watched until the four went into the trailer.

"We got time for one more nick." Grinning, Dodge gave Mackie a playful jab with his elbow. "Whaddya say we show Olive how to do a proper smash and grab?"

Mackie's face lit up. "You bet!"

"But there was a policeman there," Olivia said.

"He's gone now."

They crossed the street and headed for the construction site. Once there, they saw it was a dirt lot. Two cement mixers were on one side along with a tall crane, an earth mover, and the trailer with a sign on the door that said Office. The work that had been done so far amounted to placing supports and a poured concrete shell of the first floor.

"This way," Dodge said softly and led them along the tree line to the right, which was the closest cover to the SUV and car and the farthest from the trailer.

There was one streetlight casting its circle of light fairly close, so they ducked under the trees until they were well past it. Dodge stopped when the vehicles were only twenty feet away and between them and the trailer.

Mackie whispered, "What do you think, Dodge?"

Dodge stepped from the vehicle and looked to the distant trailer. Then he stepped close and tried to open the passenger-side back door, but it was locked. "Easy peasy."

"Wemon squeezy," Mackie added.

"What if it's got an alarm?" Olivia asked.

"It's a top-of-the-line Mercedes. You can bet there's an alarm." Dodge pulled the hammer from his jacket. "It's why this nick is called a smash and grab. Should call it a smash and grab and run. See, Olive, that trailer is pretty far. It'll take 'em a few seconds to react when they hear the alarm. As much as ten seconds or more. Still, even if they start running as soon as they hear the alarm, we'll be long gone by the time they get here. I'll smash the window and reach in to unlock it. Olivia, you open the door. Mackie, get the briefcase and pass it to me." He pointed into the woods. "We'll run at an angle through the trees to the road. We signal Mr. Teacher and get out of here."

Mackie stood, eyes alight. "Weady, Fweddy?"

"Let's go, Joe." Dodge grabbed Mackie's arm and moved him to the left and then nodded for Olivia to stand to his right. Lifting the hammer, he slammed it hard against the window, the safety glass falling in thousands of little pieces. The first thing through Olivia's mind was how quiet the breaking glass had been, and then the alarm started in a loud, whistling scream. As soon as Dodge reached into the SUV, Olivia grabbed the door handle, opened it, and Mackie dove in. Her adrenaline pumping, Olivia stared wide-eyed, taking a step back as she waited for Mackie to emerge. She took another backward step and another until she was past the front of the SUV. Movement caught her attention, and she saw two men running for them. They were way closer than they should have been. She realized that they had already left the trailer before Dodge swung the hammer, that they must have been returning to the vehicles when the alarm started to shriek.

"They're almost here!" Olivia screamed.

"What?" Dodge asked.

"They were already close!"

"Get out of there, Mackie!" Dodge shouted.

A second later, the briefcase fell from the door.

Dodge grabbed it and shouted at Olivia, "Run!"

She started in the direction of the trees. Dodge was behind her, and she turned to see Mackie jump from the door. She focused on the woods and hoped that Tink was right and that her fairy wings would help her run faster. Her heart pounded in exertion and fear.

"Get 'em!" someone shouted.

And then Olivia was in the trees.

"Wait," Dodge shouted, and she stopped and turned. He shoved the briefcase into her hands. "Get out to Mr. Teacher. Tell him we need help."

Olivia stared with terrified eyes. "What?"

"Something's wrong. Mackie's still back there. Go get Mr. Teacher." Dodge turned and ran back through the trees.

Olivia could just hear someone shout, "Call Trask and tell him to get his ass back here."

Olivia turned and headed deeper into the trees and hopefully toward the road. The briefcase had enough weight that she carried it with both hands. It got tangled in her legs once, and she fell. Tree limbs ripped the fairy wings from her back. Twice, the briefcase got snagged in brush, and she had to yank it free. One moment, she was in the dark in the trees, and a second later, she was standing on blacktop, a streetlight glowing in the distance. Between her and the light was Mr. Teacher's car. She put down the briefcase and waved her arms. The VW coughed to life, and the headlights switched on.

The car stopped next to her, and Olivia pushed the briefcase through the open window onto the floorboard. "I think Mackie got caught. Dodge went back for him."

"Damn it!" He leaned over and opened the passenger door. "Get in!"

She got in the seat next to him. He leaned so that his face was inches from hers. "What happened?"

She cried as she quickly told him.

"Well, this is a proper cock-up," Mr. Teacher muttered. "One of you should have had eyes on the trailer the whole time."

An engine roared, and Mr. Teacher cut off his headlights. Down the road, the car flew from the parking lot and turned right. A second later, the SUV sped out, turned left, and raced past them. Olivia turned in the seat, hoping to somehow catch a glimpse of Mackie or Dodge.

"I'm guessing they're in the SUV. Hold on to something," Mr. Teacher ordered, and she grabbed the armrest.

He pulled a U-turn, and the right-side wheels bumped over the curb. He quickly ran through the gears, but the SUV was steadily gaining distance.

"Come on, you piece of junk, go. Go, go, go, go."

Like a mantra, Olivia joined in. "Go, go, go, go."

The SUV slowed when it got to San Marco. A police car pulled in behind it, and Olivia repeated what she'd already told Mr. Teacher about a policeman being in the construction site parking lot. Mr. Teacher cut the speed of the VW, dropped back, and followed the SUV and police car all the way out to the Mount and Penny Road.

Chapter 7

Hiding in the brush, Olivia and Mr. Teacher watched one of the people from the SUV talking to the policeman as they stood atop an overpass. Both were illuminated by the headlights of the SUV.

"You were hired to provide security," one of them said, loud enough for Olivia to hear.

The cop gripped his belt with both hands. "You said you wanted me there for the transfer. The transfer was made, and I left. I did what you paid me for."

"Chicago is not going to be happy."

The policeman looked away, removed his hat, and wiped at his forehead with the back of his hand. He put the hat back on. "We'll get it back."

"Damn right we will. Go get the little one."

The policeman walked through the beam of the headlights to the side of the SUV, where a big man in a suit held Dodge and Mackie by the necks of their jackets. The policeman grabbed Mackie by his upper arm and dragged him into the headlight illumination.

"They're monsters, aren't they?" Olivia asked in a whisper.

Mr. Teacher put a finger to his lips and nodded. He leaned close and spoke softly in her ear. "Wait here." In the next second, he was gone.

As Olivia watched, her lips moved silently, mouthing the word *monster, monster, monster.*

This monster dragged Mackie to the side of the overpass and sat him on top of a railing above the drop. Mackie and the monster were opposites. As usual, Mackie was filthy. The monster, however, was clean and wearing clothes that Olivia guessed were expensive. Olivia strained to hear what they were saying.

"Where is it, kid?" The monster spoke calmly. "Come on, you can tell me."

Scared, Mackie shook his head.

The policeman approached and stepped close to him. "Son, I'm a policeman. I'm here to help. You can tell me. Where is it?"

Mackie shook his head again. The monster slapped him, and Olivia gasped. Tears started down Mackie's cheeks, yet his expression showed anger. The monster let loose with a backhand that started a nosebleed.

"Hey, now," the policeman said. The monster glared at him, and the cop took a couple of steps back.

Mackie wiped at his face. He glanced at the blood on his fingers before gripping the railing again.

From her perspective, Olivia would have been able to see much of the drop below the overpass if it wasn't night. Right now, though, it looked as if Mackie was perched over a black sea.

A train whistle blew in the distance, sounding like a lonely night bird.

The monster spoke in a friendly, matter-of-fact tone. "Look, kid. You and your friends stole something from that SUV tonight. Right?" The monster motioned toward the vehicle and then began brushing Mackie's shoulders as if clearing away dandruff. "In fact, this police officer could arrest you right now. But he's not going to because we're going to work this out ourselves. What you took is not mine. It belongs to some associates." The monster looked one way and then the other and got close as if to share a secret. "I'll be honest with you. These associates are very dangerous men, which is why I'll do whatever it takes to get it back."

The train whistle, louder now, blew again.

"In fact, you should consider us your best friends right now, me"—the monster held out a hand to the policeman—"and Officer

Friendly. You help us get it back, and we'll work it out with those dangerous men, tell them it was all just a big mistake, and they won't hunt you down and hurt you or your friends." The monster studied the child while smiling. "Or worse."

Olivia wanted to believe what the monster was telling her friend, believe that the monster and the policeman would let Mackie and Dodge go.

The monster winked and appeared all buddy-buddy. "At least tell me your name."

His voice was hoarse, but he managed, "Mackie."

The monster nodded toward the SUV. "And him? What's your friend's name?"

"Dodge."

"Dodge? Like the car?"

"No. Not wike the cah. When someone's aftah him, he's good at dodging them."

The monster laughed. "Dodge didn't dodge us though, did he?"

Mackie blushed and looked down. "That's 'cause he came back foh me."

The monster patted Mackie's cheek. "So, whaddya say, Mackie? Tell me where I can find that other friend of yours, the little black girl, and we'll get our briefcase, and everybody will get out of this without getting hurt."

Mackie stared into the monster's eyes. Olivia wondered if he saw lies mixed with bad. By now, Olivia could hear the clickety-clack of steel wheels. The train was getting closer.

The monster scowled and pulled out a pistol, pressing it under Mackie's chin, forcing his head back. The policeman stepped forward, a hand out, but a glance from the monster stopped him.

Turning to Mackie, the monster growled like a wild animal. "Tell me where it is."

Though there was a gun at his throat, Mackie did the strangest thing. He laughed.

No, Mackie. Don't make the monster mad.

Mackie spoke without a trace of fear in his voice. "You awen't gonna shoot a kid."

The monster looked surprised, finally saying, "Yeah, Mackie, you're right. It was a bluff."

Olivia grinned. Mackie was so brave to laugh with a gun under his chin. He was the bravest kid in all the world.

The ground started to shake as the train rounded a distant curve. The locomotive's headlight lit up the area beneath Mackie, illuminating a train track twenty feet below.

The train was loud, but Olivia could still hear as the monster turned toward the SUV and called to the big man, "Make sure that one is paying attention."

The train was seconds from passing underneath them.

Releasing Mackie, the monster put away the gun, placed both hands on Mackie's chest, and shoved him like a bully trying to provoke a fight. Mackie launched backward in the air, his eyes wide and mouth open.

"No!" the policeman yelled and grabbed at the empty space that had been occupied by Mackie a second earlier.

The boy's feet trailed behind him as his arms windmilled. Arcing back, he was lit by the train's headlight, a single fiery eye of a giant, angry, stampeding bull. Olivia looked away too late. She saw the locomotive strike her friend.

"What did you do?" the policeman asked.

"Shut up," the monster said. "Go get the other one."

No, no, no. Not Dodge too.

A hand clamped over Olivia's mouth. Close to her ear, Mr. Teacher whispered, "We have to go now."

He released her, and she turned to see Mr. Teacher and Dodge start through the overgrowth, away from the site of Mackie's murder. She looked back at the policeman, who stepped past the headlights and opened one of the SUV's doors, which turned on the interior light. It illuminated the big man lying on the ground, eyes closed.

The policeman said, "Well, shit."

Olivia turned and crept silently after Mr. Teacher and Dodge.

"**F**uck! Fuck! Fuck!"

Everyone stared in stunned surprise as Mr. Teacher stormed in, trailed by Olivia and Dodge, who were both in tears. Mr. Teacher flung the briefcase across the room, just missing Geronimo. He threw his hat to the ground, spun, and grabbed Dodge by his jacket lapels, pulling him up so that he stood on tiptoes. Face twisted with rage, Mr. Teacher shouted, "Why didn't you look after him? Why did you risk something so stupid?"

Dodge's mouth gaped, and twin rivulets of tears ran down his cheeks. Mr. Teacher's expression softened, and he pulled Dodge into a fierce hug. "I'm sorry. I'm sorry. I'm sorry," Mr. Teacher repeated, and he, too, openly cried.

Some of the small ones started crying as well.

Though she whispered, Nancy's voice carried through the room. "Where's Mackie?"

Mr. Teacher collapsed into the brick chair. He quietly relayed what had happened. When he was done, everyone cried, even Tarzan.

Mr. Teacher jumped up and paced around Thieves Kitchen, stepping outside now and then, only to return to pace more. Every time he passed by the briefcase, he stopped to stare down at it.

"Attention!" he called. Every face turned his way. "We'll need security. Tarzan, come up with a schedule. The older ones shall take turns. Position them in the woods where the roads intersect." He paced the other way. "If you are on watch and see someone, anyone at all, approaching, signal like this." Mr. Teacher placed two fingers in his mouth and whistled three times with long blasts. Mr. Teacher went from kid to kid, looking them in the eyes. "If you hear that, run away from Thieves Kitchen as fast as you can. You older kids help the smaller ones."

"Run where?" Dodge asked.

Pacing again, Mr. Teacher said, "We'll meet up under the San Marco Pier."

At the briefcase, he stopped and picked it up, the firelight producing an oversize shadow of him on the wall.

"Our sweet little Mackie died because of this." Mr. Teacher held up the briefcase. He tried to open it. "Locked. Lend me your hammer, Dodge."

Mr. Teacher placed the case on a stack of bricks by the fire and rained down angry blows. Setting down the hammer, he lifted the lid to expose stacks of banded one-hundred-dollar bills filling the case. Cries of surprise echoed throughout the room, and everybody gathered round the briefcase. Some of the children reached to touch the money as if to see if it was real.

Olivia turned away. The money didn't mean anything to her. She only cared about Mackie.

Chapter 8

Saturday Night

I would rather have been in the audience than onstage in front of a hundred or so people clad in tuxedos and gowns. No one would call me a shy person. I'm far from it. The discomfort came from the fact that the woman speaking into the microphone on the ballroom dais in the Garrido Art Museum was heaping too much praise on me. I looked down at Nick, who stood near the stage, and I could tell he was enjoying this. I shot him a dirty look, which made him laugh out loud.

Marjorie Katherine Hamilton, the woman who'd hired me to find *Cold Green Spring* for the exhibit we were celebrating with tonight's grand opening, continued her one-person Lise Norwood fan club routine. "I, like many of you, followed the sordid case of Michelangelo. Not the great artist but the serial killer who cast a reign of terror over San Marco last year. So when I found I was in need of a private investigator, I immediately thought of that plucky Lise Norwood and how she single-handedly ended Michelangelo's killing spree."

If I wasn't in such a visible spot, I would have done a facepalm. Plucky was bad enough, but giving me sole credit without mentioning the San Marco PD was not good. A quick glance at Detective Baker demonstrated that. He looked like a volcano that was seconds from erupting.

"And it gives me great pleasure that Lise has once again brought a case to a successful conclusion. That being the case of the missing

Frieseke. Without which our exhibition, *Florida, Masters in Passing,* would have been incomplete."

Full of piss and vinegar, Marjorie had enough confidence for a dozen CEOs. If she proclaimed you a rock star, then by God, there was nothing to do but strap on the Stratocaster and crank the amplifier to ten. So I stood there trying to look humble as she declared me the finest sleuth this side of Sherlock Holmes. Awkward, yes, but the slightest grin played on my lips as I thought how her endorsement would throw good business my way.

"Ladies and gentlemen, please welcome investigator, private eye, sleuth, gumshoe Lise Norwood," Mrs. Hamilton said and then turned to me, applauding.

I had a split second of panic that I'm sure showed on my face, but I quickly got it under control. Not only had she not told me I would be publicly thanked, she hadn't informed me that I would be giving a speech. As I headed toward the podium, I scrabbled for what to say.

I got to the podium and demonstrated my fantastic oratory skills. "Okay, then." *Skreeee.* Oh great. The obligatory feedback. I backed off the microphone and blathered some more. "Marjorie said... she said... and I want to..." Hundreds of eyes stared up at me, and I was babbling like an idiot. "Well, that is to say... maybe I... what I mean is..." I was going to say something, but what? I swallowed, and just to get the ball rolling, I started talking. "Marjorie... uh... was kind enough to hire me to try and find Frieseke's *Cold Green Spring.*" An idea hit me. I envisioned a lightbulb clicking on over my head. I would just tell them about the case. And I did. The crowd loved it. I paused when Pete entered the story, so I could introduce him.

"Where are you, Pete?"

He whistled from one of the bars, where he had his arm around his wife. He held up his other hand to show a napkin-wrapped bottle of beer. I had told him it was a black-tie affair, so he wore one of those black T-shirts made to look like a tuxedo. Kudos to him for wearing black jeans, and it looked like he'd polished his steel-toed boots.

"That's Pete. He wasn't sure he could make it until I told him it was an open bar." The crowd laughed at that. "That's Pete's wife of twenty-six years, Wicked Wendy."

She called up to me, "Wicked Wendy was way back in my youth. These days, Wendy will do." She was stunning in her black skirt and blouse.

I got a great reaction, lots of gasps, and sounds of disbelief when I told the crowd what Wendy had paid for the painting at the Ormond Beach estate sale.

"While I thank Marjorie for crediting Annalise Norwood Investigations for bringing *Cold Green Spring* to the Garrido Museum, I thank the real heroes in our story"—I held out my hand to the bar—"Pete and Wendy!"

The crowd broke into enthusiastic applause.

Once the obligatory speeches were done, a band started playing and guests started milling. I approached Marjorie and told her, "Next time, let me know in advance if I have to give a speech."

Marjorie gave me a mischievous grin. "I knew you wouldn't let me down. That was so amusing." She took my arm and leaned close to speak confidentially. "I want to introduce you to someone who'd like to hire you."

"Somebody here?" I asked.

"Yes. His name is Edward Burke, a delightful gentleman. He's a businessman."

"I look forward to meeting him."

"I'll go hunt him down." Marjorie disappeared into the crowd.

Wandering the ballroom, I took in the Christmas décor. The ballroom had been festooned in a Victorian Christmas theme with a half-dozen tall trees dusted in white and decorated with antique ornaments. Wreaths and ribbons were everywhere, while strands of holly and ivy ringed doorways and windows. Dangling sprigs of mistletoe inspired lots of casual smooching, which put me on the lookout for Nick so we could get in on the action. Instead of Nick, I saw Baker and his wife in the buffet line, so I headed in the opposite direction. Finally, I spotted my date, looking sexy as hell. Sexy because he handed me a short glass of bourbon with simple syrup, bitters, cherry, orange peel, and one big-ass ice cube.

Nick bowed as I took it. "Your old-fashioned."

"No, you're old-fashioned." He didn't laugh, pretending he didn't get the joke. Sighing, I gave Nick a peck on the lips because, well, he brought me bourbon. It was my third and—I vowed—final for the evening. Then I took his hand, led him under the mistletoe, and gave him a proper kiss.

The band ended a song and then kicked in with a few bars of "Hark the Herald Angels Sing" before slipping into a lively Bruno Mars tune. The members of the nine-piece band were bedecked in white tuxedos, and they had a killer horn section.

Nick emptied his glass and placed it on the tray of a passing wait-ress. He started doing a funky dance. I so wanted to tease him, but darn it, he danced well.

"Care to cut the rug?" he asked.

"Maybe later." I held up my nearly full glass. "I want to spend quality time with this. You go ahead, and I'll catch up later."

"Your loss," he said and headed for the dance floor.

I wandered and sipped my old-fashioned, taking in the artwork as well as the attendees. After one last pleasurable sip, only the cherry was left underneath the dwindling ice cube. I tried to pick it out, but it kept slipping away from my finger.

Getting frustrated, I did my Margaret Hamilton impersonation. "I'll get you, my pretty, and your little stem too." I brought the glass up to eye level and put in two more fingers to assist the first. It worked, and I cornered the cherry.

"Annalise Norwood?" I looked from my glass to find a man who rivaled Hugh Jackman in the handsome department. He spoke in a deep, soothing voice, "My name is Edward Burke." He held out a hand.

I realized my fingers were still in the glass. Without breaking eye contact, I took them out, wiped them on my gown, and shook his hand. It wasn't calloused, nor was it smooth. His hand was firm, warm, and dry. He released me, took the glass from my other hand, plucked the cherry from it, and handed the glass to a passing waiter.

"Did Marjorie tell you I was hoping to speak with you?"

"Yes, she did."

He handed me the cherry. "Pleased to meet you, Lise." He had pale-blue eyes, and his six-foot-four frame was adorned in a black tuxedo, tailored to best show off two hundred pounds of firm muscle. I wasn't sure if I was appraising him with my private investigator's keen sense of observation or because he was smokin' hot.

"Ah, good. You two have met." Marjorie moved to join us.

"We were just making introductions," Edward said.

"Allow me to make it official," Marjorie said. "Lise Norwood, private investigator, meet Edward Burke of Burke Industries."

"Burke Industries?" I looked at Marjorie. "You said he was a businessman. You didn't say he owned the company."

"Companies, Lise. Plural. You could say that Edward's business is owning businesses," Marjorie said.

"How many do you own?" I asked.

"Enough that I'd be bragging if I told you."

"Edward is also CEO," Marjorie said. "He's very active in all of his businesses."

"So it pays well?" I meant it as a joke, but it sounded tacky.

Still, Edward laughed.

I noticed a woman standing nearby. She stood out because she was athletic, as in the hard-core-bodybuilder, mixed-martial-arts type of athletic. As in she could take the gold in an Olympic freestyle ass-kicking competition.

Seeing who had my attention, Edward said, "This is my head of security, Eileen Warrick."

Broad in the shoulders, thick in the neck, and hair cut short, she wore a black suit and had huge hands.

"Pleased to meet you too," I said.

She nodded once.

Curious, I asked, "Is there a reason you need security at the Garrido?"

"She's serving as my bodyguard." He held up a hand. "Before you ask why, it's more of a precautionary thing."

"Okay."

Marjorie said, "Edward is from Chicago but is currently residing in San Marco as one of his construction companies is building the new San Marco Performing Arts Center."

"I've been reading about that. It's a wonderful thing for the community."

Edward glanced past me and beckoned to someone. I turned to see a woman approaching and wondered if it was his wife. She was tall and thin, beautifully attired in a peach gown and wearing dangling silver earrings. She peered at us through thick glasses. Oddly, her glasses added to her attractiveness. Her blond hair tumbled in curled locks to her shoulders.

"Lise, let me introduce you to Burke Industries' chief financial officer, Patricia Meyers."

"Hi." I held out my hand and realized I still held the cherry from my old-fashioned. I popped it into my mouth and took Meyers's hand. She shook vigorously.

"Call me Trish. I'm so happy to meet you." With a wide smile, she spoke in a rush. "I've heard wonderful things about you. That's crazy about *Cold Green Spring*. I love San Marco and am so happy to spend winter here instead of in Chicago. I mean, the weather is so mild."

I started to tell her that we were having an unseasonably warm winter, but she'd already taken off in a new direction.

"I hope we can become friends, Lise," she said. "I'd love for you to show me the sights. Maybe you could introduce me to some interesting locals. We think your knowledge of art could be of great benefit."

When she finally stopped, I said, "Um, yeah."

Though I sounded like an idiot, Edward seemed not to notice. "Along those lines," he said, "we'd like to discuss something with you soon."

"And I'm so excited about it," Trish said. "If you'll excuse me?" Trish made her way into the crowd.

Edward chuckled. "What do you think of Trish?"

"Ummm... Exuberant?"

"Oh yeah. Bubbly personality," Edward said. "She's like that when she meets someone who's on our radar. As unique as she is, her financial acumen is unrivaled by anyone I've ever met. I like to think I have a good head for finance, but Trish is head and shoulders above me. And, as you just witnessed, she approaches everything with a full-speed-ahead attitude." He looked like an idea had just occurred to him. "I hope she didn't come across as annoying."

"What? No. I like her." I spun my hands counterclockwise around each other. "Can we back up a little bit? You said 'someone who's on our radar.' What'd you mean by that?"

"I'd like to hire you, but here's not the place to discuss it. Can I stop by your office?"

"Sure. Monday?"

"Monday is fine. Do you have a business card?"

I looked down at what I was wearing. "I'd gladly give you one, but apparently, the designer of this gown didn't think pockets were important."

"I suppose the sole purpose of a gown is to highlight a woman's beauty," Edward said. He leaned a couple inches closer. "And in your case, it works."

I felt a blush heating my cheeks. "Thanks."

Marjorie said, "I can give you Lise's contact information, Edward."

"Excellent." He took my hand in both of his. "A pleasure, Lise."

"A pleasure."

"Don't forget. Monday."

"Monday," I echoed.

I stared after him as he and Marjorie walked away.

A moment later, a hand gripped my shoulder none too gently. "Hi there, Norwood."

I turned around to see Baker scrutinizing me. His wife, Delores, stood next to him, watching with both a smile and a look of concern.

"I got a bone to pick with you," Baker said.

Delores swatted his arm. "Be nice."

Baker turned to watch Burke work his way through the crowd. "You're gonna make your boyfriend jealous."

"Nick and I don't do jealousy."

"Uh huh."

"That man is movie-star handsome and then some," Delores said.

"Hey, I'm right here," Baker said. "Who is he?"

"Edward Burke, owner and CEO of Burke Industries. A possible client. He's in charge of building the new San Marco Performing Arts Center," I informed them.

Baker took in that knowledge and then narrowed his eyes. "But he isn't why I tracked you down."

"Honey, go easy on her."

I gave him an expression that could go into an illustrated dictionary under the word *remorse*. "Sorry about Marjorie's 'single-handedly ended Michelangelo's killing spree' thing."

"Oh? Because I didn't hear you say anything about it when you were up at the microphone."

"I'm really sorry."

"Uh-huh." Baker glared a few seconds more and strode off.

"Sorry, Lise. You know how he gets," Delores said and went after her husband.

Chapter 9

I went looking for Nick so we could leave, but I was intercepted by Pete and Wendy.

Pete gave me a hug, his beard tickling my neck. "Hey, Lise. Thanks for the invite. Food's good, and the booze is great."

"Meaning free," Wendy said.

"Speaking of... be right back." Pete vanished into the crowd.

"Sorry I was such a hard-ass about lending my painting to the museum," Wendy said.

"Cool to see it here, isn't it?" I gestured in the direction of the room that held the three Frieseke pieces.

"Definitely. I can't believe I had it in that plastic frame. It really goes great with that frame they put around it." The museum had put the painting in a frame made from a thick piece of driftwood that had been sanded and stained. "And it's so cool knowing the history of it. Hard to believe a masterpiece has been taking up space behind the bar all these years."

"Have you decided what you'll do with it after the exhibition?"

"I'm going to sell it."

I raised my eyebrows in surprise.

Wendy looked around and stepped closer to me. "I have a secret, Lise. Please keep it to yourself."

"Of course."

"I have something in common with a famous baseball player."

"Huh?"

"Lou Gehrig."

"Oh? Oh! Oh, Wendy, I'm so sorry. How long have you known?"

"Well, an ALS diagnosis is a tricky thing. It's mainly ruling out other diseases, and that's what my doctor's been doing these past several months. We've known it's probably ALS, but he didn't make the diagnosis official until my last appointment. That was the day I met you. That's why I was in such a shitty mood that night."

"And Pete doesn't know?"

"Nah. You know those five stages of grief?"

"Yeah."

"Pete will work through them, but he'll get hung up on that anger part. He'll brood a lot and get into fights."

"You've got to tell him sometime."

"I know. But I have an idea. If I sell the painting, I can take Pete on a trip somewhere. One last big hurrah while I can still function. Something to make memories."

"That sounds wonderful."

Wendy smiled at the prospect. "Maybe tour Europe or Japan or something. After that, I'll tell him." She turned to look at her husband, waiting by the bar. "I met him thirty years ago when he was fresh out of the marines. He had a buzz cut and a baby face. I thought we'd have a fling, and that would be that. Now look at us."

"How long does your doctor think... you know?"

"Probably not long. Stephen Hawking was a rarity. They say two to five years from diagnosis. I'm only telling you because I want you to help me sell the painting. I'll pay you whatever you charge for your services."

"Are you kidding? My services are on the house for lending us *Cold Green Spring.*"

Pete approached holding three whiskey glasses. "Can you believe they don't have shot glasses at this shindig?" Pete asked, handing us both a glass. "They have good booze, though. This is Blanton's. Cheers."

I'd promised myself that my final alcohol intake for the night would be that last old-fashioned, but I didn't want to be rude... and it was Blanton's. We raised our glasses, clinked them, and drained them.

I handed the glass back to Pete and told Wendy, "Next time you're in town, call me and we'll do lunch." My code for *we'll get the ball rolling on getting your painting to auction.*

I found Nick on the dance floor, shaking his money maker. I pulled him away from his dance partner, a woman twice his age. He was breathing hard and had a light sheen of sweat.

"How about we get out of here?" I said.

"Can we hit the buffet first? I danced off dinner."

On the way there, we bumped into Trish, and I introduced her to Nick. Then we ran into Adolph Hurst, a friend and local gallery owner who joined us at the buffet table and put a half dozen steamed Mayport shrimp and a spoonful of cocktail sauce on a plate. Looking for a place to sit, I led them to a table where Baker sat and nursed a beer.

"How come someone as charming as you is sitting all alone?" I asked.

"Shut up, Norwood."

"See? Charm in abundance."

He pushed out a chair with his foot. "Have a seat."

"Where's Delores?" I asked.

"Socializing."

I found myself seated with three of my favorite men, all of whom were connected to the Michelangelo case. Nick had been my boyfriend not once but twice. He took over as the dean of the Department of Art and Art History at San Marco University when his mentor, Gabe Turner, killed himself. Gabe also turned out to be the misogynistic serial killer in question. I worked as a consultant with the San Marco PD on that case, identifying the Michelangelo masterworks Turner was copying when he left his victims posed. That was how I met Baker, half of the homicide team of Baker and Ortega. Samuel Ortega was murdered by Michelangelo. And my friend and gallery owner, Adolph Hurst, had helped me solve another case going on at that same time, though he'd come to my attention as a suspect in the Michelangelo case.

"So, what's occupying your time, Baker?" I asked.

"Homicide. It's always homicide."

"Is there that much violent death in San Marco?" a woman's voice asked, and I looked to see Marjorie standing behind me.

Baker stood and shrugged. "I exaggerated when I said 'always homicide.' San Marco isn't big enough for the police to have an exclusive homicide division. Not enough budget and not enough homicides. When there aren't any murders to look into, I lend myself to robbery or vice. As of now, I'm the only homicide detective." He pulled out a chair. "Have a seat, Mrs. Hamilton."

"I wish I could, but as I'm considered one of the hosts, I have to be the social butterfly." She held up a finger at a passing waiter and took a flute of champagne from his tray. "But I will stay long enough to recharge myself." She took a sip and then said to Baker, "I don't know how you do it, dealing with violent crimes so much."

Baker nodded. "This job can break your heart. Spent the day working a tragic case. Poor kid hit by a train."

"Oh no, how terrible." Marjorie's voice took on a tremulous note. She had a soft spot for kids and even headed up the charity Safe Homes for Children, which worked with orphaned kids or kids from homeless and low-income families. "Since you're working on it, does that mean it was murder?"

Baker shrugged. "A lot of what I do is try to figure out if a death is a homicide to begin with. Ruling out natural causes means there are three possibilities. Accident—or what we call death by misadventure—homicide, or suicide. Right now, I'm leaning towards a stupid, horrible, needless accident."

"That poor boy," Marjorie said. "His family must be devastated."

"If they knew. Right now, he's unidentified, so no notification." Baker took a swig from his beer bottle. "We're lucky because normally someone hit by a freight train sustains substantial damage. However, we think he was struck at a glancing angle, and while he was killed instantly, his body was intact. His face, though damaged, is in good enough condition to identify."

"Dear God," Marjorie muttered.

"I'm sorry. I'm going into too much gruesome detail. What I'm getting at is that we've been showing his picture around, and no one knows him. No one's called to report a missing child."

Marjorie moved closer to Baker. "Promise me you won't give up. Promise you'll find out who he is and, if it was a homicide, who's responsible."

Baker started to respond, but I jumped in. "I can speak from experience that Baker will put his all into it. He's a curmudgeon, but he's still one of the good guys."

"Thanks? I think," Baker said.

Marjorie put down her champagne and waggled a finger at us. "I have a good idea. Why don't you hire Lise to help you learn who the boy is?"

Baker had been drinking from his beer when she said this, and he sputtered, nearly spraying beer. He carefully put the bottle down and gave Marjorie a smile that did not show in his eyes. "Mrs. Hamilton, I appreciate your suggestion, but the police department doesn't hire private investigators."

"But you did hire her for the Michelangelo case, right?"

It was my nature to prod a sleeping bear, so I said, "Yeah. What about that?"

Baker flashed me his homicide detective glower of doom and then turned to Marjorie with a forced smile. "Mrs. Hamilton, we hired Lise as a consultant because of her art knowledge, not because she was a private investigator. The fact that she poked her nose into the investigation nearly got her PI license revoked."

"Well, I think she would do wonderfully and that you should consider it."

Baker shook Marjorie's hand. "I will take that under advisement. Now, if you will excuse me, I need to find my wife."

I stood and told Baker, "I'll help you look." I then got Nick's attention, giving a subtle nod to the door.

Halfway across the room, I took Baker's arm. "You know I had nothing to do with what she said just now or on the dais."

"Yeah, yeah, I know. But first, she gives you full credit on Michelangelo, and then"—he made quote fingers—"'why don't you hire Lise to find out who the boy is?'" He shook his head. "When we screw up, everybody is quick to point fingers, but when we do good, no one gives us credit."

I stopped him. "I do. You're good. San Marco is lucky to have you."

Baker sighed. "Thanks, Norwood. And for what it's worth, San Marco is lucky to have you too." I started to get a little verklempt and had an urge to hug Baker, an urge he quickly squashed. "But I guarantee you there's no way in hell that you'll ever work another San Marco PD case."

"Hey now. We did work well together with the Michelangelo case, though it was tumultuous at times."

"Tumultuous." He chuckled. "Well, we'll be teaming up soon enough come March."

My cousin had been murdered in a Panama City park back when I was in college, and the crime was never solved. Baker had agreed to help me look into it. I attributed his agreement to the fact that he had been in the hospital at the time and under the influence of pain medication. Still, he had two weeks of vacation coming up in March. He would spend five days with me, poking around in Panama City, and the rest of the time on vacation with his family in Orlando at the house of mouse.

"And thanks in advance for that," I said.

"I gotta call in to one of the detectives who worked your cousin's case. I'll get back to you after I talk to him."

"There's Delores." I pointed at a group of women looking up at a portrait of a Black conquistador.

"Time to blow this popsicle stand," Baker said and left.

Nick walked up. "Ready to slip out?"

"Like a couple of teenagers from a school dance for some necking and heavy petting."

Nick wiggled his eyebrows. "Your place?"

I started to agree, but I felt really good and ready to face my demons that lurked in the shadows at Nick's house. It was there that I'd witnessed and experienced terrible things and was why we almost always stayed at my place. Feeling strong and bold, I took Nick's arm. "Let's stay at your house tonight."

Chapter 10

We talked about the evening as Nick drove to his house. He did an exaggerated impression of how I looked when I realized I would have to give a speech, eyes and mouth wide open in horror. I swatted his arm, and we laughed. As we entered his neighborhood, however, I grew quiet. When he slowed for his house, my stomach tightened. Nick's house had once been a sanctuary for me, but it had turned into reminders of a bloody night that had taken place almost a year ago. I leaned my head against the passenger window as we pulled into the driveway, and like always, I noted the spot where an FBI agent named Kyle Teague had been murdered while assigned to protect me.

Nick parked and, knowing I was apprehensive, got out, came around the car and opened my door. He took my hand and helped me out. "We can still go stay at your place."

"Nah, I'm hunky-dory." I tried to sound like all was right with the world.

For all my bravado, my eyes were drawn to the wall near the bottom of the staircase when we stepped into the foyer. That was where Gabe Turner, one-time dean of the art history department at San Marco University, had blown his brains out, painting the wall with gore as I watched. Though the drywall had been replaced, my memory superimposed the carnage there.

Nick pulled me past the spot and toward the kitchen. "I propose a nightcap dessert of Baileys Irish Cream."

"I second that proposal."

In the kitchen, Nick poured the Baileys into two German schnapps glasses that he'd picked up the previous year in Vienna. He handed one to me and raised the other. "To Lise Norwood, super sleuth and finder of lost art."

We clinked our glasses and drank our Baileys.

Nick refilled the glasses and leaned against the counter. "Did you have fun tonight?"

A simple question, and I meant to give a casual response, but my voice broke when I said, "I did. I really needed that tonight."

Nick took my glass and put it and his on the table and pulled me into a hug. "Thinking about your mother?"

I nodded against his shoulder. "For a moment, after I gave my speech, it hit me how much I wished Mom could have been there." I started crying. "She'd have been so proud of me."

I didn't want him to let go of me, so we stood there a long time. It had been almost three months since my mother died, and it still hurt. Her passing hadn't been a surprise. Years earlier, she had been diagnosed with early-onset Alzheimer's. She'd been in the final stages these last couple of years, and it was brutal. She was well looked after in a home that specialized in dementia and Alzheimer's care, but it was so hard to see someone you've known and loved all your life stop being themselves and stop remembering their lives. One of the nurses once told me that she believed somewhere deep down, they could still hear and understand us. I held on to that philosophy like a drowning woman holds on to a life buoy.

I visited Mom regularly, and we would have one-sided conversations while I brushed her hair or applied nail polish. Whenever Nick and I were going through a rough patch or when I thought my business would fail or if I was just feeling down, I told Mom about it and asked her what she thought. I knew her well enough to know what she would probably say, and though the responses were in my head, I pretended the advice came from her. In reality, I'd been mourning Mom since she moved into Alzheimer's latter stages, but now that she had finally passed, I welcomed the closure. I hoped that didn't make me a bad daughter.

I pulled from Nick's arms, went to wash my face at the kitchen sink, and dried myself with paper towels. Without a word, I took Nick's hand and led him upstairs to his bed, where we made love. For that time, my mind was at peace, taking joy in our bodies coming together.

Afterward, as the glow from our union ebbed, I asked Nick, "Are you asleep?"

"Hmm, no."

"How's the search going?"

Nick was a member of the committee seeking someone to take his old position since he'd been moved up to dean of the Department of Art and Art History.

He yawned and rubbed at his eyes. "Pretty good. We have it narrowed down to three candidates. One is a professor at SCAD." That was the Savannah College of Art and Design. "Another is at the University of South Florida. He's a surfer, and there's not much opportunity for that on the Gulf Coast. I get the feeling he wants to come more for the waves than the job. The third is someone you went to school with."

I rolled onto my side and rested my head on my hand. "Really? Who?"

"Remember Meredith Frazier?"

"Of course I do. She was the little slut you consoled yourself with when I kicked you to the curb."

That got Nick laughing so hard that it triggered a coughing fit. He sat up. "Who kicked who to the curb?"

I first dated Nick when he was a grad student and I was a mere junior. As lovers, we started red-hot, but we quickly deteriorated to petty bickering and stupid drama. When talking about it these days, we figured that we had needed to mature a little bit, which we had, and that was why things were working so well this go-round. That first time didn't even last six months, after which he started going out with Meredith Frazier, who, by the way, wasn't really a slut. Meredith and I had taken classes together, lived in the same dorm, and were friendly, if not friends. I liked her and could see what Nick saw in her.

"I suppose she's married now with eight or nine kids?"

"Nope, she's still single." Nick played innocent as he rolled over and added, "Still has a killer figure."

I threw myself on him and said with a grin, "You do know the hell that shall fall upon you if you hire your old girlfriend."

"Oh yeah, that's definitely being taken into consideration."

"And she's really a possibility?"

"Yeah. There's a lot to be said for being an alumna, but her CV is outstanding. When she left here—"

"After kicking you to the curb," I said.

"In this case, yeah. One night, we're rolling in the clover, and the next morning, she was telling me it wasn't working," Nick said.

"That's what happens when your skills in the sack are sadly lacking."

He hit me with a pillow. "Anyway, she took her graduate studies at Dartmouth."

"Wow."

"She taught three years at Chipola College in the panhandle, but ever since, she's been teaching at Emory University."

"Another wow."

"She loves San Marco and wants to return." He fluffed a pillow and lay back down. "You wouldn't really mind if we brought her on board, would you?"

"Of course not. We don't do jealous, remember?"

He wiggled a bit, settling in, and put his arm over me. "That's right. We don't do"—he yawned—"what you said."

"One more question. It's important."

"Hmm?"

"What are you getting me for Christmas?"

"That's for Santa and me to know and you to find out," he mumbled and soon fell asleep.

I knew the majority of people didn't like sleeping with a snorer. But the timbre of Nick's snores was low and soft. People paid good money for white-noise machines to help them sleep. Nick was my white-noise machine, and his rhythmic purr soon had me catching some Zs.

Unfortunately, sleep wasn't long-lasting. I found myself awake, gasping for air and clutching the sheets. My heart pounded. I forced myself to take deep, calming breaths as Nick snored softly next to me. I lay on my back and stared up, the tin ceiling tiles just visible in the dark. I sighed in surrender. Knowing that sleep wouldn't arrive anytime soon, I got up and tiptoed from the room. I intended to go downstairs for a glass of orange juice—had in fact taken a step in that direction—but I was frozen to the spot by what was behind me.

Not wanting to, I turned to take in the door at the end of the hallway. Thanks to the nightlight, I had a clear view. Nick had affixed a large padlock to it, which wasn't unusual. It had been his home office, and if he brought home a valuable piece of art to study, he would padlock the door. But now it was padlocked for a different reason. I approached like a sleepwalker. The room beckoned me, called me to see where evil had taken place, where I'd almost been butchered. Where Gabe, as Michelangelo, had killed one of his latter victims before taking her corpse to pose at another location. In that same room, he'd bound me and told me how he would cut me into dozens of pieces, only to put me back together as a beautiful and bloody mosaic. It was in that room I'd watched him kill Baker's partner with a knife.

I stood a foot from the door, willing my hand to reach and touch it, but my hand wouldn't respond. The more I stared at the door, the more the wood grain seemed to shift from one dark image to another. My heart pounded, and my breathing was loud.

I sensed a presence behind me and spun to see a figure there. I screamed and shrank back against the door.

"Lise, it's me."

"Nick? What the—" Nick stood back, hands up in a placating manner, wearing only his plaid boxer shorts. I fought the urge to punch him in the arm. "Damn it, Nick. You scared the crap out of me."

"I'm sorry. I didn't mean to." He looked me over. "It's bothering you again, isn't it?"

I shrugged. "I couldn't sleep. And the house... well, you know." I turned and pointed at the locked door. "And that room, it's like it calls to me, wants me to go in."

"You can go in anytime you want. I'll go with you."

I shook my head. "I don't want to go in, but I feel—I don't know—compelled." I could see the helplessness that Nick felt at my animus toward his home. I told him, "Hey, it's not your fault. It's not your house's fault. It's Gabe's fault, the bastard." I stepped into Nick's arms. "I can't help how I feel."

Holding me tight, he said, "I wish I could cut out that room, delete it from the rest of the house." Stepping back, he put hands on either side of my face. "I've told you before. I can sell the house and get another place."

"Don't be silly. But thanks." I kissed his nose. "I can't sleep here. I'd better head home."

We walked back up the hallway, and Nick said, "Don't. Not yet. Come lie down with me for a little bit."

I wanted to tell him it would be futile, but I returned to his room, crawled into bed, and amazingly, I fell asleep.

Chapter 11

Sunday

I woke early and felt pretty good, considering I'd indulged in one drink too many at last night's gala and had that sleepless bout in Nick's bed.

I decided to head home to shower. My plumbing was more reliable. Nick's house had been an old, rundown Florida cracker house when he purchased it years before. He was slowly resurrecting it by himself, but on a scale from one to ten, his home repair skills came in at around negative three. Spending time under his showerhead included a lot of random water flow starts and stops, plus instantaneous and dramatic changes in temperature.

By the time I got home and showered, it was a little after seven. I had on my short terry-cloth robe and was waiting for my coffee maker to work its magic. I was engaged in a mental debate as to whether to attend Mass or not when a car horn honked.

"That's rude," I mumbled, thinking of my sleeping neighbors.

The car honked again, three short bursts and one long. Curious as to who the ingrate was, I secured my robe and went out onto the deck. I had a stilt house a few blocks from the beach, and a dark-gray sedan was sitting half in my driveway and half in the street. Baker stood by the open driver's-side window looking up at me, a to-go coffee cup in one hand. The other reached through the window and pressed the horn again.

"Hey! Knock it off. You're going to get me in trouble with the neighbors."

"Come on, Lise. Time to go."

"Go where?"

Baker made a show of looking at his watch. "Get dressed. I'll give you ten minutes." He got in the car before I could ask more questions.

Eight minutes later, I slid onto his passenger seat and closed the door. Given my limited time, I dressed in jeans, a blue long-sleeve T-shirt, and worn sneakers.

I stared at the homicide detective as he drove. "So, to what do I owe this pleasure?"

Baker snorted. "Pleasure?" He shook his head. "You're getting this *pleasure* because I had the *pleasure* of getting my ass reamed by the lieutenant at about eleven-thirty last night, after he had the *pleasure* of having his ass reamed by the captain. All because the chief got a late-night call from Marjorie Katherine Hamilton."

"Really?"

"Really. All those ass reamings bounced down the chain of command like a steel ball in a pinball machine and passed right between the flippers and into my lap. All because Mrs. Hamilton, of deep pockets and endless connections, felt it would be in the city of San Marco's best interest if *you* were brought on to help *me* work the case of the mystery boy killed by the train."

Trying to deflect the blame, I pointed out, "She was hitting the champagne a little hard last night."

Baker glanced at me in disappointment and shook his head. "This morning, you are undoubtedly the least popular person among the entirety of the San Marco Police Department hierarchy. That's quite a feat."

I swallowed, and it sounded loud in my ears. Hoping to mellow him out, I tapped the Christmas-tree-shaped air freshener hanging from his rearview, setting it to swinging. "Love your holiday décor. It's so piney."

Without taking his eyes from the road, Baker grabbed a couple sheets of paper next to him and dropped them in my lap. "Here. Your 1099 tax form so you can work as an independent contractor for the PD."

"I didn't fill any out last time."

"Yeah. Well, if it's going to be a habit, might as well get it in the files."

I sat a minute before telling Baker, "I don't even want to work it."

"I'll let you tell Mrs. Hamilton that."

We headed west, past the Prince and Panther Golf Course. Buildings and houses started to thin out.

I thought a moment. "Here's what I'll do. We're heading out to go over the scene, right?"

Baker grunted.

"Will Reuben be there?"

Reuben Busby was the PD's crime scene technician. He was nice enough, a little squirrely, and considered himself a top-notch dancer and ladies' man.

"Busby's gonna meet us, let us know his findings. Pretty sure he'll call it an accident."

"Tell you what, we'll look around, hear what Busby has to say. You take me back to my house, and I'll call Marjorie and tell her all about coming out here and how my services aren't necessary."

Baker smiled. "I like it."

"Where we headed specifically?"

"The Mount." At the western edge of San Marco, just before leaving the city limits, was an area that had an elevation of eighty-six feet above sea level. Considering most of San Marco was right around the six-foot mark, the Mount was real nosebleed territory for a Floridian. A number of caution signs advised that logging trucks used the road. We turned from it onto a narrow, badly paved road with tall pines on either side.

"Penny Road," Baker muttered.

Baker's sedan could use some suspension work, that fact driven home by broken pavement and potholes.

"Any closer to learning the boy's identity?" I asked.

"Nah. Coroner says the boy is somewhere between seven and ten. Apparently, he suffered physical abuse."

"Poor kid."

"Yeah, but there's scarring that could aid in identifying him. So I'll be checking pediatricians, hospitals, schools, Department of Children and Families, that kind of thing. And we have initials. Kid was wearing an old military jacket of some kind. His initials were written on the inside of the collar with a marker, F.C.T., so I'm guessing he's a Fred or a Frank."

Around a curve, the crime scene van was parked twenty yards from the overpass bridge. Just past that was a T intersection with the road disappearing into trees on both sides.

"Wonder how the kid got out here," I said. "It's pretty far from town, not a lot around. Did you find a bike?"

"Nope. And we canvassed the few houses out this way. He wasn't from any of them. In fact, Busby thinks the boy might have been a runaway or homeless or both."

"Why's that?"

"How dirty the kid was. His clothes too."

Baker parked behind the van, and we got out. The bridge was barely wide enough that two cars could pass without exchanging paint. I walked out on the fifty-foot-long structure. Underneath, both sides angled sharply down to railroad tracks.

"Hey, Lise! How are you?" Reuben Busby hiked up one side, grabbing at scrub and growth to help him ascend.

"Hey twinkle toes, how's the ballroom dancing coming?" I called to him.

He craned his neck to look at me and grinned. "As romantic as always. You should join me sometime." Reuben was small statured with neatly trimmed dark hair combed straight back. I had to admit that I liked his pencil-thin moustache. As a certified black-and-white film buff, he kind of reminded me of a small William Powell from the Thin Man movies.

"I would if I didn't have a boyfriend who takes offense at me engaging in anything romantic with other men."

Busby got to the top and stood there a moment, brushing his hands together. "I won't tell if you don't."

"Knock it off, Busby," Baker said. "Run us through what you got."

Busby unrolled his sleeves and smiled at me with thousand-watt teeth and then turned serious. "The kid was still falling when the train hit him."

The abrupt shift to this gruesome topic made me groan.

Blood spatter from the collision traveled high and to the right of the train," Busby continued. "If he'd been on the ground, there'd have been more blood on the tracks. Plus, we found the point of impact on the locomotive. It was a little over eight feet up toward the right side." Busby gave his index finger a "follow me" wiggle and led us to the railing on one side of the bridge. "I know we were leaning toward accidental death, but here's something I find curious." He put the edge of each hand on the railing about a foot apart. "That rusty patch there is blood. And it's a handprint. Fingerprints match the boy, and the blood type is the same. That tells us two things. One was that he was bleeding before he was hit by the train."

I wondered if the blood could be from the physical abuse that Baker had mentioned on the ride here.

"Coulda been anything," Baker said. "Kids are always getting a skinned knee or a nosebleed."

Busby nodded. "True, but it could also point to violence."

"What's the second thing?" I asked.

"The way the handprint is facing shows he was sitting on the railing, facing us and not the drop. A suicide would sit on the railing facing the drop before letting go."

"As I still believe, accidental death," Baker said.

"Think about it. We have a child, sitting on the railing, facing in, not out. He hears and feels the train approaching but doesn't hop down to turn around to watch the train approach. A kid, in my estimation, would turn around to watch."

"Maybe that was it," I said. "Maybe he was facing in, heard the train, tried to turn around while staying seated on the railing, lost his balance, and fell."

"I don't think so." Busby held up his index, middle, and ring fingers. "We've been able to match three areas of impact of where the train met the front of the boy's body."

"And?" Baker said.

"Where the impact points line up means that the boy was upside down when struck, while still eight feet in the air, facing the train."

I started to imagine what that might look like and then decided I didn't want that in my head.

"Still don't know what you're getting at," Baker said.

"Upside down but facing the train indicates he was sitting on the railing facing in but fell backward. Was the boy sitting with his back to the approaching train, going against every kid's instinct of turning around to watch it, and then slipped backward? Or did someone have the boy's attention on the bridge and..." Busby used his hands to outline a boy sitting on the railing and then gave the imaginary boy a shove.

"Hmm," Baker intoned.

"Who would want to kill a boy in such a horrible way? And why?" I asked.

"My findings are based on facts, science, and patterns, but supposition and intuition play a role as well," Busby said. "I'm not going to say this was a homicide, but I plan to sign off on it being a suspicious death."

Baker gave him an irritated look but didn't speak.

Busby pointed toward the van. "Since the last rainfall five days ago, a vehicle parked in the middle of the road right before the bridge and in front of where I'm parked. The prints weren't great, but we're still going to see if we can figure out the brand of tire by tread. Judging by the size, it was either a truck, SUV, or van. Between there and here, we found a juvenile shoe print that matched the shoes the boy wore. We also got a print of size-eleven shoes—suggesting an adult male—right next to the boy's print."

"But there's no indication that the adult shoe print and tire marks have anything to do with the kid," Baker said.

"No."

"Baker told me the boy had been abused. If this was a crime, could the two be related?" I asked.

Busby thrust out his bottom lip in thought. "Anything's possible. However, the scars on his body are not recent. The coroner thinks the abuse stopped ten to twelve months ago."

Baker walked the scene again, and then we got back in his car and headed back to my house.

I looked out the passenger window, feeling slightly sickened. I knew it was because I'd trod the ground where a child had died in such an ugly fashion. "Not a lot to go on. At least you've got the boy's initials to work with."

"And photos. The kid's face wasn't as messed up as you'd expect, and the guy we use as a forensic artist is going to do a visual reconstruction with editing software."

I nodded. "It's strange his family hasn't contacted the police yet."

"Yeah, it is."

Earlier, I'd told Baker that I didn't want to work this case. Now, I wasn't so sure. But it wasn't up to me. After pulling into my driveway, Baker held up his now-empty coffee cup. He tried for sad puppy dog eyes, but it came off like feral bulldog.

I snatched the cup. "Back in a minute." Up in my kitchen, I pawed through my basket of coffee pods, found the most potent brew, and re-filled his cup.

When I took it back down and handed it through the driver's-side window, he sniffed it. "Heaven in a cup." He pointed at me and added, "Don't forget to call Hamilton."

"I won't. Promise."

Chapter 12

Monday

I started the day at the gym. I then blew whatever caloric burn I'd achieved by stopping at my favorite food truck, Gordo's, for their Behemoth Breakfast Burrito. Not only filling and spicy, the burrito was sexy in a way that only other burrito lovers could understand.

My office was at the end of a strip mall that contained a convenience store, yoga studio, a good pizza joint, and right next door, a tattoo shop. I was multitasking, handling paperwork, prepping for a divorce court case at which I'd have to testify, and going over some photos I took of Elliot the Slim serving papers on a witness in a low-level embezzlement scam. This was the second set of papers the man had been served, though he claimed he'd not been served the first time, which was why he didn't show up in court. That first process server, Fitz Fitzgerald, was a local private detective who was a fallen member of the San Marco PD and a known drunk. His reputation almost certainly played a role in the judge taking the witness's side. That was why, whenever possible, I took photos while serving.

The phone rang twice that morning. Both times, people who'd been at Saturday night's shindig at the Garrido Museum were seeking my services. I set dates and times for initial interviews while mentally thanking Marjorie for getting me more work. The third time the phone rang, the woman herself was on the other end.

"Good morning, Marjorie. How are you?"

"Busy, busy. I've been interviewing potential groundskeepers. Mine retires soon. He's worked for me thirty years and will be hard to replace. But now I've moved on to the next item on my to-do list, which is calling you. By the way, I trust you had a good time Saturday night?"

"I did indeed." Now was the time to get in Baker's good graces. "Hey, thanks for hooking me up with the San Marco PD."

"You're welcome."

"Baker took me out to the scene, shared all they had, and I decided I'd just be a fifth wheel, so I bowed out of the investigation."

"If you think that's best, but that's not why I'm calling. I understand Edward is visiting you today."

"It's tentative. We didn't select a specific time."

"Do you mind if I sit in on your meeting?" Marjorie asked.

"Fine with me if it's fine with Edward. But like I said, not sure when."

"I'll give him a ring, see when he's coming. See you later today."

I started into the paperwork, and at noontime, I considered lunch, but the breakfast burrito still sat heavily in my gut, so I hung my Back Soon sign on the door and took a walk instead. Coming back, I started at the far end of the strip mall and stopped in each business to say hello to my neighbors and compliment the Christmas decorations of those who'd put them up. I worked my way down to the tattoo parlor, Divine Ink, where the owner, Divinity Moss, had erected a Christmas tree in one window. In the other, she had taken countless strands of Christmas lights and woven them into a dream catcher. I went in and talked with Divinity and the other artist working, Tall Paul. Back at my office, I got lost in more paperwork, and as I was adding up my hours for the process-serving invoice, I heard the door open. Looking up, I saw Edward.

"There she is," he said and entered.

"Here I am." I stood and came around the desk. We shook. Nick was only a little taller than me, so we were almost eye to eye, but Edward towered over me by eight inches. So I was definitely looking up to meet his gaze.

"Hello, you two." Marjorie stood by the door.

Edward released my hand. "Hello, Marjorie."

"Hi, Marjorie," I said. "Can I get you guys some coffee, water, Diet Coke?"

"Nothing for me, dear," Marjorie said.

"I'll take water," Edward said.

I went to the back room, which had been the stockroom when my office was a small convenience store. I kept my Keurig and a small refrigerator back there next to a sink.

Edward and Marjorie were already seated when I returned, and I gave him his water and sat.

"Where's your muscle?" I asked.

Edward chuckled. "Eileen's in the car. I guess she doesn't consider you much of a threat."

"I don't know whether to be insulted or not."

Edward took a swallow of water, put the cap back on, and placed it on the floor by his chair. "Congratulations again on the honor from the museum."

"I wasn't expecting it," Lise said.

"I sprang it on her as a surprise," Marjorie said. "But really, she did an incredible job finding *Cold Green Spring*."

Edward crossed his legs. "And I heard about that awful affair last year with the serial killer. I'm sorry you had to go through all that."

"At least she put an end to that nightmare," Marjorie said.

"It was a joint effort with the San Marco PD," I said.

"And she's humble," Marjorie said to Edward.

"A hero," he added.

"Good lord, no. Now stop embarrassing me, and tell me what I can do for you."

Marjorie nodded and got down to business. "It has to do with the new San Marco Performing Arts Center."

Edward took over. "If things go as planned, we should open our doors right about a year from now. It's tucked away on a nice bit of property in the Breakers neighborhood northeast of the university."

"That's a great area for a performing arts center."

"I know." Edward smiled, probably having picked the site himself.

"And since he's going to be here for a while, he's joined several of our local charitable boards, which is how we met." Marjorie leaned in my direction, as if imparting a secret. "He's a philanthropist."

"To quote Lise, 'Good lord, no.' Believe me, my company is getting paid and paid well for the project. I've found it helps to get to know the movers and shakers of a city by volunteering with different community groups and charitable organizations. Anyway, Marjorie told me about you and your art history background. I'd like to hire you for something a bit out of the ordinary for a private investigator."

"This is exciting, Lise," Marjorie jumped in. "It is a performing arts center but will also feature visual arts."

"It'll have a gallery?" I asked.

"There will be a small gallery," Edward said. "And we'd like to place artwork throughout the lobby, in the lounges, and even in the bathrooms, which, by the way, will be magnificent."

"I like it," I said. "But what's this have to do with me?"

"We're nine months out from hiring a staff. One of those positions will be a person who will collect the pieces to put on display. We're thinking initially of changing the exhibits every six months. Until we get a person for that, I'd like to hire you to arrange the first year's exhibits. And to dangle a carrot, if you like the job, it would put you as a front-runner for the permanent position. Would you be interested?"

I thought a few seconds. "I guess Marjorie told you I worked at galleries in Tampa, Jacksonville, and Savannah?"

"Yes, she did."

"A lot of galleries and museums share their artwork with each other. Often, a museum will send their works to others for a price. There are also traveling exhibits we could tap into."

Marjorie reached to pat Edward's hand. "See, she's already warming to the idea."

I sat back. "Private collectors also loan their artwork."

"And I can get you an initial list of names to start with," Marjorie said.

"I can as well," Edward said.

"How about local and regional artists included in the mix?"

"I think that would be wonderful," Edward said.

I leaned forward and got down to business. "I'd charge what I do as a PI, though I'd waive the retainer."

"Perfectly reasonable," Edward said.

"Can you give me a day to think on it?" I asked.

Edward smiled. "I'll be generous and give you two." He stood and removed a card from a jacket pocket and put it on my desk. "Call me when you decide. Now, if you'll excuse me, I've got to scoot. Marjorie, always a pleasure." He took her hand in both of his. He turned to me, and we shook. "I'm delighted to see you again."

Marjorie and I walked him to the door and watched as he headed to his car.

"Is he married?" I asked.

"Why? You interested?" Marjorie asked with a sly grin.

I laughed. "Just curious. He seems to be a truly nice person, he's as handsome as Hugh Jackman—"

"More handsome than Hugh Jackman."

"Okay, more handsome, and he seems to be extremely rich. Seems he'd have his choice of women."

Marjorie shrugged. "He probably does, but he's not married, nor is he seeing anybody on a regular basis that I know about."

Edward got in a black Tesla. From the look of it, it was the priciest model. The car started silently, backed up, and drove off without a sound, Eileen Warrick in the passenger seat.

I turned to Marjorie. "Why does he need a bodyguard?"

Marjorie blinked and looked away. "Oh, some things have recently come up, and he feels active security is pragmatic. More of a deterrent than anything else."

"Intriguing."

"Mm-hmm."

"Interesting guy."

"I know." Marjorie sighed. "If only to be young again."

"He wouldn't stand a chance."

Marjorie laughed and then said, "You're young."

It took me a moment to figure out what she meant. "What? Me and Edward? A couple?"

Marjorie gave me a smug look.

"You know I'm taken."

She took my left hand and made a show of examining it. "I don't see a ring." Laughing, she went out the door.

Chapter 13

After the departure of Marjorie and Edward, I headed home. I wasn't calling it a day, but I wanted to explore Edward's offer. In my years of working at art galleries, I'd made notes on different galleries and collected contact information. I kept those files at home. I mainly wanted to go over them and see what I had to start with if I took the job.

My mind turned to the mystery boy who died on the train tracks. Who was he? Why had he been there? Children could be exceedingly cruel under the right—or wrong—circumstances. Had that been the case here? A bully or bullies who went too far? And why was the kid wearing an old military jacket? I kept telling myself it was a good thing that I wouldn't be working this. It took a special person to look into how and why a child died, and I seriously wondered if I had the emotional fortitude needed.

I got to Old Town, San Marco's historic district. There were even more cars with out-of-state plates, so I decided it would be quicker to skim the border of Old Town, and I took a left onto Spanish Trail Lane. One side of the street was taken up with a large motel, and the other had a few homes, the offices for the San Marco Family Council, and the First Coast Theatre. I noticed as I drove past that the first letters of each word in the theater's sign were oversized. Nick and I had gone there to see the musical *Once* a couple months back. I started singing my favorite song from it, "Falling Slowly." I was only a few lines in when I forgot the rest of the lyrics but ad-libbed *dah-duh-dahs* and *dooh-dah-doohs*. Out of the blue, a thought occurred to me, and I pulled over. For a long moment, I stared at the theater's sign in my rearview mirror.

First Coast Theatre.

"No way," I mumbled. Slipping into reverse, I backed all the way to the community theater and into its lot. I parked, got out, and found the front door locked. I checked the box office hours of operation and saw that it should have been open.

Deciding to tell Baker about my possible discovery, I started for my car but stopped when a bright-red Kia Soul with a black racing stripe turned into the lot and slipped into the parking space next to Minnie. The driver's door opened, releasing a thick plume of cigarette smoke, and a woman in her seventies got out.

"Excuse me," I said.

The woman answered with a raspy voice and thick Southern accent. "Here, catch."

She threw something at me, and thanks to good reflexes, I caught a ring of keys. When I turned my attention back to her, she had opened the back of her car and picked up countless clothing articles, holding them in place with a bear hug. It was a funny sight. The short woman held so many costume pieces that all I could see of her was her dyed red hair, styled high on her head.

"Would you get the door? It's the copper key next to the War Eagle pendant."

That made sense since "War Eagle" was the battle cry for the Auburn Tigers. Her accent was definitely Alabama-born. I opened the door as a moving mass of clothes shuffled up the three steps and pushed through the entrance.

"I'll be right back," she said and vanished through another doorway.

Five minutes later, she returned holding two First Coast Theatre coffee cups and handed one to me. "I was jonesing for a cup. I hope you take it black."

"I do. Thanks." I nodded to the door she'd gone through. "Costumes?"

"Yep, fresh from the laundry." She wore brown, high-waisted slacks with cuffs and pleats, a fashion hit back in the sixties. Her rose button-down blouse was open over a black T-shirt with First Coast Theatre spelled out in glitter. A pair of purple cat-eye glasses with faux diamond chips hung from a strap around her neck.

"Are you the costume designer?" Thanks to a period in high school when I thought I wanted to be a Broadway star, I took some drama classes and knew that was the proper term.

"Nope, but believe me, I've done and still do my fair share of costuming. I'm Patsy Butler, executive director." She held out her hand.

I took it. "Lise Norwood, private investigator."

Her eyes lit up. "It must be fun to say that."

I leaned close to her as if imparting a secret. "It really is."

"Follow me. I'll give you a tour while you tell me what you want." She led me through the doors that opened to the actual theater.

"I've seen some shows here. My boyfriend and I saw *Once*."

"Then you know this room." We walked down the aisle. She gestured to the maroon seats. "A capacity for an audience of one hundred twenty-eight." We stepped up on the stage that had a couple flats painted to look like cabins. "We're tearing down the set for *Duck Hunter Shoots Angel*." She turned and looked at me over the rim of her coffee cup, eyebrows raised. "So, what can I do for you?"

"Actually, it has to do with costumes."

"I see."

"Do you mark them?" I asked. "You know, with the theater's name, initials, something like that?"

She smiled, emptied her coffee with a big swallow, and put the cup down on a papier-mâché rock. "Follow me." She led me through the women's dressing room, the men's dressing room, the green room, through the workshop—pausing to point out the prop closet—and then to the costume shop. "We share costumes, sets, and props with other theaters in north and central Florida, not to mention with San

Marco University's theater department, all the high schools, and some middle schools. So you bet we mark them."

The costume shop was twenty feet long and ten feet wide, and it was crammed full of clothing. A high ceiling allowed the theater to have three levels for costumes to be hung, and a ladder next to the door was used to access the high stuff. I noticed that men's costumes were on one side and women's on the other. Hats and shoes took up all the wall space at either end. Under the lowest-hanging garments, Tupperware bins were stacked.

Patsy took a shirt from a hanger, put on her glasses, and peered into the collar. She held the shirt out to me. It had the same initials, appearing to be in the same writing, as those in the military jacket the dead boy had been wearing. "We use Sharpies to put F.C.T. inside the collars of shirts, jackets, and blouses. Same thing for pants and skirts, but along the inside of the waistline. On the back of belts, in shoes, inside hats. If there's a place for it, you'll find F.C.T. I'm not saying people steal costumes, but not everything that's borrowed makes it back."

"Do you have any costume pieces out on loan now?"

Patsy cackled. "Good lord, yes. Stuff loaned out, stuff overdue, stuff that just vanished off the face of the earth."

My mind was racing. "If I took a photo of a jacket and texted it to you, could you tell me if it was one of yours?"

"Maybe. Or you could bring it over."

"I can't. The police have possession of it," I told her.

"Excuse me?"

"It was found on a deceased body. A boy, actually."

"Oh. Well, that's terrible. Wait a minute. Is this the boy I read about in the paper, the one hit by a train?"

I nodded and put down my coffee cup. "Yes. The initials F.C.T. were written in the collar."

She cast her gaze to the long table in the middle of the costume shop.

"Patsy?" I said.

"Hmm? I'm sorry." In her eyes, I saw compassion for the boy coupled with a fierce determination to help.. "Would they let me look at it if we went to the police station?"

Chapter 14

I put in a call to Detective Baker, but it went directly to voicemail.

I left a message. "You were barking up the wrong tree thinking F.C.T. were the boy's initials. I'm bringing someone to the station who can ID the jacket."

I next called Reuben Busby. He answered and agreed to meet us at the station. Patsy rode with me, and both Busby and Baker were waiting for us in the parking lot.

I introduced everyone and said, "Patsy is head honcho over at First Coast Theatre."

"Damn." Baker shook his head as the realization hit him. "First Coast Theatre."

"F.C.T.," Busby said.

Baker, a file folder in one hand, took Patsy's hand with his other. "Thank you for coming. I assume you know about the boy killed by the train?"

Patsy nodded. "From what I read in the newspaper and what Lise told me."

"We haven't been able to identify the boy, so any help you can provide would be great," Busby said and led us inside, down a floor, and then down hallways to the back of the building.

We entered a large room with row after row of metal shelves. Busby disappeared between two shelving units.

Baker held up the file he was carrying. "I was wondering if you could take a look at a photo of the boy. See if you recognize him."

Patsy put up her hands. "Please don't make me look. I don't know if I could stomach it."

"It's not his death photo. Our forensic artist came up with a reconstructed photo of what the boy would have looked like."

"Oh, very well." Patsy still didn't sound pleased.

Baker opened the file, took out the eight by ten, and passed it to her.

Patsy looked at it for a long time, finally muttering, "You poor, poor boy." She handed the photo back to Baker. "I've never seen him before."

Busby came back with a plastic container, opened it, and took out a large Ziploc plastic bag that contained the jacket the boy had been wearing. Busby put on latex gloves, removed the jacket, and laid it on a table. Though the fabric was a light khaki color, a third of it was stained with dried blood.

Patsy approached the table. "That's one of our costume pieces. Can you open the collar?"

"Sure," Busby said and stretched open the collar.

Patsy examined it. "That's my writing. F.C.T."

"What style is it?" I asked. "I mean, military, no doubt."

Patsy nodded. "It's a World War II German Wehrmacht jacket. Specifically, the Afrika Korps." She looked it over. "It was worn by a low-ranking officer in the infantry. We actually got a half dozen of these and pants to go with them. Originally an olive green, they've faded over time." Patsy smiled. "We did a run of *The Sound of Music*. Needed Nazi soldiers. It was a big cast, and not a lot of people auditioned. One of the Nazi soldiers was a thirteen-year-old named Natalie Schwartz. Now if that isn't a flagrant case of irony, I don't know what is. This was the smallest we had, so she wore it."

"Afrika Korps?" Baker said. "Didn't *The Sound of Music* take place in Austria?"

Patsy grinned. "In community theater, you use what you can get."

I knelt and scrutinized the fabric, as if it would give me insight. "How'd the boy get it?"

"I can answer that," Patsy said. She turned to Baker. "Can we get some coffee?"

We retired to a break room to sip hot coffee out of cracked mugs while seated around a small Formica table.

Patsy told us what she knew. "The theater got burgled a few months ago. The thieves got box office for that night, around twenty-five hundred. We have a safe someone donated as a set piece for a show years ago. It now sits in my office, and we use it to lock up each night's box office take. The thing is older than I am, and whoever broke in had no trouble opening it. Detective Ramirez told me that even though the police got prints off the safe, they didn't match any in a police database."

"I've worked with Detective Ramirez. Last year, she helped me recover a valuable sketch that was drawn by both Picasso and Dali." We'd since become friends and got together every few weeks for margaritas and bowling.

"Detective Ramirez did learn one thing from the prints," Patsy said. "The safecracker was a child."

"What?" I did a classic double take.

"And it was more than just one child. We had several big bags of those little Halloween-size chocolate candy bars in the green room. They tore into those, plus they knocked over the sugar container for our cast's coffee drinkers. They left several different shoe prints in the sugar, all children's sizes." Patsy blew into her mug. "And chocolate-smeared handprints and fingerprints. Besides the money, they vandalized the prop room and costume closet."

"And the deceased boy was in one of your jackets," I said.

Patsy nodded sadly.

Busby looked at Baker. "We should have made that connection."

"Ya think?" Baker said and then asked Patsy, "Did you know they'd taken costumes?"

"I'm not surprised, but there's really no way of knowing if anything was taken unless I go look for something and it's not there. Makes sense that they took stuff because they went through the prop room and costume closet like tornadoes. When I spoke with Detective Ramirez, I was mainly concerned about getting the money back and didn't even consider that they'd stolen anything else."

"It's safe to assume the boy was part of this group," Baker said.

Busby added, "Just to be sure, I'll compare his prints to those acquired at the theater."

"I'll talk to Detective Ramirez, see what she learned about this gang," I said and noticed Baker stiffen. "I mean, if it's all right with you."

Baker looked at me and pursed his lips. "I'd like to talk to Norwood alone."

"Sure," Busby said. "I have plenty to do."

"Can you take Patsy to the lobby, Reuben?"

"Sure."

I turned to Patsy. "I'll meet you there in a few."

Baker stood, shook her hand, and thanked her for coming in. When we were alone, Baker leaned against a countertop and crossed his arms. "Pisses me off we missed the connection between the theater burglary and the jacket on the boy."

"You've got it now," I said.

"Thanks to you, Norwood." Baker moved his head from one side to the other as if working out kinks in his neck. "What you got on your table these days?"

"Couple of background checks, papers to serve, a domestic, and maybe a job acquiring artwork for San Marco's new arts center."

"Here's the thing. I have a truck-versus-bicycle hit-and-run from last night and a body found in a retention pond that looks hinky. I know I said I didn't want you on the case, and you said you didn't want to work it. But you got some traction going, and since you already got permission to work with us, I was hoping you'd look into it some more. See if you can learn the boy's ID."

"Really?"

"At least until I can devote more time to it. I'm really swamped."

Earlier, I'd thought about how difficult it would be working a case that involved a child's death. Yeah, it would be hard. It might even be heartrending, but didn't I become a private investigator in the hopes of doing important work? "Now that I think about it, I'd like to help find out who this poor kid is."

Baker looked at me with gratitude, an expression rarely seen on his face. We went to his office, and he passed along a file with two photos of the boy, one of the deceased on the autopsy table. It was hard to look at. The other was the visual reconstruction made by the forensic artist.

"I'll call IT and get you a temporary username and password to get you into missing children databases."

I told him I would poke around and get back to him in a day or two and then went to meet up with Patsy. Back on the road, I asked her, "Do you think a group of kids was messing around outside the theater and found a door unlocked?"

"That's what I wondered, but Detective Ramirez found evidence that our actors' access door had its lock picked."

"Crazy stuff. We're talking about kids picking locks and cracking safes."

Chapter 15

Tuesday

Before leaving for the office, I called Eve Ramirez, and we agreed to meet that evening at the bowling alley so I could pick her brain about the burglary at First Coast Theatre. I then proceeded to punch in the number on the card that Edward Burke had left me.

"Hello, Lise."

"Hi, Edward. Thought I'd give you my answer on the job."

"Over the phone? That's no way to accept the position."

"Who says I'm accepting?"

"Then definitely not how to turn it down. That'd be like breaking up with someone via text."

"Well, then let's get face-to-face." I realized that I was looking forward to spending time with the man.

"What's your favorite breakfast spot?" he asked me.

"I have a few. You'll find I'm not a picky eater. How about we meet up at Granbys in Old Town. It's on Malaga Avenue."

"How soon can you make it?" Edward asked.

"Soon."

"I bet you're a competitive woman. Am I right?"

"I can be."

"Good. Let's race. Last one there buys breakfast."

I started to respond, but he'd already ended the call. I ran for the door, scooping up my handbag in the process, raced across the deck, down the stairs, and planted myself behind Minnie's steering wheel. I was lucky I didn't get a ticket as I wove through traffic. That luck held as a car pulled from the curb a half block from Granbys.

I parked and got out of Minnie, assured of victory, but then I spotted Edward, in jeans and a teal golf shirt, across the street from Granbys, his bodyguard a few steps behind him. I sighed, accepting defeat. As I headed to the restaurant, I noticed that Edward was still on the other side of the street, talking to someone who was definitely down on his luck. The man's clothes were filthy, and his untamed gray beard and hair were a contrast to his dark skin. I slowed my approach and watched Edward take out his wallet, pull out a bill, and hand it to the man. He stared down at the money and then up to Edward. I stopped walking as Edward took out a business card and a pen, scribbled something on the back, and handed it to the man. Edward shook the man's hand, turned, crossed the street, and entered Granbys.

I no longer cared that I'd lost the race. Curiosity had a hold of me. I crossed the street, taking a five-dollar bill from my purse, and approached the homeless man as he started to walk away.

"Excuse me," I said.

He stopped and turned.

I held out the five. "Good morning."

He smiled warmly and took the money. "Thank you, ma'am." This close, I saw that he was between forty and fifty-five years old and badly in need of a shower.

"I just saw you talking with a friend of mine."

"Mr. Burke? A fine man."

"So, you know him?"

"No, ma'am. We just met."

"Oh? What did he want? If you don't mind me asking."

The man got the business card Edward had given him from a pocket and held it up. "He told me to take this to the foreman at a construction site in town. Said they'd give me a job if I wanted." He put the card back in his pocket.

"Must be the new performing arts center."

"Yes, ma'am. And he gave me enough money for some new clothes and something to eat. It's gonna be a blessed day. Enjoy it."

"You too." I watched the man head down the street, thinking how my already good opinion of Edward had risen another several notches.

I opened the restaurant door, and Edward turned from the hostess to smile a greeting. "Sorry, Lise, looks like breakfast is on you."

"It'll be my pleasure." I noticed his security nearby. "Morning, Eileen," I said cheerily.

In return, I got a scowl and a small nod.

Edward and I sat at a small four top. Warrick took a nearby two top.

I leaned over the table while pointing Warrick's way. "Was it something I said?"

Edward chuckled. "What she lacks in charm, she more than makes up for in skill. She served as an MP in the army, did four tours in the Middle East, and came home a total badass. She stays close enough to protect me but far enough to give us privacy."

The waitress brought our menus, and we asked for coffee and mimosas. I turned my attention to the menu. I was hungry and ordered steak and eggs when the waitress returned with our drinks. Edward ordered a fruit plate and croissant.

"A healthy breakfast, huh? If you're trying to make me feel guilty, it won't work."

"I happen to like fruit and croissants."

We discussed the merits of different breakfast foods, turned the topic to the warm winter weather, and then he abruptly changed the discussion to business.

"So, Lise, will you take the job?"

"Do I have to call you boss if I do?"

He grinned. "Edward will be fine."

I held out my hand. "Consider me hired." We shook. "I've already been in contact with some galleries. I plan to start talking with private collectors soon."

"To that end, I have a half-dozen names and contact info of friends and colleagues who would be more than happy to lend some of their collections." He pulled an envelope from a jacket pocket and passed it to me.

"Excellent. Marjorie said she had some contacts as well."

Edward looked past me. "Ah, Trish. Impeccable timing."

"Good morning, Edward."

Edward stood as Trish arrived at the table. She looked much more like a CFO this morning than she had at the museum gala. She wore a dark-gray business suit, low heels, and a more-businesslike pair of glasses, with her hair tightly pulled back. Her earrings were a single pearl in each lobe.

Trish sat, and I noticed she held a file folder. "Congratulations on the new job."

"How did you know? I only just took it."

She laughed and looked at Edward. "He was sure you'd take it."

"Ever the optimist," he said.

Trish slid the file folder towards me. "Since our human resources department is up in Chicago, I get the honors of handling your paperwork. Some things for you to fill out and sign. My card's in the file. Call me when you're done, and I'll pick it up."

"Thanks," I said. "Hey, at the museum, you said you were hoping I could introduce you to some locals. I'm bowling with a friend tonight, if you want to join us. I'll make sure to fill out the paperwork and bring it with me."

"That'd be great. Are you sure I wouldn't be imposing?"

"Not at all. We're meeting at San Marco Lanes at six. It's on the beach road."

"Wait a minute. You guys aren't like professional bowlers or something, are you? I haven't bowled in years."

"I'm not, but Eve is the strike queen. Last year, I saw her use a bowling ball to make an arrest. She's a cop, by the way."

"And made an arrest with a bowling ball?"

"Took his feet right out from under a fleeing suspect. Count on losing to her, but you have a chance against me."

"Great. I'll be there."

"Want some breakfast? I'm paying."

"You're paying?" She turned her attention to Edward and grinned. "Don't be such a cheapskate."

He crossed his arms and sat back. "We had a race here, fair and square. To the swift go the rewards."

Trish nodded. "Be careful making wagers with Mr. Competitive here. I'll pass on breakfast. I have a Zoom meeting to attend. But if we get a chance tonight, let's toss around some ideas for financing the loaned artwork. Edward and I have already talked about black-tie fundraisers with each new opening."

He shrugged. "Any excuse for a party."

As our food arrived, Trish got to her feet. "See you this evening, Lise."

When she'd gone, Edward said, "Thanks for inviting her along. She's really business focused and doesn't have much of a social life. It'll be good for her to get out."

We started in on our food. Edward sparingly picked at his fruit while I attacked my steak and eggs. Focused on my food, I hadn't realized we'd been silent for a few minutes. I looked up at Edward and could tell he was uncomfortable.

Worried that I had a chunk of meat stuck in my teeth, I felt along my incisors with the tip of my tongue.

Edward cleared his throat. "I hope that we can do this again, Lise. Only the next time, let's make it dinner."

"A business dinner?"

He stared at me for several seconds before answering, "Call it what you like."

I thought that was an odd comment and didn't reply.

"Marjorie tells me that you're seeing someone."

"Yes, I am."

Edward nodded. "I understand he's a professor at the university."

"He's dean of the Department of Art and Art History."

"Impressive. How long have the two of you been together?"

"That's kind of complicated. The short version is a couple years, but we also dated for a few months when we were in college a long time ago."

Edward sat back and wiped at his lips with a napkin. "Are the two of you—" He stopped.

"What?"

"Oh, nothing. I was being nosy without really thinking about what I was saying."

"Go ahead and be nosy."

"Well, I was going to ask if your relationship is serious."

I sat back and put down my silverware. I understood why he'd hesitated. It was an uncomfortable question. A simple yes or no didn't cover it, and I didn't want to get into details with someone I'd only recently met. I decided to deflect the question with a joke. "As serious as you can be with a couple of people who are members of the Three Stooges Fan Club."

"You're pulling my leg."

I locked eyes with him, reached into my purse, retrieved my billfold, and removed my official Three Stooges membership card. As I held it out to him, I said, "Nyuck, nyuck, nyuck."

He laughed. "I can say with confidence that you are the first member of the Three Stooges Fan Club I've ever met."

As I put away my membership card, I said, "Now let me ask you something."

"Shoot."

"When I got to Granbys, I saw you talking with a homeless man. What was up with that?"

"Why do you ask?"

"You talked with him for a while, and it looked pretty serious. I guess I'm curious."

A look of concern came to his face. "Are you wary of the homeless?"

"Huh? No. In fact, my one part-time employee is a homeless man named Elliot the Slim. Like I said, curiosity."

Edward nodded. "We were just discussing the weather and what was on tap for us both on this beautiful day."

I'd given him a chance to talk about what a nice guy he was, giving the guy money and possible employment, and he kept it to himself. I liked that about him. I liked it a lot.

"So, how about we have that business dinner?" Edward asked. "Tomorrow night?"

"Sure."

"Pick you up at seven?"

I held up a finger. "Business dinner. I'll meet you there."

He nodded. "Business dinner."

My cellphone buzzed. I looked down to see the call was from the San Marco PD.

"I've got to take this, Edward." I got up, stepped away, and answered, "Annalise Norwood Investigations."

It was the IT guy with my username and password that would get me into three missing children databases. Eager to get right on it, I found our waitress, quickly settled the tab, and asked her to tell Edward that I had to leave. She looked at me like I was crazy for ditching such a handsome man. What could I say? Sure, he was Hugh Jackman handsome, but my boyfriend was young Michael Caine handsome. That was good enough for me.

Chapter 16

I launched a pinball, and two seconds later, it fell right between the flippers, which started Eve, Trish, and me laughing again. I'd met the two other women at the little bar in the bowling lanes and introduced them to each other over a pitcher of margaritas.

"Lise said you were with the police, but she didn't say you were a detective," Trish said.

Eve said, "Yeah, it's a cool job. But look at you, a CFO of a multi-million-dollar corporation."

"To be honest," Trish said, "it's a multibillion-dollar corporation."

"I've got a PI license," I said but only received pitying looks. Then they had cracked up laughing.

When we were down a half pitcher, we took the pitcher and our glasses to the counter but were informed that, as it was league night, no lanes were available. We went to the game room instead and played a few rounds on the Ghostbusters pinball machine. Eve played like the pinball wizard from *Tommy*. I played pretty well but generally trailed by half. Poor Trish had no hand-eye coordination.

When the pitcher was empty, Trish asked, "Do they put any tequila in their margaritas? I'm as sober as a judge."

I looked at Eve. "Let's take Trish to Pescados."

Eve's eyes flashed. "Great idea."

A couple of minutes later, we stood at the side of A1A in front of the bowling alley.

I looked left, right, and left again. "Okay."

We crossed the beach road at a jog to Pescados, a fish taco joint on the ocean side of A1A. The building looked like something you would find on the coast in a small Mexican village, a mix of materials, including brick, plaster, stucco, and sheet metal, painted in vibrant purple, blue, yellow, and orange.

I held the door for Eve and Trish, and we entered. The lights were always low at Pescados, with plenty of neon lights along the walls. Some were Mexican neon beer signs. Others were figures of charging bulls, flamenco dancers, and sugar skulls. The east wall had three wide garage doors that were kept open when the weather was nice, which was ninety percent of the time. You could hear the nearby surf crash and smell the salt air as it blew over the dunes.

Trish grinned. "Now this place has character."

"Let's go out on the deck," Eve said and led the way out. We bypassed the narrow boardwalk of weathered wood that crossed over the dunes to the beach and grabbed a high-top.

"I can't believe Christmas is only three weeks away and we're sitting outside in short sleeves," Trish said. "High in Chicago today was twenty-two degrees."

"This isn't a normal winter for us," Eve said. "Northeast Florida is usually pretty cold this time of year."

I added, "Cold enough that even people from Chicago will throw on a jacket before venturing outside."

"But twenty-two degrees?" Trish asked.

"That's a stretch, though we usually get a couple of hard freezes each winter," I said.

The waitress showed up, and I ordered triggerfish tacos, Eve got the mahi-mahi, and Trish ordered one of each.

After adding a small pitcher of the house margaritas to our order, the waitress left, and I told Trish, "Small instead of large. They aren't stingy with their tequila."

"No mix either," Eve pointed out. "They make their simple syrup from piloncillo, a Mexican brown sugar. Add to that fresh-squeezed lime juice and a Gran Marnier floater."

"Sounds amazing. By the way, which way to the ladies' room?"

After Trish excused herself, I told Eve, "I am living large today. Tacos and tequila with friends tonight. Earlier today, it was steak, eggs, and mimosas with a handsome, charming, and super-wealthy businessman."

"Hmm. Nick could be classified as handsome, and he's charming. But he's not a businessman, and he's definitely not super wealthy. You stepping out on him?"

"What? No. Not at all. Edward Burke, her"—I nodded in the direction Trish had gone—"boss, hired me to gather artwork on loan for the new performing arts center. It was a business breakfast."

Eve stared at me with steely eyes. "Mm-hmm."

"Really."

She laughed. "Just yanking your chain. So, he's handsome, charming, and rich. What else?"

"He's a nice guy. Truly. I saw him give a homeless guy enough money for new clothes and a meal, and then he gave him someone's name to see about a job."

"That's going above and beyond. Maybe he was just showing off since you were there."

"I was across the street. He didn't know I saw. When I asked Edward about it later, he said they were just discussing the weather."

"Humble and modest too. He's got to be taken."

"You'd think, but from what I heard, he's unattached," I said.

Eve narrowed her eyes. "Are you getting feelings for this guy?"

"What? No. I'm a one-man woman," I said. "I only just met him at the museum gala on Saturday. We spent a little time together at my office when he made the job offer and then had breakfast this morning, which was so I could accept the offer. But now that you mention it..."

"What?"

"We're having dinner tomorrow night."

"Really? Maybe he has feelings for you," Eve said.

"It's a business dinner or... well, he said something odd. He asked about dinner, and I asked if it was a business dinner, and he said 'call it what you like.'"

"Hmm, maybe you have a rich admirer."

I stared off as I recalled something else. "He asked if I was seeing anyone, and when I told him about Nick, he asked if our relationship was serious, which I thought was a little too personal."

"What'd you say?"

"Nothing, really. I didn't want to talk about Nick with him, so I made a joke and changed the subject."

"Maybe it's the romantic in me, but I think he's attracted to you." Eve crossed her arms on the table and leaned toward me. "If you'd have answered his question honestly, would you have said that you and Nick are serious?"

"Well... sure."

"Why?"

"Because we're in love, we spend a lot of time together, have the same interests, and our... um... intimate moments are really good," I answered.

"Those are all good things," Eve said. "How about the future? You guys ever talk about getting married or moving in together?"

"No, not really. Now and then, one of us will say something about how we need to talk about whether we want to take our relationship to the proverbial next level. We've never really had that talk, though."

"You want my advice, or do you want me to mind my own business?" Eve asked with a smile.

"I'll take your advice if you think I need it."

"If it was me, I'd be tempted to ask my boyfriend how serious he considered our relationship, because it sounds like this Burke guy has a lot going for him. It'd be a shame to pass him by for a relationship going nowhere."

"Geez, you make it sound like Nick and I are stuck in a quagmire," I said and then mentally added, *Are we?*

Eve held up her hands. "Hey, just telling you what I think, which could explain why I'm currently single."

The waitress arrived with our pitcher of bliss, which was perfect timing because I thought I needed a slug of tequila right about then.

When she departed, I downed a mouthful and pointed to the ocean. "A storm's coming in."

Trish returned then. "Storm?"

Most of our storms started inland and worked their way east over the coast, but this one had started over the water and was headed in. Lightning flashed over the ocean. Afterward, stars were visible west of the storm, but I could delineate the line of the storm from where the stars disappeared. Thunder reached us.

"Hey, I met your security head at the department," Eve said to Trish.

"Eileen Warrick," Trish said.

"She and Sergeant Trask, our public relations officer, will act as liaisons between your boss's company and the police department."

"Why?" I asked.

Eve shrugged. "In the event that traffic needs to be rerouted during construction. Then when the center opens, they'll be hiring officers to help with security for shows and performances, as well as traffic in and out."

I asked Trish, "Now that we're on the topic of cops, do you mind if I talk shop with Eve?"

"A private investigator talking shop with a detective? Not at all. Oh, wait. Would you like me to give you two some privacy?"

I looked to Eve.

She thought a second. "Not necessary. However, it concerns an ongoing investigation, so no running to the *San Marco Ledger* with details."

"Lips are sealed," Trish said, and she mimed locking her lips.

Eve took a sip of her drink then asked me, "You have some questions about what Herman calls the case of the juvenile magpies?"

I told Trish, "Her partner likes to name the cases they work in a noir-like fashion." Turning my attention to Eve, I said, "You know that poor kid killed by the train was wearing one of First Coast Theatre's costume pieces."

"I read about that boy who was killed," Trish said.

Eve nodded. "Yeah, the captain chewed me and Baker out. Said we should have made the connection between the juvenile magpies and the dead kid. Which I would have if Patsy had told me about putting the theater's initials in all their costumes."

"It wasn't your fault," I pointed out. "She said she wasn't even sure if anything other than the box office money was taken."

"Yeah, but still. Anyway, it's official. Busby says the kid's prints match some we got at the theater."

"Baker has asked me to help identify the boy, and I'm not having much luck."

"I'm sorry to interrupt, but who's Baker?" Trish asked.

"Homicide detective."

Eve said, "All we had to go on at First Coast Theatre were fingerprints and shoe prints— oh, and one of them was barefoot—so we have a bare footprint. You can't pinpoint an age from a fingerprint, but you can get a good idea. Busby thinks, from the size and sharp definition of the friction ridges, as young as eight to ten. He also thinks some of the larger footprints indicate older kids and maybe adults. It's an odd case. One of my theories is that they're part of a large extended criminal family."

Lightning flashed again, and the storm was noticeably closer.

"Do you mean First Coast Theatre isn't the only place they've hit?" I asked.

"Yep. There's been an uptick in burglaries the past several months, and that includes cars getting broken into. Children's fingerprints recovered. It's the same group of kids. Prints from one crime match prints from others. Old City Pawn was after First Coast Theatre. They have a security camera out front, and there's footage of a group of kids, all ages, wandering by. All of them, every single one, had their faces turned from the cameras. And they were dressed like they were going to a masquerade party."

"Costume pieces?" I asked.

"We know that's the case now. The time stamp showed it was a little past two in the morning. Ten minutes later, a strange figure approached the camera and aimed a can of spray paint at the lens. Next morning, the owner shows up to find his doors open and a lot of missing items. It was obvious that someone tried breaking into a safe where he keeps the really valuable jewelry, but they didn't get it open. That safe is a lot more sophisticated than the one they opened at First Coast Theatre."

"What do you mean by *strange figure*?"

"You can only see it for a second before it blasted the lens with black spray paint. It came from under the camera, wearing a long coat—no head, the body wobbling this way and that— and then up comes the spray paint. Herman and I think it's one kid on another's shoulders, the coat worn over them, heads tucked in so they can't be identified."

I gave a quick laugh, as much out of bafflement as amusement.

"Does this kind of thing happen a lot?" Trish asked. "A juvenile crime syndicate?"

"Maybe in the big cities but not here," Eve said.

The tacos arrived as the wind started to pick up, so we moved inside, and the waitress closed the garage doors.

I took a bite of my triggerfish taco. Juices ran down my chin, but I waited for another bite before I wiped my face. "God, that's good."

Trish took a bite. "Wow."

Mouth full, Eve nodded while chewing.

After swallowing, Trish asked, "So, you have a crime spree here in San Marco being perpetrated by a gang of children?"

Wiping her chin dry, Eve said, "Yeah. All take place late at night, which led me to wonder why parents would let their kids, some of them obviously very young, stay out so late. That led to my theory that they're all from a large family. Brothers, sisters, cousins, parents, aunts, and uncles. On the other hand, though we couldn't make out much on the security footage, we could tell there were some different ethnicities."

Our conversation returned to the more mundane. After our plates were empty and our pitcher dry, Trish said, "Let's do this again. Only we'll Uber so we can tackle a large pitcher of margaritas."

"It's a date," Eve said.

We ran through the storm, across A1A, to our cars in the bowling alley parking lot. By the time I sat in Minnie's driver's seat and closed the door, I was drenched, but I had one more stop to make before heading home and drying off.

Chapter 17

Thinking back to my heart-to-heart with Eve, I realized she was the second person in the same day to question the seriousness of my relationship with Nick. Why? Was there a reason? Did other people see something that I didn't? Lightning flashed, followed by rumbling thunder. I decided I better put Nick out of my mind and concentrate on driving in the rain.

The storm would actually make my chore easier. I wanted to find my sometime-employee, Elliot the Slim. Elliot assisted me in a number of ways, including surveillance and serving papers. A few jobs back, I was trying to find a teen runaway, and I learned of the value of Elliot's street connections. A lot of information was transferred through the city's homeless population. Through Elliot's contacts, we located the runaway in less than a week. Elliot earned a fat bonus for that one.

That particular month, I made Elliot the Lise Norwood Investigations Employee of the Month. Yeah, he was my only pseudo employee, but he got a kick out of it. Ours was a cash-only, handshake relationship. No contracts were between us and no tax forms to fill out. Most people would classify Elliot as homeless, which he claimed was absurd. Since he considered San Marco, Florida, his home, he wasn't homeless as long as he was within the city limits. Hard to debate that rationale. Elliot suffered from a condition that was the opposite of agoraphobia. Sort of. My research on the subject pinpointed claustrophobia as agoraphobia's opposite, but that wasn't exactly Elliot's problem. He broke out in a cold sweat by being indoors and under a roof.

He once confided the reason to me. He had been in the army during the Iraqi war surge, part of a squad that went from house to house to flush out insurgents. He came to think that, with every house he went into, every door he went through, the odds increased that he would be killed. It got harder and harder for him to go into buildings, and he started having panic attacks. When he got back Stateside, he couldn't go indoors anymore. Simple as that. Just thinking about crossing a threshold gave him the heebie-jeebies. I knew that if it was stormy, his favorite place to sleep was under the Carroll Street Drawbridge on the west side of the Intracoastal Waterway.

I pulled into the lot of a closed furniture store and parked Minnie. I grabbed one of the two burner phones from the glove compartment. When Elliot worked with me, I gave him a burner phone so we could keep in touch and so he could take photos if the job required it. At the end of each job, Elliot sold the phone for a few extra bucks. I didn't mind giving him a new one for each job. I considered it a business expense.

I reached for the small umbrella I kept behind the passenger seat and got out of the car into the downpour, but at least I had some protection. The bridgetender blasted his horn, announcing that the bridge would be rising. There was easy access to the water on both the west and east sides of the span to accommodate fishermen, and I quickly made my way down and under it. Once at the waterside, I collapsed my umbrella and looked up at the bottom of the Carroll Street Drawbridge twenty feet overhead. The rain was still loud, though muffled.

"Elliot?" I called out.

A beat later, "That you, Lise?"

"Yeah."

A small flashlight clicked on ten feet up the slope to the underside of the span. "Up here."

I hiked myself up and sat next to him. "Figured I'd find you here."

"Yep, quite the storm."

Farther out from us, the drawbridge was up, and a thirty-foot boat with its sails tied off motored toward the gap, heading north. Besides their red port sidelights, Christmas lights were entwined in the mast. Once the boat was through, the bridgetender blasted his horn again to announce the drawbridge was going down.

"It's nice here, out of the rain," I said, watching the boat continue its northward trek.

"Yeah. I like it."

I turned to him. "If you're ever in my neighborhood and the weather turns, feel free to hunker down in the carport under the house."

"Thanks, Lise, you're good people." Elliot reclined with his hands behind his head and stared up at the underbelly of the bridge. "Got a job for me?"

"Yep."

"Good. Things have been boring of late."

I filled Elliot in on the kid killed by the train, how his jacket connected him to a crew of children committing burglaries. "Detective Ramirez wonders if they're all part of a large family, lots of siblings and cousins, that kind of thing."

"You don't agree?"

"It's possible, but I'm wondering if it's more of a street-level kind of thing. If the kids are out all night stealing stuff, then they probably don't have to be up bright and early to go to school."

"You thinking homeless kids?"

"Something along those lines. Homeless kids, kids from homeless families joining together, something like that. Can you put your ear to the ground, ask around, see if you hear anything?"

"Can do, boss." He held out his hand, and I passed him the burner phone.

Chapter 18

Wednesday

It wasn't even ten a.m., and I'd already made two promising calls concerning artwork acquisition for the arts center. I next called the director of the Garrido Art Museum, Lorenzo Locke. He was a man with three fiery passions. One was art, another was his beautiful wife, and the third was Florida's African American history. He could trace his family roots back to the late 1600s, when his ancestors—a husband, wife, and baby—were among the first fourteen slaves to escape from the English colonies and seek refuge and freedom with the Spanish who had colonized Florida. When it first opened, Locke chose the name Garrido Museum after Juan Garrido. As far as history was concerned, Garrido was the first African to step foot on American soil. Originally from the Kingdom of Kongo, he was a conquistador and arrived with Ponce de Leon in 1513. Some historians credited him with bringing wheat to America.

After talking for some time with Lorenzo, I ended the call and held up my fists in victory. "Score!" The *Florida, Masters in Passing* exhibit would be ending at about the time that the San Marco Performing Arts Center was scheduled to open to the public. Lorenzo liked my idea of moving a few of those works to the arts center for its first exhibition. It wasn't a slam dunk because he first had to get permission from the board of directors. And I needed to see if Edward liked the direction I wanted to head.

"Lise, what a pleasant surprise," Edward said when I rang. "So, if we're still on for tonight, where's the best place to get a prime rib in San Marco?"

"There're a few places, but for my money, anything in the red meat family should be consumed at Razorbacks."

"Dress code?"

I snorted a laugh. "The food is mighty fine, but it's not fine dining. Anyway, I have a quick question, Edward. I'd have waited until tonight, but things are starting to gel, and if you don't like what I'm thinking, then I can restart and take a different direction."

"Tell me about it."

"If your scheduled opening holds, the Garrido will be wrapping up *Florida, Masters in Passing* around that time. I may be able to arrange for us to get a number of those pieces on loan. I'm thinking a half dozen to serve as the anchors for the exhibit, but the main theme will be contemporary Florida artists."

"Okay. Run with it. You can tell me more at dinner."

"See you tonight."

"I'm looking forward to it."

I pressed End Call and sat there, phone in hand, thinking about what Eve had said the night before, something like, *Maybe it's because I'm a romantic, but I think he's attracted to you.* Flattering if it was true. And then there were the more troubling questions that Eve had put out there. *How about the future? Do you and Nick ever talk about getting married or even moving in together?* The quick answer was no. As I'd told her, the closest we'd come was talking about talking about it someday. Now that I put it into words, that sounded like a passive-aggressive way of avoiding the topic altogether.

Before I could put the phone down, a ringtone sounded, Barry White's "Can't Get Enough of Your Love, Babe." My specific ringtone for Nick. A second of guilt quickly gave way to irritation that he was calling while I'd been thinking about the possibility that our relationship was going nowhere. Irrational, I knew, and I was as culpable as Nick about not planning out a future.

I pressed the answer button and said, "Nick." Even to my ears, the greeting sounded cold.

"Hey, sweet thing, how are you?"

"Fine."

A moment of silence. "You sure?"

"Yep." I realized I was giving out one-syllable sentences, something Nick didn't deserve. "Sorry, Nick. I'm multitasking. How are you doing?"

"Doing great."

"What's up?"

"Some of the faculty is getting together to celebrate tonight. Want to join us?" Nick asked.

I'd already committed to dinner with Edward, so it wasn't like there was a choice—unless I wanted to be rude. But I realized I would much rather have dinner with Edward than hang with Nick and a bunch of faculty. "Um, tonight? No, I can't make it. Sorry."

"Too bad. What are you up to?"

And once again, that guilt/irritation thing hit me, only this time, irritation came first, as I felt he was being nosy. Then the guilt followed because it was a simple question.

"Lise?"

"I have a business dinner tonight."

"Which case?"

"It's not really a case, per se. I've been hired to put together an exhibition of artwork for the new San Marco Performing Arts Center when it opens and another six months after that."

"Hey, that's cool. Why didn't you tell me? I'll be happy to help any way I can."

"Thanks. It only became official yesterday, and I was waiting to tell you in person."

"We'll drink a toast in honor of Lise Norwood and the case of putting together an exhibit. Text when the dinner is over. You can join us later."

"Depends how late it goes."

"Love you, kiddo."

"Yeah, you too."

After I hit End Call, I sat there and replayed our conversation in my head. *Yeah, you too?* That was my response to Nick saying he loved me? I did love him. I knew that. All in all, I thought I'd been bitchy on that call. Luckily, Nick didn't seem to notice. And then I realized that he had said they were going out to celebrate and I hadn't even asked what they were celebrating. That switched my call ranking to bitchy *and* selfish.

A hint of panic struck. Nick said they were going out to celebrate. That meant there was a good chance they'd be heading to Razorbacks, which was popular among faculty and students. It would be uncomfortable running into Nick while dining with Edward. Now that I thought about it, Razorbacks was a stupid choice in general. Nick and I knew most of the servers by name and definitely all the bartenders. A lot of our friends went there on a regular basis. Oh, the gossip that would be fueled if I showed up with Hugh Jackman instead of young Michael Caine.

I immediately called Edward, but it went to voicemail. I left him a message. "You know what? Razorbacks gets pretty loud, so maybe we should go to a quieter establishment. The Chop House is another meat-leaning restaurant with wonderful prime rib. It's near the university, which means it's also near where you're building the performing arts center. We will need reservations at the Chop House. Can I leave that up to you? Call me if there's a problem. Otherwise, see you there."

Possible disaster averted, I got up and went to get a cup of coffee. As the Keurig machine filled my cup with black gold, I decided to start hitting the missing children databases and hopefully find something to help Baker's investigation. My cup full, I returned to my office, where Baker was sitting in one of the chairs.

"Speak of the devil," I said.

"Huh?"

I went to my desk and sat. "More like, think of the devil. I was just thinking about you. I'm getting ready to hit the missing children databases."

"Then I won't keep you long. I was driving by and thought I'd let you know that I've been talking with a retired detective in Panama City. Guy named Cruz."

"Cruz? Yeah, I met him once. He was one of the detectives who worked Gracie's murder. I was still at the university, but I visited my aunt a lot during that time. I met Cruz's partner too." I paused as I tried to remember his name.

"Richards," Baker supplied.

"Right. They came over to update my aunt on their progress, which if I remember right, was nil. Keep in mind that this was over fifteen years ago." I thought a moment. "I think they also showed her some photos of a couple of druggies to see if my aunt knew them."

"What was your impression of Cruz and Richards?"

I looked up as I tried to recall. "Cruz was, I remember, intense. Focused. Richards, on the other hand, I got the impression that he wasn't too serious about the case."

"He was an asshat?" Baker asked.

"What?"

"That's what Cruz called him. Said he could be an asshat and had no sympathy for crime victims if he considered them lowlifes, figured they asked for what they got. So he didn't like to put too much effort into solving those cases, and since your cousin was a known addict..." Baker shrugged. "Richards was senior detective, which didn't allow Cruz a lot of leeway to look into things more aggressively."

"Asshat," I grumbled.

"Cruz said their captain was of the same mindset as his partner. He felt that they had more leads to chase down when the captain brought the investigation to an end. Cruz said he'd be happy to talk with us when we go to Panama City in March. He said he'd do what he could to get us copies of the files on the case."

I had the urge to run around the desk and kiss his cheek, but he was highly embarrassed by such displays of affection, so I settled for, "Thanks, Baker. That's really great."

Chapter 19

Sometimes, my mind settles on something and gnaws on it like a dog with a marrow bone. As I got ready for the evening, that mental mastication went into overdrive concerning a certain private investigator, her boyfriend, and a new man in her life. Wait, that sounded so wrong. Make that a new client.

"After all, it's just a business dinner," I said out loud as I looked in the bathroom mirror, trying to decide how to wear my hair.

My conscience retorted. *Oh yeah? Then why are you working so hard to be attractive?*

"I'm trying to look professional."

I think he's attracted to you. Great, just great, now Eve was cluttering up my mind with her opinion. Okay, so let's assume, for argument's sake, that he was attracted to me. So what? Then I thought to look at it from a different perspective. How would I handle Edward if I didn't have Nick in my life? I froze, brush halfway through my hair.

Goose bumps rose on my arms, and my eyes locked with their mirrored counterparts as I admitted to myself, "Oh crap, I am attracted to Edward."

I resumed brushing my hair, though more aggressively. Why the attraction? There were the superficial reasons, like he was off the charts in both the handsome and rich departments. But I'd noticed other qualities, such as his humility and his kindness. He also had a sense of humor, something that was very important to me. And I was a firm believer in pheromones, those unique, invisible chemical messengers that triggered sexual or romantic attraction toward some people but not others. And in those cases where both parties were attracted to the other's pheromones, an intense magnetism could draw the couple together. Were my pheromones and Edward's in synch somehow?

My mood wavered. Eager anticipation one minute, remorse the next. I picked up my phone a couple times to call Edward and cancel our business dinner. And then I would think that I was engaged in the ol' mountain/molehill thing and making too much of Edward's friendliness.

A couple of times, I thought to call Nick and talk it through. He was my best friend, after all, and could help me figure this out. But in all honesty, I knew that wasn't going to happen.

"Shut up," I muttered to my brain.

The mental ping-pong between anticipation and guilt was tiring me out, so I brought up loud music on Spotify. I got to work on my makeup while jamming to Greta Van Fleet. Now my mind was occupied with the question of how Josh Kiszka could sing like that without his throat exploding. I dressed in a tan skirt just an inch high from modest, a black blouse with sleeves rolled up, and red pumps. For bling, I wore a silver bracelet and a silver cross and chain. Some discordant notes started to sound, and I realized it wasn't the music but my cell phone. I paused Greta and answered.

"Lise, hi. It's Elliot."

"Hi, Elliot. Got some news for me?"

"There's word on the street about those kids you're looking for."

"What do you have?"

"Not a lot, to be honest."

"Every little bit helps."

"I guess so. Anyway, it's around a dozen kids, from young to mid-teens. They're runaways and orphans. Some people have tried to talk to them, but they stick to themselves, don't want to have anything to do with adults. No one sees 'em during the day. They come out at night, and they're dressed weird. Funny hats, wings, loincloths, pirates, cowboys, and Indians."

"Costumes?"

"Yeah, I guess so."

"Any idea where they go during the day?" I asked.

"All I've found out is that when they leave downtown or Old Town, they head west."

"And they're on their own?"

"Not exactly. There's a man who's been seen with them. From what I've heard, he's like the ringleader. Their boss."

"What's he look like?"

"Long hair and beard. Old enough that he has some gray. Wears a black hat and an overcoat."

"Any way we can find out where they live?"

"I'm ahead of you. I told a few guys I trust that you'll give a hundred dollars to the person who finds out where they hole up during the day. Hope that was all right."

"That's fine. I'll just add it to the consulting fee. Thanks, Elliot."

"There's one more thing." Elliot's voice got low and soft, which usually indicated something serious. "Someone else is looking for them too."

"Who?"

"Don't know, specifically, but word is they're heavy hitters. Criminals, but the kind that dress in nice clothes and drive fancy cars. They've been talking to street folk, asking questions, offering bribes, threatening some."

"Does anyone know why they're looking for them?"

"Nope. Usually comes down to money, though, don't it? All I know for sure is that we're in a race. I'm gonna get back to it."

"Let me know when you learn anything. Right away, no matter the time."

I ended the call and looked at myself in the mirror. I didn't like what I saw. Elliot was heading back into the trenches, and I was going out to have dinner with a man who may or may not be attracted to me, and who I may or may not be attracted to. Sighing, I strode through the living room, picked up my bag, and headed for Minnie.

My mind was on heavy hitters as I drove to the Chop House. Elliot called them criminals in nice clothes driving fancy cars. Why would they be looking for these kids? I came up with some possibilities. They were human traffickers, and the kids had escaped. Maybe the kids had something these people wanted, or the kids knew too much about them. Could be this group of underage thieves owed them something and were in default. And then there was the leader of the kids. What kind of man would force children to burglarize and steal? What had he done to them? What would he do to them? If the kid's death wasn't an accident, had this ringleader pushed him in front of the train? Had the heavy hitters done that?

Steering with my left hand, I scrolled my contacts with my right, called Detective Baker, and filled him in on what Elliot had told me.

He paused a long moment then said, "Let me know if you learn anything else."

"Okay."

"I'll call Eve and fill her in."

"Thanks, Baker."

After a grunt, he ended the call.

Chapter 20

"Hello, Chop House," I mumbled as I turned Minnie into the parking lot. I didn't normally greet the restaurants I patronized, but after talking with Baker, I got my mind straight. I was going to have dinner with a man who had hired me for a job. Quite different from my other PI jobs but a job just the same. I liked Edward and enjoyed spending time with him. No crime there. Plus, I loved good food, and that was what the Chop House offered. There was no reason, I decided, that I should feel guilty.

I got out of Minnie and breathed in the wonderful aroma of grilled meats. Originally a 1930s house on a large lot a block from the university, it had been a restaurant longer than I'd been alive. While chops were the focus, the menu offerings went well beyond.

I entered the restaurant carrying a file of information about contemporary Florida artists and photos of their work. I told the hostess, a pretty young woman I assumed was a student at San Marco University, who I was meeting. She informed me I was the first to arrive and led me through one dining room, past the bar, and into the back dining room. She showed me to a table and offered to get me a drink. I ordered a buttery Chardonnay and a glass of water.

The table was in the more elegant of the two dining rooms, which was dimly lit with a burning candle on each linen-covered table. The chairs were wooden with stuffed brown leather on the seats and backs. Our table was next to a window that looked out at the back patio, which featured benches among a well-manicured garden and a koi pond. Strings of soft white Christmas lights gave the patio a dreamlike quality.

A server—"Hello, my name is Gavin"—brought me my wine and water. I took a sip of the Chardonnay and closed my eyes in appreciation. Opening them, I saw Edward approach, wearing dark slacks and a matching jacket over a black V-neck shirt. His bodyguard stalked him, her eyes casting around the room.

He took my hand as if intending to shake it, but instead, he covered it with his other hand and held it for a moment. "Sorry I'm late." He released my hand and sat in the chair across the table.

Eileen Warrick took a seat at the next table over.

The hand he'd gripped seemed to radiate warmth. "No problem. The wine and I were just getting acquainted."

Gavin approached, introducing himself again, and Edward said, "I'd like to get acquainted with a good Cabernet."

When Gavin returned with Edward's wine, the server launched into the evening's specials.

Edward held up his hand. "Gavin, let me stop you there. Tonight, we're on an expedition in the pursuit of good prime rib. Can you hook us up?"

"Yes, sir. We have the best prime rib in San Marco."

Under my breath but still loud enough to hear, I said in a singsong voice, "Razorbacks."

Gavin blushed and amended his statement. "We have prime rib as good as anywhere else in San Marco."

"Excellent. We'll have two prime rib dinners."

Watching our server depart, I said, "Leave him a good tip to make up for me interrupting his pitch."

Edward pointed at the file folder by my place setting. "Is that the business part of our dinner?"

"It is." I slid the file to him. "So, these are some of the notable artists from mid-Florida up to southern Georgia. I'd like your opinion on which you'd like me to pursue."

Edward nodded and spent several minutes flipping through the photos. When Gavin arrived with our salads, Edward put down the file. "Lise, I have a confession to make."

I took a few seconds to chew and swallow microgreens and vinaigrette. "Wow, I haven't known you that long and already you're confessing. I hope it's embarrassing."

He gave me a serious look. "My success is due in large part because I hire the best people and let them do their jobs without micromanaging. You go ahead and set up this exhibit in the way you choose, and don't worry about getting approval."

"I appreciate your confidence in me. But as far as confessions go, I was hoping for something more salacious."

He speared some salad on his fork. "I'm saving those for a little later in our..." He paused, and I thought he was on the verge of saying *relationship*. Instead, he finished with "friendship."

Friendship was not as intimate but a good deal warmer than association. *Stop overanalyzing,* I thought to myself in the same singsong voice I'd used on the waiter. I took a sip of wine.

He seemed to sense my discomfort and brought up his plans for initial performances at the arts center. From there, topics shifted to San Marco's rich history, of which I loved to share my knowledge to an eager listener, which he turned out to be. He asked questions about my past—nothing too personal—and I filled him in on my history. Our prime ribs arrived at the same time a merry band of revelers took over the bar area. Laughter and loud conversation replaced the serene quiet we'd enjoyed.

After we'd both had a glass of wine too many and packed away as much prime rib as we could muster, curiosity overrode my common sense. "So, how about the women in your life? Past and present."

"Well, I'll start with present. Currently, the women in my life include Trish and Eileen. And since Marjorie has taken me under her wing and is introducing me to the city's movers and shakers, I'll include her."

"I was thinking of women besides a CFO, bodyguard, or senior citizen." My timing was perfect because everyone in the bar laughed at something, and I felt like I had my own personal laugh track.

Edward, however, didn't laugh. He didn't even smile but in all seriousness said, "And there's you, Lise. You are, at present, a woman in my life." His blue-eyed gaze locked on me, and I found it hard to turn away. "I hope that you will be a woman in my life in the future as well."

Through sheer force of will, I glanced away. "You know what I mean."

He smiled, the intensity in his eyes gone. "Indeed, I do." He seemed to collect his thoughts. "I've never been married. I've never found someone I wanted to marry. I guess it's as simple as that. I've had a couple of long-term relationships, and I'm still friends with both women. I date when I meet someone who interests me, and I'm open-minded about where it will lead. But eventually, things end." Edward took a sip of wine. "I think, in the past, my mind was focused on my businesses too much for me to maintain a stable relationship. But I hope that at this stage in my life, if I find the right woman, I'd work on that and shift more of my focus on her." With that statement hanging in the air between us, the fire in his eyes reignited.

I felt my cheeks start to blush. "When I first met you and saw Trish at the Garrido, I thought she might be your significant other."

Edward grinned at that assumption. "She is significant in my life, but not like that. No, a long time ago, I made the conscious choice to never date an employee or coworker. That can go wrong on so many levels."

I felt a great deal of relief and also some regret. For good or ill, I was off the hook.

Edward leaned forward and placed his arm on the table in front of him. "That being said, what do we call our professional relationship?"

"Huh?"

He slid his right hand along the tabletop, past his plate and wine-glass, until it was within easy reach.

"You're neither a coworker nor employee. You are a private investigator, and I am your client. Right?"

I suddenly heard Scooby Doo in my mind. *Ruh-roh.* The bar area erupted in more laughter.

My left hand, seemingly of its own desire, settled on the table next to his right, my little finger brushing his thumb. Edward moved his hand slowly and settled it gently on top of my own. I stared from our hands to my plate and then to his handsome face. I thought to pull my hand away, but I was frozen by a fluttery nervousness in my chest. I also suffered from that inability to draw anything but a shallow breath that only showed up at the beginning of a new relationship. He squeezed my hand in a way that was both firm and gentle.

"Well, look who's here," a familiar voice said from behind me.

I turned in time to see Warrick place herself between Nick and our table. She put a hand to Nick's chest, stopping his progress.

In a perturbed voice, Nick said, "Excuse me." He attempted to push her hand away. She grabbed his wrist, spun him around, and a second later, had his arm pinned behind his back.

Chapter 21

I stood and blurted, "Nick!" Though I only said his name, I used many different inflections, including an *Oh my God, you're being attacked* variation. Another indicated *Yikes, you caught me having dinner with another man.* A third interpretation was the ol' *What are you doing here?* And of course *It's not what it looks like,* which usually means *It's so what it looks like.*

When Edward realized who Nick was, he called off Eileen. "That's enough."

She cocked an eyebrow at her boss.

"He's a friend of Lise."

She released Nick but stood at the ready.

Nick distanced himself from her. "What was that?" he asked dazedly as he straightened his shirt.

"I'm sorry," Edward said.

A feminine voice called, "Nick! Are you all right?"

The question should have come from me, but it didn't. A woman with a mane of fiery red hair hurried toward us. As if the night's surreal turn couldn't get any stranger, there was Nick's old girlfriend.

"Meredith Frazier?" I said, like I feared I might be suffering from a strange hallucination.

"Lise, hi."

Every eye in the dining room was fixed on our little group.

"It's okay," Edward said to Warrick, and she returned to her table. Edward then got up and pulled out a chair for Meredith. After she sat, he held out a hand to Nick. "Edward Burke."

Nick, still looking stunned, shook his hand. "Nick Weldon."

"Yes, I've heard of you."

He next took Meredith's hand.

"Meredith Frazier," she said and gazed up at him, an awestruck expression on her face. A lot of women probably wore that same look when they first met him.

"Please sit," Edward said to Nick and me.

Nick and I exchanged glances as we sat, his confusion evident. And did I see some hurt in his eyes? I quickly looked away. I was dumbstruck, and judging from the lengthy silence, the situation was uncomfortable for everyone.

Nick finally spoke. "So, what's with..." He looked over to Warrick at the next table.

"I'm sorry about that," Edward said. "She's my bodyguard. It's her job to stop anyone she doesn't know from approaching me."

Nick nodded as if in thought and then said loud enough for Eileen to hear, "I was approaching my girlfriend, not you."

"Nick, don't start," I said.

"Start what?"

Edward held up a hand. "No, it's all right. I'm still getting used to having a bodyguard myself. I've never had security before, but because of certain recent events, and at the encouragement of Burke Industries' board of directors, I now have Eileen looking out for me."

"So, what do you do that requires security? Organized crime? In the witness protection program?"

"Nothing nefarious, I assure you. But sometimes, successful businesspeople find themselves targets for some reason or another."

"You've hired Lise?"

"Yes. She's collecting artwork for display at the new San Marco Performing Arts Center."

Nick fixed me with a gaze. "So this is your business dinner?"

"Yes, it is. What are you and Meredith doing here?" I asked.

"Hear that?" Nick lifted his eyebrows and pointed a finger up as raucous laughter came from the bar. "That's the celebration you couldn't make because you had a business dinner."

The only way he could have made *business dinner* sound more pretentious would be by adding air quotes.

"At the Chop House?" I could think of a bunch of places more suited to a faculty celebration, specifically Razorbacks.

"My choice," Meredith said. "This was my favorite restaurant back in our school days." Meredith smiled at me and shrugged. "I was told to pick a place."

Edward gave Meredith a hundred-watt smile. "What are you celebrating?"

Before she could answer, everything clicked into place. "You hired Meredith for your old position."

"I didn't hire her," Nick said. "The university hired her, but yes, that's what we're celebrating tonight."

"Congratulations," Edward said.

"Thanks," she said, staring into his eyes.

As if things weren't strange enough, we tried to have a normal conversation, which Edward helped along with questions. We talked about when Meredith and I had been students and what she had been doing since she left town.

Finally, Nick stood. "We'll leave you guys to your business dinner." Again, the unwanted emphasis on *business dinner*.

"Hey, come join us for a drink when you're done," Meredith said.

"Sounds good." Edward stood and shook her hand. When he took Nick's, they both looked each other in the eye for longer than necessary.

As Nick and Meredith made their way back to the bar, Edward said, "That was interesting."

I glared at him. "I'm so glad we could amuse you."

"No, Lise, that's not what I meant."

I tuned him out and dropped my gaze to the tabletop to try to analyze what I felt. Confusion, guilt, embarrassment, and an odd sense of displacement that I was here instead of with Nick.

I stood abruptly. "It's been real."

Edward stood. "Are you all right?"

I snagged my purse hanging from the chairback. "Yep."

"Would you like me to walk you to your car?"

I picked up the file folder. "Nope."

I walked out the French doors onto the back patio. I would take the time to go around the restaurant rather than pass by the bar.

Chapter 22

Thursday Night

"Olivia, my dear, let's take a walk," Mr. Teacher said. "I have a chore to run with Dodge and Tarzan, but I would like to chat with you first."

"Okay," Olivia said.

They strolled around the campus of the old abandoned college, their way lit by tiki torches. They stopped to listen to Nancy sing a beautiful ballad of lost love while Tarzan strummed his guitar. When the song ended, they started off again. Mr. Teacher walked erectly with his hands behind his back. She stayed by his side but kept her gaze downcast. Mr. Teacher pointed to a building with a wide window low to the ground that had long ago had its glass broken out. They sat on the window jamb, side by side, like it was a bench.

"How are you holding up, my dear?"

Olivia's feet were a few inches off the ground, and she squirmed about to balance herself. "I'm still sad about Mackie."

"And you will be for a long time. It's called grieving, and there's nothing wrong with feeling like you do. I want you to look at it from another perspective, however. Do you consider yourself lucky to have had him in your life, as short a time as it was?"

"Oh yes."

"Then, when grief strikes, remember that it was a blessing to have his friendship." Mr. Teacher smiled sadly. "Do you know what a eulogy is, my dear?"

Olivia shook her head.

"It is a speech written about a person that is read at their funeral. I want to have a memorial service for Mackie. Would you write a eulogy for him that I may read aloud to the others?"

"Yes."

"Thank you, my dear." Mr. Teacher bent down to look into Olivia's eyes. "Did you chronicle Mackie's death yet?"

"Yes."

"May I read it?"

She opened the journal to the correct page and passed it to him. He read it over and then gazed into the distance. After a couple of minutes, he reread it, closed the journal, and passed it back to her.

"Very good, Olivia." After a moment, he tapped the journal. "Put in there that I failed to save Mackie."

"No, Mr. Teacher."

He gave her a stern look. "Put it in just as I told you." He stood and walked off.

She wrote for thirty seconds and hoped Mr. Teacher wouldn't be mad if he ever read what she really wrote. *The monster killed Mackie, but Mr. Teacher saved Dodge.*

She worked on the eulogy for a while and heard an engine start. She looked up to see Mr. Teacher, Tarzan, and Dodge head out in the old VW. They returned an hour later, opened the hood—which in old VW bugs was the trunk—and removed a large coquina rock big enough that it took all three of them to lift. They carried it past the old swimming pool to an area where, earlier that day, they'd all cleaned out brush and debris. They dropped the rock at the center of the clearing.

"Bring all the lanterns," Mr. Teacher instructed. To Dodge, he said, "Get me the briefcase."

Fifteen minutes later, they all sat in a circle around the big rock, the clearing lit by multiple lanterns.

Mr. Teacher had taken the small Santa ornament from the Christmas tree and placed it on the rock. "My dear friends, tonight, we honor dear Mackie with a memorial, and this rock will stand as his headstone." He looked to Olivia, and she held out the journal, opened to the proper page. Mr. Teacher took it, cleared his throat, and read to the group.

Mackie was a smile,
Mackie was laughter,
He was a sweet, funny voice,
He was sunshine,
He was a candle in the dark,
Mackie was our friend.

"Mackie," Mr. Teacher said.

"Mackie," Dodge said.

"Mackie."

"Mackie."

"Mackie."

One by one, the clan of children spoke his name, Olivia the last to do so.

Mr. Teacher closed the journal and returned it to her. Clasping his hands together, he extended both index fingers and tapped them against his lips. He walked within the ring of children, orbiting several times before he finally spoke.

"My friends, my family, I have made the difficult decision that it is time for us to leave San Marco."

Groans and expressions of disappointment sounded from the children.

Mr. Teacher held up his hands. "I know. I feel the same as you. San Marco has become our home." He strode to the stone and placed his hand on top. "And yet, our home has betrayed us and taken our Mackie. Because of the briefcase, I fear that all of us are in danger. And for good reason. Dodge and I carefully counted the money last night, and it comes to one million dollars."

Whoas, wows, and whistles came from the group.

"One million dollars exactly. Certainly the most momentous pay-off we've had but not nearly enough to compensate for the loss of our little brother." Mr. Teacher raised an arm and pointed to the sky, speaking like a hellfire-and-brimstone preacher. "The very thing that brought this curse upon us will now give us wings so that we may take flight." He sat in the dirt. "Tomorrow morning, we will pack up the school bus and depart, beginning new adventures."

"Where will we go?" Nancy asked.

"I'm thinking of the Gulf Coast but out of state, far enough that we'll be safe from the people looking for us. I think our family would fit in well in New Orleans. Perhaps we could expand our repertoire. Besides thieving, we could take on the mantle of street performers as well. Some of you could use your musical skills, particularly Tarzan and Nancy. We could develop a whole act around Tink's juggling and Bet's magic. Charly could do stand-up comedy. Yes, I do believe that New Orleans is our destination. Is everybody all right with that?"

Olivia thought that the children, for the first time since Mackie's death, seemed excited. They cheered.

"One more thing," Mr. Teacher shouted, getting everyone's attention. "Do not discuss our plans with anyone who is not part of this family. If they find out— and you know who I mean—they'd no doubt follow us to the Big Easy."

"What's the Big Easy, Mr. Teacher?" Bet asked.

"That, my dear, is a nickname for—"

From a distance came a long whistle, followed by another, and then a third.

"The warning signal," Mr. Teacher said. "Quick, quick, gather round."

Olivia and the rest of the kids rushed to encircle him. His eyes blazed as he spoke in a low voice. "Tomorrow. Under the pier." He took a second to take in their faces and then he shouted, "*Run!*"

Instant chaos erupted as kids rushed everywhere. Mackie's Santa ornament was knocked from the rock and shattered on the ground. Dodge ran past Mr. Teacher and tossed him the briefcase before disappearing into the brush. Olivia watched it all, so scared she couldn't move. Suddenly, the clearing was empty, and she thought she was alone. Grabbed from behind, Olivia screamed. She was spun around and found herself face-to-face with Nancy.

"Come on, Olivia." Nancy took her by the hand, and they ran into the woods. After several minutes, they stopped. "Are you okay?"

Panting, Olivia nodded.

"You wait here. I want to scout ahead."

Olivia didn't want to be left alone and started to protest, but Nancy was already gone. Olivia didn't know what else to do, so she knelt on the ground and tried to make herself as small as possible. Ahead of her, it sounded like large animals were moving through the woods, but then lights swept back and forth. Someone spoke, and someone answered. Men with flashlights. She stood and fled in the opposite direction of the voices. More flashlights appeared to the right of her, and she veered left.

Someone grabbed her and picked her up. She screamed, and a hand covered her mouth. "Shh, Olive. It's me, Tarzan." He put her down, grabbed her hand, and they ran from the lights.

It was all happening so fast. She pushed through the woods behind Tarzan, who would go straight for a while and then take random turns. He stopped, knelt, and pulled her down. Up ahead were three flashlights swinging back and forth, accompanied by the noise of men stepping on sticks and leaves and pushing through undergrowth. They were heading directly toward Tarzan and Olivia.

Tarzan put his mouth near Olivia's ear. "I'm going to draw them away." He pointed to the right. "When they come after me, you run that way." He aimed his finger in the opposite direction of the approaching men.

"Tarzan, no."

He grinned at her. "See ya, Olive." He was off, running noisily through the brush. When he got twenty feet from her, he let loose a ululating howl that sounded like a great jungle animal.

"There!" someone yelled, and three men with flashlights went after him.

Olivia ran in the direction Tarzan had instructed, and soon, her breathing was rapid and shallow. She nearly dashed into a small clearing where several men were talking but dropped to the ground behind a tree instead.

"I think she went that way," one of the men said.

"Then go after her," another man ordered, and the first man took off in pursuit.

"Shit, the little squirrely one got away."

Olivia recognized the third voice, peeked around the tree, and saw the policeman who'd been there when the monster killed Mackie.

"Come on, how hard can it be to grab some stupid kids, huh?" the first man asked.

When the two men stumbled off into the dark woods, she ran in the opposite direction and learned the best thing to do was to run a little bit and then crouch down and listen. She avoided two groups of hunters that way.

Someone behind her yelled, "Ouch! Fuckin' trees!"

She took off. Her lungs hurt with each breath, but she didn't dare slow down. More minutes of blind flight passed, and then she realized a road was just ahead. Through the trees, she saw the Thieves Kitchen school bus drive past.

"Wait!" she yelled and ran for the road.

She got snagged by a thorny vine, and by the time she worked herself free and bolted into the street, the bus was rounding a curve, heading away from her. She waved her arms and shouted. The road lit up, and her shadow loomed in front of her. She turned to see two headlights quickly approaching. Olivia screamed and fell. Brakes squealed, and a car stopped mere feet from her, blinding her with its headlights.

She heard the door open. "Oh my God, are you all right, sweetheart?"

A great wave of relief surged through Olivia at the sound of the woman's voice.

"Are you hurt?" The woman rushed to Olivia and picked her up with strong arms.

` "Monsters," Olivia said. "Monsters are chasing us."

The woman carried Olivia to the back of the car. "There's no such thing as monsters, sweetie. Let me get you a blanket."

Confused as to why the woman thought she needed a blanket on a warm night, Olivia watched the woman open the trunk with her key fob.

The trunk opened and the trunk light came on, illuminating the woman's face. *Monster!* Olivia thought.

The woman threw Olivia in the trunk and closed the lid, plunging her into darkness.

Olivia heard the woman shout, "Hey! I got one of them!"

Chapter 23

Early Friday Morning

I'm a side sleeper. If I have trouble sleeping, it was left side, right side, left side, and repeat. As my business dinner with Edward went so atrociously wrong, I was wearing a groove in my mattress with all my side-to-side back and forth. Oh yeah, I had a fully stocked anxiety bar. First was my embarrassment in front of Edward, and I think that stemmed from how poorly I handled the whole thing. And had Nick seen Edward's hand on mine? Throwing Meredith into the mix hadn't helped the situation.

"Fuck, fuck, fuck," I muttered, cursing the fates that put my dinner and Nick's celebration at the same restaurant.

If my mother were still alive, I would have driven to San Marco Eldercare first thing in the morning. It didn't matter that she wouldn't have been capable of speaking or that she wouldn't have recognized me. I would be in her presence, and I could unload all my baggage, and then I would hear her voice in my head offering the best advice a mother could give.

I sat up, swung my legs off the bed, and decided to chase a melatonin pill with a shot of Irish whiskey. Then I heard someone climbing the wooden stairs up to the deck of my stilt house. A person could sneak up undetected, which had been proven the previous year when the serial killer, Michelangelo, prowled through my house while I slept.

Whoever was ascending the stairs this time wasn't trying to be stealthy but walking with heavy steps.

"Nick," I mumbled. I'd been hoping to get my thoughts straight before we had our inevitable talk, but if he was here, then so be it.

I turned on the light and looked at the clock, which showed it was just after one. I stepped into my flip-flops as he crossed the deck, and I walked out of my bedroom when he knocked on the door. In purple cotton pajama bottoms and a white tank top, I went to let him in.

When I turned on the porch light, though, I saw it wasn't Nick. I opened the door. "Pete?" I looked past him to an old pickup truck parked at the curb in front of my house.

He pulled open the screen door and pushed past me. "You fucked us over, Lise." His face was dark and twisted with rage. Wendy had told me how angry he could get, which led to lots of fights. Watching him pace in a worn black jacket and heavy boots, I was worried.

I spoke calmly. "I have no idea what you're talking about, Pete."

He stopped pacing and glared at me, one hand tugging at his lengthy beard. In a low, accusing voice, he said, "You didn't tell us this could happen."

"Are you sober?"

His glare got even more hostile, and then his gaze turned to my hand still on the knob of the open door. He looked back to my face as if daring me to stop him, and he pulled the door from my grasp and closed it.

"I'm not drunk." His volume doubled. "What I am is pissed." And like someone flipped a switch, his anger was gone, and he softly said, "And I'm scared."

"Come here," I said and led him to the kitchen. I got my bottle of Jameson from a cabinet, along with two short glasses. I put them on the butcher block. "First this, and then I want you to tell me what's going on."

He reached into a jacket pocket for a hair tie and secured his long locks in a ponytail. "Yeah, okay."

I poured us both a couple fingers of whiskey. He brought his glass up to his lips, and I could tell he was going to shoot the whole thing down.

"Wait," I said, and he paused with the glass halfway to his mouth. "No shots. Sip it. And when you're ready, talk to me."

He nodded and took a sip. I did as well, keeping my eyes on him the whole time. After a couple more sips, his breathing went from bear-like pants to slow and even.

Pete started for another sip but put the glass down instead. "I need the painting back. Tonight. Now."

"I don't have it, Pete. The museum does. You know that. Wendy loaned it to them."

He drained the remaining whiskey. "Yeah, well, the museum has to give it back."

"Wendy signed paperwork. She agreed that it would be shown for a certain length of time, after which you guys will get it back." I watched his face, waiting for a reaction. "Besides, legally speaking, Wendy is the owner, and she's probably the only person who can request its return."

He grabbed the bottle, poured more whiskey into his glass, went into the living room, and dropped onto my sofa. "I am so screwed, Lise."

And then it clicked. "Where's Wendy?"

Pete held my gaze but didn't answer.

"Does this have to do with Wendy's—" I almost said *Wendy's ALS*. "Have to do with Wendy's health? Do you need money for medical bills?"

He looked at me as if I had spoken in Mandarin. "What the hell are you talking about?"

I sat in a chair, the coffee table between us. "Tell me what's going on."

"I can't."

"Why?"

"They told me I couldn't tell anybody." He drank what was left in his glass and set it on the coffee table.

I was sure confusion was evident in my expression. "Who's they?"

He shook his head.

I leaned forward, elbows on my knees. "I can't help you if you don't tell me what's going on."

He kept his face cast down. After a full minute, he said, "I'll tell you, but you first have to promise you won't tell anyone else."

"Okay."

He looked at me. "And that includes the police."

"Oh. I'm not sure I should—"

Pointing at me, he said, "We're in this mess because you tracked down the painting and convinced Wendy to put it in the museum. It's because of you it made the news." He brought his fist down onto the coffee table.

I jumped and took a moment to think. "I promise not to tell anyone, unless you agree that I can."

He nodded slowly and reached into an inside jacket pocket, retrieving a folded piece of paper. He handed it to me.

I unfolded it and read it. Then I read it again. I felt goose bumps rise on my flesh. "It's a ransom note."

Chapter 24

Olivia wanted to scream but was too scared. During the short ride, she ran her hands all over the interior of the trunk, feeling only the rough carpet she lay on and the trunk lid overhead. She was small enough that she could easily move inside the trunk, but the ride was over before she could find anything useful.

From outside the trunk, she heard the woman's voice. "In there."

A moment later, the trunk opened, and two flashlights blinded her. Strong hands grabbed her and lifted her, banging her head against the trunk lid in the process. Somebody carried her about twenty feet while she struggled. At a police car, she was draped across the hood, belly down. She could feel the heat of the engine as someone pulled her hands behind her back. She twisted her head and saw the policeman, who secured her wrists together with a zip tie. A number of men wearing suits were standing around, and one of them lifted her, carried her to an SUV, placed her in the back seat, and shut the door.

"Hello, Olive."

She turned at the sound of the familiar voice. Tarzan sat, cramped against the other back door. Between them were Dodge and Dag. All three of the other children sat slightly forward because their hands, like Olivia's, were zip tied behind their backs.

"Where are we?" Olivia asked.

"Road into Thieves Kitchen," Dodge said, anger in his voice.

Dag swung his head to the side to get his curly locks out of his eyes. "So far, we're all they've caught."

"What will they do to us?" Olivia asked.

"Don't worry, Olivia," Dodge said. "Mr. Teacher will get us out of this."

Dag laid his head back against the seat back and muttered, "Like he saved Mackie?"

Dodge stiffened, and his face darkened, but it was Olivia who shouted, "Don't say that!"

They all stared at her in surprise, probably because they'd never heard her speak much louder than a whisper.

Dag nodded. "You're right, Olive. I'm sorry. Mr. Teacher *will* save us."

For the next half hour, they watched the goings-on around them. Their attackers included nine men, one of them a policeman, and one woman. There were three SUVs, all black and the same make and model, the police car, and the sedan that the woman had driven when she captured Olivia. The men occasionally returned to the SUVs, talked with one another, and then disappeared back into the woods.

"Did you see the lady?" Dodge asked Olivia.

She nodded. "You mean the monster," Olivia said, her voice trembling. "The monster who killed Mackie."

Eventually, all the men who'd hunted them down returned. Tarzan said, "I think everyone else got away."

A couple of minutes later, Dag said, "I wish at least one of us had our hands free."

"To help us escape?" Dodge asked.

"No. To scratch my nose. It's itching like crazy." Dag shoved his nose against Dodge's tuxedo coat and moved his head left to right and up and down.

Snickering, Dodge said, "Cut it out."

Dag shifted and rubbed his nose against Olivia's shoulder.

She giggled. "Quit it."

All four of them chuckled then let loose with gut-wrenching laughter. Maybe it was nervous energy that had built out of fear and anxiety, but they were laughing just the same. One of the rear doors was yanked open, and the interior light made them squint.

A man bent to look inside the car at them. His face was wide and flat while his nose crooked at an angle. "Shut the fuck up!" he bellowed.

They went quiet, but Olivia took comfort in the confusion that showed on the man's face. He slammed the door, shook his head, and walked to join a couple of other men.

Olivia, Dag, Dodge, and Tarzan grinned at each other. Olivia had witnessed courage when Mackie laughed at the woman who had held a gun under his chin. She'd seen it again when they had all laughed while the bad guys tried to scare them. Olivia's smile faded when she remembered that Mackie's brave moment ended when he was pushed into the path of a train.

The door by Olivia opened again, and the woman said, "Him."

A second later, the pie-faced man reached across Olivia and Dag, grabbed Dodge, and yanked him from the car. Dodge struggled but only managed to kick Dag in the chin. Outside, the big man held Dodge against the SUV.

The woman stepped up to him. "Dodge, isn't it?"

Dodge glared at the woman and then spat in her face. Looking shocked, the woman stepped back a couple paces and wiped at her cheek with the sleeve of her jacket. She nodded at the man, and he punched Dodge in the face. Dodge slumped to the ground.

"You idiot," the woman said. "I meant in the stomach. He needs a clear head to remember the instructions."

"Sorry," the man said.

"Pick him up."

The man held Dodge against the SUV with one hand, and with the other, he patted Dodge's cheeks.

After a minute, Dodge jerked his head back and yelled, "Stop doing that!"

"Ah, good. You're back with us," the woman said.

Dodge fought against the man's grasp and, through gritted teeth, said, "Let me go."

"That's just it, Dodge. That's what I'm going to do," the woman said.

He stopped thrashing. "Huh?"

She got close to his face. "First off, if you spit on me again"—she looked up at the man holding Dodge—"I'll have him snap your spine over his knee." She took a moment to gauge Dodge's reaction and then went on. "I'm going to let you go, and you're going to deliver a message to your boss."

Dodge stared at her through narrowed eyes then motioned a thumb over his shoulder toward the back seat. "What about them?"

"They stay with me. You get the message to your boss. If he does what I say, I'll free them. If, however, you don't get the message to him or he doesn't do what I say, they'll die just like your little friend. What was his name? Maxie, right?"

"Mackie," Dodge said in a low tone.

"Whatever," the woman said. She leaned until her nose was only a couple inches from Dodge's. "Tell your boss that he can save your little friends if he returns the briefcase. Tell him we'll count the money, so he better make sure it's all there. When we get it, we'll free them." She looked at the kids in the back seat and then at Dodge. "Easy, right?"

"How do we find you? How do we get the briefcase to you?" Dodge asked.

"Tell your boss that he needs to find a woman in town, a private investigator named Lise Norwood. Now, repeat the name to me."

"Lise Norwood," Dodge said.

"And then you'll tell Lise that we'll call her and give her instructions. Understand?"

"Got it."

She pointed at the policeman. "And don't even think about going to the police. They're on our side."

Dodge glared at the officer. "We don't go to the cops. Ever."

The woman stood to her full height. "Oh, and take too long..." She drew a line across her throat with a long-nailed finger.

She turned, stalked back to the sedan, and got in. The flat-faced man shoved Dodge away from the SUV, got in the driver's seat, closed the door, and started the engine.

Olivia looked out the window of the SUV at Dodge as they drove off.

Chapter 25

The ransom note read, *We have your wife. Do as we say, or she will die. Don't tell anyone. No police. Will exchange her for Cold Green Spring. Will be in contact.* The note looked as if it had been printed on twenty-pound copy paper on an average home printer. I looked up from the note to the worry on Pete's face.

"I've already fucked up, Lise. I told someone else. You."

"Maybe. But we won't let them know that." I reread the note. "Tell me how you got this."

"Bowser, one of the bartenders, the big guy you met, was closing the bar tonight. Wendy was supposed to be home by nine. I waited another hour and then called the bar. Bowser said she'd left a little after eight. I called around, but no one had seen her. I was gonna go hit some other nightspots, see if she was at one, but I found that note stuck in the screen door. I freaked and drove up to San Marco. At first, I was gonna break into the museum and get the painting back, but I cooled down enough to realize I'd get caught, which wouldn't help Wendy. Then I thought you'd be the best person to help me get the painting out of the museum."

Figuring this took precedence over the late hour, I got my phone and called Marjorie's home. I first had to convince her butler it was important that I talk to her. It took a few minutes for him to go and wake her and for her to pick up the phone. Pete paced the whole time.

"Lise?" Marjorie sounded confused and sleepy.

"Marjorie, I can't offer any explanation, but the owners of *Cold Green Spring* need the painting back right now. It's very important."

I expected some argument or a demand to know more. Instead, sounding wide awake, she said, "Come over in an hour, Lise. Bring whoever is with you."

"**I** never knew this was here," Pete said.

Even though Marjorie lived in the heart of San Marco's Old City, few people realized how extensive her property was. It covered a full city block, but it was ringed by stores, galleries, restaurants, and a bed-and-breakfast, and was, therefore, hidden. The back of her main house sat on Cordova Avenue, but the rest of her property was virtually invisible to the casual observer. A restaurant shared the driveway to her estate, and restaurant employees and the drivers of food delivery trucks turned into a lot just past the restaurant. Those who continued going straight got to Marjorie's gate. Visitors had to press an intercom to gain entrance unless they knew the code, which Marjorie had provided me when she first hired me. I punched in the numbers, and the gate slid to the side.

Marjorie had recently told me that every year, she had a crew put up Christmas decorations and thousands of colored lights to illuminate the estate. The main house was directly across the property from the gate. We drove past a guest house that was almost as big, through manicured gardens and lawns, and past several outbuildings, including a seven-car garage. We finally came to the mansion that had been designed and built in 1889 by Thomas Hastings as one of his Florida homes. Hastings was one of the architects responsible for the New York Public Library, as well as several luxury hotels built in the late nineteenth century in Florida. When I'd first visited, Marjorie had given me a tour of the home built in what she called the beaux arts architectural style, a combination of French neoclassicism with renaissance and baroque elements. She had even laughed at my "if it's baroque, don't fix it" joke. Suffice to say the house was huge and old but still in great shape.

"Please come in, Ms. Norwood," Kent said. A tall man in his fifties with a full head of gray hair, he wore a navy-blue bathrobe made of silk with gold edging. His pajamas were matching. I thought of him as a butler, but Marjorie called him her house manager.

"Thanks, Kent. This is my friend Pete," I said.

"Pleased to meet you, sir."

"Yeah, back at you," Pete said, eyeing him cautiously.

"Would you like me to take your jacket?" Kent asked, indicating Pete's leather jacket.

"No." Pete brushed past him.

"Mrs. Hamilton is in the sitting room. I'll bring some coffee."

I leaned toward him. "Can you also bring something brown, Irish, and in a bottle?"

Kent gave a brief nod and departed. I knew the way to the sitting room and led Pete there. It may only have been a little past three a.m., but the house was lit from top to bottom. Pete's head was swiveling left and right as he took in the fine furnishings, artwork, and overall luxuriousness.

"Swanky," he said.

"That it is."

We got to the door leading to the sitting room. Before entering, I asked, "How're you holding up?"

"Not well." He took several deep breaths. "Let's find out what the old lady has to say." Pete went through the door. "What? No. Who's that?"

I stepped in after him. Marjorie was sitting on a large sofa, wearing a raspberry-colored housecoat and slippers. Edward Burke, in faded jeans and a plain white T-shirt, sat next to her. His CFO, Trish Meyers, was in a chair. Like Edward, she wore jeans but had paired them with a well-worn peasant blouse. Her eyes appeared haunted, and she fidgeted, rubbing at her fingers. Pete looked back at the doorway, and I could tell he was thinking about leaving.

"Marjorie, you've already met Pete," I said.

"At the museum, yes."

"Pete, this is Edward and Trish." I shifted my attention to Marjorie. "I asked you not to tell anyone."

"I'm out of here." Pete turned and headed for the door.

"Someone you love is being held for ransom," Marjorie said. "That ransom being *Cold Green Spring*."

Pete stopped as abruptly as if he'd walked into a wall.

Marjorie fixed me with her serious gaze. "When you called and told me the Steadmans needed it back, no questions, I knew right away what had happened." She locked eyes with Pete. "You see, it's happened to us as well."

Pete walked robotically to a chair and sat. I sat too. Kent came in with a tray that held five cups, a carafe of coffee, a small pitcher of milk, a sugar bowl, and an open bottle of Redbreast 21 Irish Whiskey.

Kent poured our coffees and then left the room.

We took a moment to fix our coffee to our liking, during which I asked Edward, "Where's Hildegard the bodyguard?"

Edward gave me a small smile and accentuated her name. "*Eileen* wasn't home when I got a call from Marjorie. I called her phone and left a voicemail but haven't heard from her yet. Neither of us knew I'd be leaving the house again tonight or this morning or whatever."

Everyone added a splash of the Redbreast. Marjorie was last to do so, but after watching us, she muttered, "When in Rome." She sipped and then said, "Edward, please go first."

Edward put his cup on the coffee table and placed a hand on Trish's forearm. "Nine months ago, not long before I came to San Marco to oversee construction, Trish didn't show up for a meeting. It had been important, and I was furious." He focused on Pete. "But that was before I found the note."

Pete leaned forward. "Like this one?" He pulled the ransom note from his jacket pocket, unfolded it, and handed it to Edward, who read it and passed it back.

"Just like that one, except where yours says *Cold Green Spring*, mine said *Three Women Walking*."

"You own a Willem de Kooning?" I asked.

"Owned, past tense. Fine art is one of the things I invest in. In order to get Trish returned unharmed, I had to hand it over. *Three Women Walking* was the ransom."

Looking close to tears, Trish said, "I'm so sorry, Edward."

"And like I've told you before, it's not your fault. I was targeted, but they used you to get to me. I should apologize to you." He sipped his coffee and leaned back. "Two days after receiving the note, Trish called with instructions from the kidnappers. They sent me from one location to the other, making sure I was alone and wasn't followed. They eventually had Trish tell me where to leave the painting."

Trish spoke to Pete. "I know you're terribly worried, but take solace in the fact that I was not harmed."

"This was while you were still in Chicago?" I asked.

"Yes," Edward answered.

"Can you describe the people who did it?" I asked Trish.

"They kept me blindfolded."

I glanced at Pete, and he glowered as if thinking of Wendy having to endure that. I asked Trish, "How about voices? What'd they sound like?"

She shook her head. "They whispered and muttered and only spoke in short sentences. I really couldn't tell anything from their voices."

"I'm sorry you had to go through all that," I said.

Trish gave a sad smile. "Me too. Luckily, I have the best boss in the world." She turned her smile to Edward.

"What happened after they got the painting?" Pete asked.

Trish said, "They took me for a long drive and released me out in the country. They said to count to one hundred before taking off my blindfold, which I did. I walked until I found a small store and called Edward."

Marjorie cleared her throat, getting our attention. "They took my niece, Alicia."

I blinked in surprise. "You too?"

Marjorie nodded slowly.

"Here. In San Marco?"

"Yes. They took her while she was riding her bike. It cost me my David Hockney painting to get her released." She leaned closer to Pete. "If your situation is the same as ours, you should get a call in a day or two. It will be Wendy with instructions on how to get her back."

"Did either of you involve the police?" I asked.

"No, dear, I was too frightened," Marjorie said.

"I didn't want to risk Trish's life," Edward added. "After she was returned, I told my board of directors what had happened, and they insisted I get a bodyguard for the foreseeable future, which is why Eileen goes wherever I go."

"Except for tonight," I pointed out.

"Like I said, we hadn't planned on going out tonight," Edward said.

"Who's Eileen?" Pete asked.

Edward leaned toward Pete. "Eileen Warrick is the head of security for Burke Industries. When I asked Eileen to get me her best person to serve as my bodyguard, she told me she was the best. She's been my shadow ever since."

I sipped my coffee, which was now tepid, but the Redbreast still packed a punch. "If both of you kept these incidents quiet, how did you learn you had this shared experience?"

"I broached the topic with Edward two days after Alicia was taken," Marjorie said. "We met to discuss a charitable project. I was going to cancel, but just sitting around and waiting was driving me mad, so I went ahead with the scheduled meeting."

"I could tell something was bothering her and asked if she was okay," Edward said.

"We had been talking about the gallery at the performing arts center and the exhibit at the Garrido. I thought about how Edward invested in artwork, how he knew countless collectors. I was at my wit's end, so when he asked if something was wrong, I asked if he'd ever heard of anyone being kidnapped and art being the ransom."

"I knew then that Marjorie was going through something that Trish and I had already lived through. I told her about Trish getting abducted, and she told me about her niece."

"Edward was so sweet and helped me get through it all."

I thought about it. "So, someone is getting artwork instead of money for ransom. And with one abduction taking place in Chicago and two here in San Marco, it has to be connected to you, Edward."

"Evidently. Though I don't know how."

"With Wendy's painting in the news, she became a target." Pete's voice broke. He cleared his throat. "I need that painting."

"And you shall get it," Marjorie said. "Later this morning. Let's say, eight a.m., an hour before the museum opens. I'll call the museum director and tell him we're returning the painting to you."

"Don't tell him why," Pete said.

"I'll tell him it's important that you have it, but the reason is private."

Pete and I agreed to meet with Marjorie at the museum, and then he and I returned to my house. Neither of us could sleep, so I lit up my backyard firepit, and we drank coffee and talked. Pete talked mostly about Wendy and some of the shenanigans they had gotten into when they were young. As he spoke, I couldn't help but feel for the guy. His wife had been kidnapped, but even if he got her back, he would soon learn that ALS would eventually take her for good.

Pete drove his truck and followed me to the museum a little before eight. Edward was waiting at the front door with a cardboard tray of coffees.

I took one first, followed by Pete, who said, "Thanks, man."

"Get any sleep?" I asked Edward.

"I dozed. That was it."

I took a slug of black gold. "You didn't have to come. We're just getting *Cold Green Spring*, and then Pete's taking it back to Daytona."

Edward took one of the two remaining coffees. "I know. I just feel invested in it, you know?"

"Appreciate your concern," Pete told him.

Through the glass walls and doors, we saw Marjorie approach from inside the museum. A uniformed guard was at her side, carrying a package wrapped in brown paper. The guard waited by the information desk, and Marjorie came to unlock the front door. Edward pulled it open as Marjorie returned to the guard for the package.

She carried it reverently and handed it to Pete. "I'm sorry that things turned out the way they did. I'll pray for Wendy's safe return."

"Thank you, ma'am," Pete said. "Thanks to all of you."

I put a hand on his arm. "If I can help you in any way, even with just advice, call me."

"Thanks, Lise."

We stood in a huddled group and watched Pete walk to his truck.

"The poor man," Marjorie said, taking the last coffee from Edward.

"I wonder if I should have worked harder to get him to call the police or at least let Baker help," I said.

Edward breathed deep. "It wasn't your decision to make. If it goes like our ransoms, he'll have his wife back in a day or two."

Marjorie went back inside, and Edward walked me to my car.

"Sorry that dinner ended like it did," he said.

"Sorry I left so abruptly. I felt cornered."

"Have you spoken with Nick about it?"

"Not yet."

We were silent for the remaining distance to my car.

I got in and headed home. As sleep had been nonexistent the night before, I collapsed on my bed, in my clothes, and plunged into a deep sleep. I only got a couple hours sleep before my phone rang, and I struggled to wake up to answer it. I was too late but saw the call was from Elliot. Staying prone, I called him back.

"Hey, Lise," he answered.

"What's up?"

"I'm heading to the island."

The barrier island was across the Intracoastal Waterway. "Okay. What does that have to do with me?"

"Got a call from a friend, Oscar Abrams. He's one of the tenders of the San Marco Bridge. I asked him to keep an eye out for kids who are uniquely dressed. He said a group of four kids just crossed the bridge, heading east. He said one wore a derby, and the other dressed like he was heading to an Apache war council."

I sat up. "When was this?"

"Hour or so ago. I started heading that way. When I got there, Oscar pointed out another group of kids who'd just crossed the bridge and were a couple of blocks east. They turned right off the main road. So now, I'm trailing Calamity Jane, Long John Silver, and John Glenn."

I swung my feet off the bed. "Don't lose them."

"I won't."

"Don't let them see you."

"I won't. They went a street in and are now going parallel to the main drag."

"Less traffic, meaning less people will see them," I said.

"That's what I think. I'll call you when we get to where they're headed."

I lay back and shut my eyes to do some serious thinking. Instead, the warm embrace of sleep welcomed me.

Chapter 26

Olivia had never lain on a bed so big and so comfortable, but because of the fear, she didn't enjoy it. She curled up next to the woman who'd told Olivia that her name was Wendy. The woman was stroking Olivia's hair, and that helped lessen her fear a bit. Olivia sat up and scooted to the edge of the bed, which was so high her feet dangled a foot from the ground.

"Are you all right?" the woman asked.

"Yes, Miss Wendy," Olivia said softly.

Their captors had searched the children after bringing them to this place, a big house out in the country. Pie Face had found Olivia's journal and pen, seemed not to consider them a threat, and dropped them to the floor at her feet. When he went on to search Dag, no one stopped Olivia when she picked them up and stuffed them back in her waistband. Pie Face took a pocketknife from Dag and turned to search Tarzan but stopped when he saw that Tarzan only wore a loincloth.

Olivia pulled her journal and pen from her waistband and looked around at the biggest bedroom she'd ever seen. The posts on the four corners of the bed almost touched the ceiling, and lush fabric hung from them, tied off on the posts. A long white chest of drawers ran along one wall, with an ornate mirror placed above its center. Around the room, there were a small table and two chairs, a loveseat, paintings, a pair of French doors, and three regular doors. The door they'd used to enter the room had been secured with a padlock and had a hasp on the other side. Another door led to a large bathroom, and the third opened to an equally big but empty closet.

Dag was asleep on his belly on the loveseat, his curly red hair a fiery contrast to the white fabric. Tarzan had pulled a chair in front of the French doors that opened onto a second-floor balcony. The doors had been secured by a thick chain run through the handles and then padlocked. When they'd first arrived, Tarzan had gone through the drawers in the bedside tables and chest of drawers and every inch of the closet and bathroom, looking for something he could use as a screwdriver. His plan was to unscrew the handles from the French doors. His search yielded empty drawers, cabinets, and one paper clip that he was using to try to pick the padlock.

Olivia got off the bed and went to Tarzan. "How's it going?"

"Not so good." Tarzan paused to wipe the back of his hand across his forehead. "Dodge is the lock picker, not me." He gestured to the gold pen in Olivia's hand. "Let me take a look at that." Olivia passed it to him and watched as he unscrewed the pen and shook out the ink barrel, spring, and push button. He examined the pieces and then reassembled the pen. He pointed at the pocket clip attached to the side of the pen. "This might help, but I'd have to break it off."

Olivia said, "Go ahead."

Tarzan grinned and ruffled her hair. "Thanks, Olive." He snapped the clip off, handed the pen back to her, and worked at inserting it in the lock's keyhole.

So quietly as to almost be whispering, Olivia said, "I'm scared."

Tarzan left his makeshift picks jammed in the keyhole and pulled Olivia into a hug. "Yeah, me too. But we can't stop trying to escape. Right?"

"Right."

He released her and started back on the lock. "And you can bet that Mr. Teacher is already planning something to help us get away."

"You think so?"

"I know so."

Olivia felt hands on her shoulders and looked up to see Wendy standing behind her. "My husband too. I can guarantee you that he's trying to find me. We just need to stay positive."

Olivia nodded and sat on the floor next to Tarzan's chair. Wendy pulled over another and sat.

Olivia opened her notebook. "What's another word for *fancy?*"

Wendy thought for a moment. "What are you describing?"

"This room."

Without stopping what he was doing, Tarzan said, "Extravagant."

"Umm, lavish," Wendy said.

"Luxurious."

"Gilded."

"That's it." Olivia put pen to paper but stopped. "How do you spell it?"

"G-i-l-d-e-d."

Olivia started writing.

We're locked inside a gilded jail,
And the monsters have the keys,
My gladness is a sadness now,
I pray that we are freed.

Tarzan jumped up, roared in frustration, and kicked at the door, but it didn't budge.

"Take a break," Wendy said. "I'll tinker with it awhile." She moved to Tarzan's chair, bent over to work on the lock, and started humming a quiet tune.

Olivia stood and hugged Tarzan.

"Aw, man," Dag said in obvious disappointment. He had awakened and was sitting up on the loveseat, rubbing his eyes. "I dreamed we were at the beach and the waves were tasty."

Chapter 27

I startled from a dream, though it didn't stay with me, other than the part where someone was banging on my door. I wasn't sure if it had been real or not. It didn't repeat in the time it took me to get up and go to the door. No one waited there.

While at the door, my cellphone ringtone started. "Damn it." The phone was back in my bedroom, and I hurried back to pick it up, still half asleep. "Hello."

"Lise, meet me at Moultrie State Park as soon as you can get here."

"Elliot?"

"Hurry, Lise. Other kids' lives are on the line." He ended the call.

Phone in hand, I stood there and felt chills at Elliot's cryptic message. I briefly wondered if maybe I was still asleep and this was part of my dream. I went to splash water on my face and considered changing the wrinkled clothes I'd napped in, but Elliot's voice had been urgent. I rushed out of the house, down the stairs, and to my car.

Moultrie State Park was just north of the city pier. It contained over fifteen hundred acres, three miles of pristine beaches, tidal marshes, sand dunes, one hundred fifty campsites, maritime hammocks holding ancient live oaks dangling Spanish moss, and shell mounds left by Native Americans centuries before. Developers looked at that land and drooled. Hopefully, bribes would never find their way to the wrong people in power.

There were two ways to get into the park. One was to drive up to the official park entrance and pay an admission. The other was to park at the pier parking lot and walk up the beach. I decided the second option was more in line with Elliot's style and barely fit Minnie into a parking space between two massive pickup trucks. I squeezed out the door and started across the parking lot, passing an old blue school bus with Grace United Baptist Church written along its length. Moultrie State Park's beach started a hundred yards past the pier. I removed my sneakers, stuck them in my handbag, and enjoyed the sand between my toes. The tide was going out, and there were about fifty yards between the water and the dunes. Past those were trees and brush and tangles of vines. As we were having a mild winter, quite a few people were walking on the beach or sunning themselves. The ocean temperature was in the sixties, but that didn't stop surfers in their wet suits.

The beach curved slowly to the left, and it wasn't until I was out of sight of the pier that I saw Elliot the Slim, sitting in the sand up toward the dunes.

As I approached, Elliot stood, turned to junglelike growth beyond the dunes, and waved.

After a few seconds, people emerged from the trees. The man in the center was tall and thin, wearing a wide felt hat with a round crown, a black ankle-length coat and—I had to double-check, but yes—finger-less gloves. It had been a long time since he'd seen either a barber or a razor, and his expression reflected a stern, perhaps dangerous, solemnity. Except for the one who looked like an Apache warrior, the others were at least a head shorter than the man, if not more.

"Wow," I muttered, taking in what I realized were children. Beside the Apache was a little girl in a white cowboy hat and boots, packing toy pistols on her hips. On the other side of the man was a fifteen- or sixteen-year-old girl wearing fairy wings that reflected the sun with sparkly rainbow hues. There was a pirate with a tricorn hat and a plastic sword at his waist. One boy wore a derby, another a spaceman's helmet. They looked feral.

The man held up a hand and said something to the kids. They all stayed at the tree line except for the man, who approached us accompanied by a boy in a green tuxedo jacket and top hat. The boy gazed at me through goggles.

As they got closer, I noticed that under his open jacket, the man wore a coarse linen shirt and dark wool pants with thin vertical stripes. His lace-up boots were so old, I would wager the soles had holes.

When they stood before us, Elliot said, "Lise, I want you to meet Mr. Teacher."

I looked him up and down and thought of the character from *Oliver Twist*. "I'd have taken you for a Mr. Fagin."

The man blinked several times and looked at me oddly. "My name is Mr. Teacher."

My first thought was that underneath the hair, beard, and filthy clothes, he was really quite handsome.

Speaking in a thick, working-class British accent, Mr. Teacher said, "Let's get in the shade, shall we?" He indicated the trees.

I looked at Elliot with furrowed brows.

"It's okay, Lise," he assured me.

We moved into the dunes, which were a protected environment that people weren't supposed to tread on. I hoped a park ranger didn't happen by. I also kept an eye out for the pygmy rattlesnakes that made their homes in the dunes. They were small, but they made up for that by being mean little buggers. Nature's Napoleon complex.

When we were halfway to the tree line, all the children turned, stepped between the trees, and vanished. We got into the junglelike growth and followed a tiny game trail to a small clearing. Mr. Teacher sat on the ground, as did Elliot and the boy in the goggles.

Mr. Teacher held out his hand to indicate a big chunk of coquina. "The seat of honor, Miss Norwood."

I sat, and he stared directly into my eyes. I returned the favor while ignoring the musky smell of body odor. Thirty seconds passed and then another thirty. But I would be damned if I turned away first.

He finally nodded. "I have been instructed to enlist your assistance."

"Me?"

"Yes, my dear. You, specifically." He glanced at Elliot and then back at me. "You see, we recently came into possession of a briefcase full of money. Quite a bit of money." He paused before adding, "A million dollars." He watched my show of surprise and then continued. "It came at a cost. A loss of life. A dear boy we called Mackie."

I sat up straight. "Killed by a train?"

He shook his head. "He was killed by an evil woman who pushed him in front of the train. A monster."

"A woman?"

Mr. Teacher looked at the boy. "Tell Miss Norwood what occurred."

The child nodded. "We had a new kid with us, Olivia. Mr. Teacher wanted me and Mackie to take her out on her first job and teach her how it's done. It was middle of the night, and we were working a neighborhood a little north and east of the university."

"What do you mean that you were working a neighborhood?" I asked.

"We were working cars. Going through them and nicking anything that had value." The boy talked about it as if they'd been out mowing lawns for a few bucks instead of committing crimes.

I glared at Mr. Teacher, wondering what sort of Svengali-like control the man had over the children.

He shrugged. "It's how we make a living."

The boy then told me about how he and his friends first saw the men with the briefcase at the construction site.

I stopped him at one point. "A policeman was with these guys? When they handed off the briefcase?"

"Yeah, in a uniform and driving a police car. He was also there later when they killed Mackie. He watched it all." The boy continued with his story, ending with, "Mr. Teacher choked out the guy who had me, and we got away."

"Can you describe the policeman?" I asked.

He looked to Mr. Teacher, as if to be sure he got the description right. "Older. Gray hair. Yellow pointed stripes on his sleeves."

"He was a sergeant with the San Marco police. Somehow, these people found out our location and raided Thieves Kitchen last night. The police sergeant was also in attendance for that melee," Mr. Teacher said.

Thieves Kitchen. That's fitting.

In high school, when I'd had dreams of becoming a Broadway actress, the drama club had taken a field trip to Jacksonville to see a touring company perform the musical *Oliver!* The parallels were surreal.

Mr. Teacher said, "They caught four of us, including..." He held out a hand to the kid in the top hat.

"Let me guess," I said. "Dodger."

The boy looked surprised. "Just Dodge."

"Tell her about last night," Mr. Teacher instructed.

Dodge took off his hat and moved his goggles up to his forehead. His cheek was deeply bruised and the eye above it swollen. "Like Mr. Teacher said, I got caught last night along with Tarzan."

"Tarzan?"

"And Dag and Olivia. They tied our hands behind our backs." He held up his arms so that the jacket sleeves dropped, revealing angry red lines around his wrists. "They took me from the others, and next thing I know, the woman who killed Mackie was up in my face."

I touched my cheek to mirror his damaged face. "Was that when that happened?"

"I spit in her face, and then one of the guys slugged me. Big guy, looked like a gorilla with a crew cut. Didn't knock me out but did knock me for a loop. Everything was all spinny and twisty for a minute or two, but when I came to, I was given instructions. She told me to tell Mr. Teacher that if he returned the briefcase, she'd return Olivia, Tarzan, and Dag."

Dodge scooted a little closer to me. "I asked how we were supposed to get the briefcase back to them, and she said that Mr. Teacher needed to find someone."

"Who?" I asked.

"You."

"What do you mean, me?"

"She said that he needed to find Lise Norwood, that you're a private investigator. She said she'll call you with instructions. Has she called you yet? How do we make the swap?" He looked at me expectantly.

They knew me? These criminals? That they had plans for me made me feel both light-headed and confused. I muttered, "I don't know. This is the first I've heard about a briefcase full of money." I thought a moment, pulling myself together. "We need to bring in the police."

Mr. Teacher shook his head. "No, we can't. There was a copper with them, helping them."

Dodge added, "And she said she'd kill 'em if we told the police."

"You may go, Dodge," Mr. Teacher said.

The boy stood, gave a dramatic bow, and disappeared among the trees.

This was crazy. I was involved in something that included a million dollars and mortal threats against children. I was out of my league and could think of only one option. Looking intently at Mr. Teacher, I said, "Look, I have a friend. He's a detective, and if we ask him to keep it quiet—"

"No, Miss Norwood. As we already know, the police are involved but not in a lawful manner. They are corrupt."

I held up an index finger. "One. One dirty cop. I can guarantee my friend isn't—"

"No! We don't know how many are involved, and if they get even a hint that we're seeking help from law enforcement, then we've condemned three children to death." He brushed his palms together twice and then flung out his hands, as if physically discarding that option altogether. He waited until I nodded and then went on. "When I received the message from Dodge, I assumed you were working with the ones who are threatening my protégées."

"I set him straight, Lise," Elliot said.

I opened my mouth to say something, closed it, and tried again. "Guys, I'm somewhere between baffled and perplexed."

"I get that, Lise," Elliot said. "Last we spoke, I told you I was following the kids. When they reached the pier, they went under it, where they met up with Dodge, and he instructed them to head north up the beach. When I got to where you found me, I saw Mr. Teacher come from the trees to greet them. He didn't see me."

"Bollocks, I saw you," Mr. Teacher said.

Undeterred, Elliot continued, "I snuck up to the tree line, silently made my way into the brush."

"Ha! You made as much bloody noise as an elephant."

"When I saw Mr. Teacher..." Elliot dipped his head and looked up at me, and I realized he was trying to tell me something without coming out and saying it. "I *recognized* a kindred spirit." Elliot would fill me in later. "We spoke, and after a while, he gave me the entire story. I told him I worked for you, and that no, you wouldn't be in cahoots with bad guys."

"The way he put it was, 'Her armor shines, and her hat is white,'" Mr. Teacher said.

My head spun. Baker had asked me to help identify the dead boy. That was it. But now I was knee-deep in something I didn't have a clue about, and I had to act as courier and deliver a briefcase of money to save the lives of three children. It was like a ransom. It was like Pete needing to give up *Cold Green Spring* to ensure Wendy's release. So that meant that there were two ransom situations underway in little ol' San Marco, and I was involved with both.

At least I had a chance to discover what Baker had asked of me. "Mr. Teacher, how did Mackie come to be with you?"

Deep sadness clouded his expression. "Oh, Mackie. What a sweet boy." He sighed deeply. "We'd been working in Tampa. Dodge was in a tough part of downtown, an area the chamber of commerce doesn't want tourists going. He was watching a pawn shop we were planning to visit, you see. A place where disreputable people can exchange items they've acquired in a questionable manner for money. Which meant it was a place where the owner would be less inclined to call the police should it be burglarized. And what should my dear Dodge see as he was engaged in his surveillance? A puppy dog of a malnourished boy came out from a nearby alley. His clothes were so old and worn that they barely hung on his small frame. It was evident by the vertical tracks through the dirt on his cheeks that he'd been crying. And running up and down both arms, like some kind of sadistic psoriasis, were cigarette burns.

"Dodge befriended the lad. Over the course of the day, his story came out. He lived with an uncle who always had a bottle at his side. An uncle who couldn't care less if the boy lived or died, but since he was there, he used the boy to kick and hit and burn. Dodge told the boy about Thieves Kitchen."

I interrupted. "I thought Thieves Kitchen was here in San Marco."

"Thieves Kitchen is wherever we are. It's not a place, but it is our home. Mackie was with us ever since."

"You just took him?" There was incredulity in my voice when I added, "Like a stray dog?"

"No, Miss Norwood, like a child in need of sanctuary."

I jabbed at the air with my index finger and loudly said, "What you should have done is reported his uncle to the authorities and let the state take Mackie."

"To place in a foster home?" Mr. Teacher sneered.

"Well, yes."

He leaned toward me. "How many times have you read about foster children being abused? Physically, sexually, or both?" He waited for an answer, and when I didn't give him one, he repeated, "How many?"

"Too many," I admitted. Still, I thought that by taking kids in off the streets and teaching them how to steal, this man was without a doubt guilty of contributing to the delinquency of minors. But I wasn't going to debate him. At that moment, I was there to get information from the man.

"When he arrived, we made him wash up. Poor boy hated a bath. And then we tended to his injuries. His arms were scarred like he had measles. Not including old burn marks, I counted up the ones that I thought he'd received recently. There were eight on his left arm and fifteen on his right.

"I got his uncle's address, and while my wonderful crew doted on the boy and gave him clean clothes, food, and friendship, I went to that neighborhood in downtown Tampa, stopping once at a cigar shop to purchase the biggest, fattest cigar they had. I visited his uncle, and by the time I left, the poor man had eight cigar burns on his left arm and fifteen on his right."

The sound of the surf was like a soundtrack as I absorbed what he'd told me. What Mr. Teacher had done in regard to Mackie was wrong, at least as far as society and legalities were concerned. But he saved the boy by taking him in and giving him a home. As for torturing the child's uncle as a form of justice, I applauded him, though I wouldn't admit that out loud.

"Mr. Teacher," I said, "do you know Mackie's real name?"

"Oh, his real name was Mackie. He chose it himself. But if you're asking about his original name, then yes, I do, as I do all my charges. His original name was Philip Reynolds. Apparently, they didn't think he was worthy of a middle name. I think he deserved a dozen."

Chapter 28

Before I left, Mr. Teacher called in his crew and introduced me to each of the children. When he pointed out Nancy, Bet, and Charly, I was sure Mr. Teacher was delusional. Those names, as well as Dodge—or Dodger—came right from *Oliver Twist*. Though he used a different name, it was obvious that Mr. Teacher thought he was Fagin.

Part of me wanted to get in his face and demand to know what gave him the right to instruct children how to steal and burglarize, to lead them into criminal activities. Another part of me recognized that he truly cared for them. They survived by the crimes they committed. It was evident, however, that he had serious mental issues. No way could I in good conscience not alert the authorities, but when and how was the conundrum.

It was decided that Elliot would stay with the lot of them and, after dark, take them to his spot underneath the Carroll Street Drawbridge. If and when I heard from the kidnappers, I would call Elliot to alert them.

"Should I go ahead and take the briefcase?" I asked.

Mr. Teacher gave me an amused grin. "I'll hang on to it for the time being."

"Let me walk you back to the pier, Lise," Elliot said.

We got to the tree line, and I turned and bid my goodbye. All the kids waved and cheerily said how nice it was to meet me.

We got to the beach, headed south, and Elliot said, "I know him."

"From the street?"

"No." Elliot stopped, and so did I. "He was in Iraq at the same time I was."

"You served with him?"

Elliot shook his head. "No, I was with the army for the surge in 2007. Our area of responsibility was southeast of Baghdad in the Babil Province. Mr. Teacher was a jarhead." We started to walk again. "His real name is Richard Charles. In the sandbox, he was kind of famous, Staff Sergeant Charles, 15th Marine Expeditionary Unit. They were already in country and, with the surge, got an extension on their deployment. Actually, it was the second extension. They worked the Anbar Province."

"Why was he famous?"

Elliot said, "He was in charge of a squad called Gertie's Grunts. Gertie was this monster truck they operated out of. We called it a Frankenstein because it was an ugly thing covered with spot-welded armor. Whatever metal they could find went on, like the body parts for Frankenstein's monster. They made a name for themselves mainly because Charles was a genius when it came to planning the kinds of operations needed for the surge. They probably cleared more buildings than any other squad."

"That doesn't explain why he's running a crew of pint-size thieves."

"Actually, it might." Elliot held up a hand to block the sun's glare. "But let's get in some shade first. Sun's cooking me."

We went to the pier gift shop, got a couple of sodas, and sat at a picnic table with a sunshade umbrella.

Elliot said, "Before we get to the kids, I should tell you what happened to Gertie's Grunts." He paused long enough to suck soda through a straw. "They weren't only well known to us but also to the insurgents, who'd had enough of their raids. An LN told them there were a bunch of insurgents basing their operations out of an old building in al-Baghdadi."

"What's an LN?" I asked.

"Local national—what we called locals who gave us intel. Informants. The building was huge, with lots of hallways and lots of rooms.

They went in at night, and the place was filled with insurgents waiting for them. The LN had set them up. It was an ambush. They killed a lot of bad guys, but in the end, Charles was the only one in the squad to make it out alive, though he was shot up pretty bad. He spent months in a hospital, and rumors started circulating that, as bad as his physical injuries were, he was more damaged up here." Elliot tapped his temple. "He couldn't handle losing his entire squad on an assault that he'd planned."

I thought about it. "That was a long time ago, Elliot. Are you sure he's Charles?"

Elliot nodded. "You learn to recognize a veteran's bearing, phrases they use. When we were alone, I asked if he'd served. He dropped that English accent, and we talked about it for a few minutes. When some kids came back, so did his accent. He said all that was a different life, and he wouldn't speak of it again." Elliot shrugged.

"So, what's with all the kids?" I asked.

"That's what makes me certain that Mr. Teacher is Charles. He and his squad volunteered at an orphanage run by an ex-nun in Haditha. They did upkeep on the building. Charles organized soccer matches for the kids and designed a website that solicited donations on behalf of the orphanage. Whenever they cleared a building of insurgents, they'd take whatever supplies and food they found and give it to the orphanage, which is how he became known as the Robin Hood of Haditha."

"And now he's the Fagin of San Marco," I muttered.

"What's with that? You called him Fagin and the boy Dodger."

"Have you ever read Charles Dickens's *Oliver Twist*?"

Elliot shook his head. "I've heard of it but never read it. I think I saw the movie when I was a kid, though I don't remember much."

"Yeah, the movie was simply called *Oliver!* There's a stage version too. There are too many parallels between the story and this Mr. Teacher. *Oliver!* takes place in London in the Victorian era. Fagin, a criminal, takes in street urchins, orphans, and runaways. He teaches them how to pick pockets. If I remember right, Fagin, in the book, is a much darker character than in the stage version. In the book, he's mainly in it for the money the kids bring in, but in the stage version and movie, he truly cares about the kids. That's what all this reminds me of. Fagin, in the story, had a kid named Dodger who was second in command at Thieves Kitchen, where they all lived. There was a Charly and Nancy and Bet too."

Elliot took a minute to process what I'd told him. "All these kids with him now, it's obvious they love him."

"I have to tell Baker about this," I said.

Elliot made a pained face. "I know you do at some point, but not now. Mr. Teacher is right. There's a dirty cop involved. Look, those thugs have already proven that they'll kill a child. If you get the police involved, even if it's just Baker, and they find out, they'll kill those three kids." He saw the wheels turning in my head. "And if Charles finds out you went to the cops, you'll never see him or those kids again. He won't trust you."

So much for alerting Baker. "Ah, shit."

Chapter 29

All the information I'd received was churning in my head like a load of wet clothes spinning in a dryer. Particularly the part where a man who had suffered trauma had become a wholly fictional character. Whether I should tell Baker now or later was also causing me mental stress. I understood that we couldn't go to the police if there was a mole in the department, but could I go to Baker and be confident it stayed with him and whoever he trusted? I'd been hired as a consultant to discover the dead child's identity. Now that I had, I should at least tell Baker. But then he would want to know how I learned the child's name, which would lead me to telling him about Mr. Teacher, also known as Richard Charles, and his band of merry thieves.

I pulled into my driveway, where a familiar car was parked. Oh, crap. I got out of my car and called, "Nick?"

"Up here, Lise." He was on my deck. His voice was flat and cheerless.

I slowly made my way up the stairs, dreading the coming conversation. Nick was in an Adirondack chair. I sat in the one next to him. We were silent a long time, during which neither of us looked at the other.

Nick broke the quiet. "What's going on with us? Everything seemed good, and then boom, you're dating a rich, handsome asshole."

"There're two things wrong with what you said. First off, Edward's not an asshole."

"A guy who goes after a woman in a relationship is an asshole to me."

"And Edward and I aren't dating."

"Looked like it to me," Nick said.

"It was a business dinner."

"Uh-huh. You two were holding hands when I walked up."

I was glad we weren't looking at each other so Nick wouldn't see my expression of guilt. "He put his hand on top of mine. I was going to take my hand away, but..."

"But what?"

"But I didn't."

Nick's voice was almost a whisper when he asked, "Why not?"

What could I say? I didn't answer.

"You like him, don't you?"

Tensions were high, emotions were on the surface, and I did the worst thing possible. I snickered.

He whipped his head in my direction. "What?"

"*You like him, don't you?* What? Are we in middle school?" I shook my head and repeated the word. "Like."

Nick leapt to his feet. "Are you attracted to him?" he asked, overenunciating. "Do you have the hots for him? Does he get your motor running?"

That was when I lost my temper, stood, and blurted, "You're the one who brought your old girlfriend back into your life." It just came out. I had never once thought he wanted to reconnect with her romantically, but it was a defensive move, and I played it to get myself out from under the spotlight.

"What? Meredith?"

"Thinking about reliving the past? Move from me to Meredith. Again."

Nick stared at me in disbelief. "I didn't bring her back. We had a committee that decided she was the best candidate overall, and the fact that she was an alumna sealed the deal."

I glared at him. "Was it unanimous?"

"Yes, it was."

"So, you did vote to bring her back into your life."

"*Gah!* Do you hear yourself?" Nick almost shouted. "And this isn't about Meredith. It's about you and that asshole." He breathed hard for several seconds and then inhaled deeply as he attempted to rein in his anger. "I didn't come here to fight, Lise. I just want to know about you and him and where that leaves you and me."

The desperation in his voice deflated my anger like a needle to a balloon. I fell back into my chair and pushed the heels of my hands hard against my eyes. "I've been thinking about you and me," I said in a soft voice. "We've been together for a couple years, and it's pretty much the same now as when we first started."

"No, it's not."

"Yes, it is. There have been times when we've said things like *we should talk about where our relationship is going,* but we never do. I think it's convenient for us both to leave things like they are."

"Then let's stop being convenient. Let's talk about it now," Nick said.

I leaned back and looked to a cloud in the sky. "I do want to talk about it, but not now." I reached out and took his hand, happy that he didn't pull away. "I have two cases right now where people's lives are at stake."

"Really?"

"Really." I squeezed his hand. "Can you give me a few days, until all this works out?"

"Of course." He squeezed back. "And don't put yourself in danger."

I didn't tell him that I wasn't sure that was possible. My cellphone ringtone sounded. I got out my phone and checked to see who was calling.

"Important?" Nick asked.

I nodded and answered, "Hang on a second, Pete." I put my hand over the phone. "We'll talk. I promise."

Nick nodded and started for the stairs. He stopped and turned. "I'm serious. Keep yourself safe. If I can help in any way, call me."

I stood and gave him a small smile, and he went on down the stairs. I brought up the phone. "What's up, Pete?"

"Wendy just called with the kidnappers' instructions."

"How'd she sound?"

"Sounded good. Like Wendy."

"Thank God. Did she say anything to indicate where she was or who had her?"

"No. She said the painting needs to be left at a specific location tomorrow. They didn't tell her where. After that's done, they'll let her go."

"Is there anything I can do?"

"That's the thing, Lise. They want you to deliver the painting."

"Me?"

"Yes. At the same time that you deliver the briefcase?" He said it like a question.

My head spun, and I reached back with my free hand for the armrest as I sat again.

"What briefcase, Lise?"

"Get up to San Marco, Pete. Bring the painting. I have to go see a friend to try to figure this out. If I'm not at my house, I'll leave a key under the red flowerpot."

Chapter 30

The sun had set by the time I got to Edward's place. I'd called him and told him we needed to talk, quickly adding that it had to do with Pete's wife so he wouldn't assume it was romance related. He gave me the address of the beachside home he was leasing. I knew it would be a big house when he told me it was in Brisas del Mar, an area of homes on either side of A1A. The smallest were around five thousand square feet and called cottages.

Edward's home was bigger than the cottages, periwinkle colored and with a metal roof, built with a passing nod to the Florida cracker architectural style. As I parked, I looked past the house to the Atlantic's crashing waves. Edward came out to greet me. He wore black linen pants held up by a drawstring, sandals, and a tight white T-shirt that clearly showed his physique.

"Tell me what's happening," Edward said.

"Shit's about to hit the fan from every direction, and I'm standing at ground zero. Somehow, this involves you, and I need your help getting a hold of it."

He looked at me with concern. "Come in, Lise." He led me into a large kitchen with an oversize refrigerator, stove, and dishwasher. "Out of all the rooms in the house, I prefer discussing business in here." We went past the cooking island underneath the hanging pots and pans, and he held out a chair for me at a rustic kitchen table made of wood and black metal trim. "Can I get you anything?"

"Yeah. Get me out of this mess," I replied as I sat.

He sat next to me. "Tell me what's going on."

I took a deep breath and started with Mr. Teacher and how the dead boy had been part of his crew. I told him about the briefcase, how the kids had stolen it, and that it was the motive for the boy's death. I then sprang it on him that the briefcase handoff had taken place at the future home of the performing arts center.

His look of shock seemed genuine. "Hold on. Why did they exchange it at my construction site?"

I shrugged. "I don't know. What do you think?"

"How should I... Wait a minute. You don't think I had something to do with it, do you?"

"You were at the Garrido Museum when the boy was murdered, so you have an alibi. But you could have had subordinates do the dirty work for you."

"Lise, I assure you—"

I held up a hand to stop him. "I will tell you that I don't think you're involved, but I am keeping all options open until I learn more."

"Fair enough."

I then told him about the raid at Thieves Kitchen and how thugs were holding three children hostage. He kneaded his forehead as I said that it appeared a woman was in charge. I could see that he had yet to reach the conclusion I'd come to about this woman. His eyes grew wide when I told him I was supposed to deliver the briefcase to the bad guys.

"That's incredible," Edward said.

To my own ears, I sounded like a TV announcer when I said, "But wait, there's more. Pete just called with the kidnappers' instructions, apparently the same kidnappers that took your CFO and Marjorie's niece. They want me to deliver the ransom, *Cold Green Spring*, at the same time I bring the briefcase."

The surprise on Edward's face matched how I'd felt when Pete told me about it.

"Maybe now's the time to involve law enforcement," Edward said.

"We can't," I said.

When I explained that a policeman was involved, he got up without a word, went to the refrigerator, and got out two bottles of cold microbrew. He opened them and placed one in front of me. "I really want something stiffer, but I think we need clear heads."

I took a long pull and put down the bottle. "They knew about me."

"Excuse me?" Edward said.

"I'm trying to put the pieces together, but this jigsaw doesn't fit. First, your CFO, Trish, is kidnapped in Chicago. You come down here to work the performance art center project and meet Marjorie, learn of her love of art, and her collection. She's targeted next."

"Next comes the museum and *Cold Green Spring.*"

"Wrong. Next comes a boy thrown in front of a train by a woman, in the company of a thug and a cop, while trying to get a briefcase filled with a million dollars. Then comes the museum gala when *Cold Green Spring* comes to the public's attention." I looked at Edward. "All these events have you in common, to one degree or another."

"Lise, I had nothing to do with the kidnappings except for paying a ransom."

"Like I said, I don't think you're involved, but I do think it's someone close to you. A woman that has the capability of killing for what she wants. A woman with connections to a crooked cop." I leveled my gaze at Edward. "Has Eileen come back?"

Edward's face expressed denial. "No." As he thought about it, that look changed to comprehension. "She knew we'd figure it out. She's gone into hiding until she gets the painting and the briefcase. But why?"

"We find her, we can find out why. Where does she live?"

"Here. She has a suite."

"We need to search it."

"Come on." Edward led me through the house, up to the second floor, and stopped before twin doors, opening them.

The suite was almost as big as my house. We entered a living room that featured a large flat-screen TV over a fireplace. A nice-size kitchen was off to the left, and two doors to the right led to bedrooms.

"You take the kitchen, and I'll go through the living room," I told Edward. "Check everything—under the trash bag in the trash can, in the sinks, every can and box in the cabinet, the ice tray in the freezer, the—"

There was a squelching sound and then a voice via radio broadcast. I spotted a police scanner on a small table next to a recliner. Apparently, unit thirty-eight was 10-7.

"Eileen keeps the scanner on," Edward said. "I think it has to with her being an ex-MP."

"And being liaison between Burke Industries and local law enforcement. She has local police connections, which could be how she found someone who'd work with her."

Edward gestured around the apartment. "Shall we get started?"

Right off the bat, we found two pistols stashed out of sight but within easy reach. One was taped under the kitchen table. I found another in the drawer of an end table. A pistol grip shotgun was mounted vertically to the wall inside the hall closet.

"She likes her toys," I said after discovering a K-bar knife taped under the coffee table.

"Tools of the trade. A little overboard maybe."

Neither of us found much else of interest, so Edward took the guest bedroom to search, and I took Eileen's. The room was big enough that she had set up a small office area in a corner, with a desk, laptop, and printer. Next to her laptop were a couple of pieces of paper. I picked them up and tried to figure out what I was looking at. Each page had the heading of Edward's company. Below that were local addresses, and to the right of them, amounts of money. Some of the monetary notations stood alone, while others had a slash after the amount followed by monthly figures. On the second page, Eileen had underlined one entry with a red felt marker.

"Edward," I called. We met up in the living room. "What are these?" I handed him the papers.

Edward looked over the paperwork. "These are properties we're leasing or have bought in San Marco."

"That many?" I asked as I glanced at the list.

"Sure. There's the land the center will be on. Homes leased for key personnel. Warehouses for equipment and supplies. We've rented a lot of storage space. Offices. Those kinds of things."

I pointed at the entry Eileen had underlined two-thirds down the page. "What's this one?"

He studied it a minute. "I don't know. It's a lease. I don't recognize the address."

"That zip code puts it out of San Marco but still in the county." I pulled out my phone, thumbed in the address, and hit directions. "Yeah, west of town, out in the country."

"Lise, I don't know of anything we've bought or leased that's not in the city limits." He ran his fingers through his hair and sighed. "Eileen, huh?"

"I'd bet on it, especially since Eileen underlined the one property you don't know about." I thought a minute. "Feel like taking a drive?"

Chapter 31

We took Edward's Tesla for surveillance because it was black, silent, and fast. Before we left, I got my binoculars from Minnie's glove compartment. Our night drive took us west, out of town, into the boonies, and finally, farm country. We'd been quiet, both of us lost in our thoughts.

Edward chuckled. "I wish we could go back to where the most I had to worry about was any problems I caused between you and Nick."

"That's something I'll have to tackle after all this." I looked at him. "But really, let's focus on the task at hand."

"Gotcha. Task at hand."

After a turn off the main road, GPS showed our destination was another ten minutes. Edward slowed down as we got to the property in question, and we glided past a driveway that passed through an opening in an eight-foot-high stone wall. The driveway was overly wide so vehicles of all sizes could fit and was blocked off by a wrought iron gate. Even though the house sat a hundred yards from the road, the gate gave us a good view of the well-lit home and property. From what we could see, the only fence was the one facing the road. The rest of the house was surrounded by thick Florida woods.

Once we were well past the driveway, Edward made a three-point turn, and we drove slowly past again. We only saw one closed-circuit camera, and it was mounted along with an intercom at the iron gate. The camera was angled downward to show whoever drove up seeking entrance.

Thirty yards past the gate, Edward pulled behind some overgrown shrubs and parked with my side of the Tesla inches from the wall. We were in a black car on a dark night. Camouflage didn't get much better than that.

"What do you think?" Edward asked.

"Large multiroom two-story house. Four to six thousand square feet. Two black SUVs parked out front. What'd you see?"

Through gritted teeth, Edward said, "A property covertly leased through my company."

A half mile up the road, where it curved, it was no longer dark. "Shit. Car's coming," I said.

The car rounded the curve, bright lights blazing, and drove past us, illuminating the brush we hid behind. Brake lights flared as it approached the gate.

"Do you think they saw us?" Edward asked, staring into the rearview mirror.

I kneeled on my seat, looking out the back window. "Only if some chrome reflected their headlights through the shrubs. If they turn around, vamoose."

The vehicle paused at the gate and then entered the property.

I picked up my binoculars from the floor. "Let's get some eyes on the place."

Edward fiddled with the control panel screen in the middle of the dash and turned off the interior lights so they wouldn't come on when we opened the doors. "You'll have to scooch over and out my side," he said as he opened his door.

"Good thing I'm flexible." I pointed at him. "And no, that's not a double entendre."

"Hey! Task at hand, remember," he said with mock seriousness, took my binoculars, and got out his door.

I crawled over the console, grabbing at the fighter-jet steering wheel, all while thinking that I wasn't as flexible as I thought. I hadn't planned my path properly and led with my upper body instead of my feet, which were still back where I'd been sitting. Edward had to support my upper body as I extricated my legs. It was not graceful.

Helping me to stand, he mumbled, "Feels like we're two-thirds of the Three Stooges."

I paused to look at him.

"What?" he asked.

"That Three Stooges comment earns you points." I looked up at the massive wall. "Shall we continue the Stooges' routine with me getting on your shoulders so I can see over the wall?"

"No." He put a hand to the wall. "I parked close so we can do this." He stepped onto the hood of his Tesla and then up onto the roof. He motioned for me to join him. "The body is aluminum, so stay close to the sides so you'll have better support from the car's frame."

I did, though the metal still made noise in protest. I stood beside him and peered over the fence. He handed me my binoculars. Like we were imitating a couple of "Kilroy was here" sketches, we peeked over the wall. Normally, out here in the countryside west of San Marco, farmhouses, ranch houses, Florida cracker homes, and maybe a cabin or two were the prevailing architectural styles. This house, however, was a monster of a Mediterranean-style McMansion, made of stucco and stone walls and topped with terra-cotta tiles.

The SUV that went past us parked in line with the others, and two men got out.

Edward asked, "You're assuming these are the people who took the kids and want their briefcase back?"

"Yep. And I'll bet you that Eileen is in there somewhere." It seemed every light in the house was on. I focused on the first floor with my binoculars and scanned each window. The last was a kitchen window, and I saw a couple of big men sitting at a table and eating.

"If we can't go to the police, then what do we do?" Edward asked.

"I don't know." I moved the binoculars up to the second floor and saw movement in the far-right window. "I think maybe—holy shit!"

"What?"

I lowered the binoculars and turned to Edward. "I just saw Wendy."

He snatched the binoculars and put them to his eyes. "Where?"

"In the far-right upstairs window."

"Hmm, I don't see any—wait. There."

He passed me the binoculars back. Wendy stood at the window and then walked out of view. "Yes, that is definitely Wendy." I studied that part of the house and saw a second-floor balcony around the side of the house. "Oh, this is good. We know where they're holding Wendy, and I'll bet you a week's salary they have the kids here too."

"What now?"

Another vehicle was approaching around the curve. "Get down."

We kneeled low on the car roof until an old pickup truck passed. It continued past the gate and disappeared in the distance.

"Keep an eye on things." I gave him the binoculars, sat on the roof of the car, and called Elliot's phone.

"Hi, Lise."

"Where are you guys?"

"Under the Carroll Street Drawbridge."

"I found where they've stashed the kids. We need to meet. Bring everyone to my place... no, wait... I'm delivering the ransoms, so they may already be watching my home." I looked at Edward. "Do you think we could meet up at your house?"

He nodded.

I gave Elliot Edward's address and told him to get there as soon as possible. Then I called Pete and told him the same thing.

Chapter 32

Saturday

The rising sun painted bright oranges and pinks above the ocean horizon so that the sky looked like something captured on canvas and hanging in the Garrido Museum. Screams, yells, and laughter came into Edward's leased house through the open patio doors. All the members of Thieves Kitchen, minus Mr. Teacher, were in the backyard swimming pool. The owners of the house had numerous swimsuits of varying sizes available for guests, though some belonged to Edward, including some shorts and, in two instances, underwear.

The arrival of Mr. Teacher and his charges had been an incredible thing to witness. A honking horn alerted us to their arrival, and Edward and I went to the door as two high and wide headlights approached up the driveway.

When the vehicle turned and parked in front of us, Edward muttered, "The neighbors are going to love this."

It was the old blue school bus I'd seen parked at the pier. The doors swung open, and Mr. Teacher, in the driver's seat, gave us a salute, and then his band of juvenile thieves had trundled off, with Elliot bringing up the rear.

I sat at the kitchen table with Mr. Teacher, Pete, and Edward. I told them, "I have a friend. He's a detective, and we can trust him."

"No cops, no way." Pete said. "They said no cops, or Wendy dies."

Mr. Teacher put a calming hand on Pete's forearm and then said to me, "I have no doubt that the man is trustworthy, but as we now know, there's a policeman involved. We cannot risk him learning that we sought help from the police. Lives are on the line. The value of any one of my protégés far outweighs a briefcase of currency. I will gladly give it back for Tarzan, Dag, and sweet Olivia."

"Ditto for the painting and Wendy," Pete said.

I nodded.

A shrill scream caused Pete to jump. Hysterical laughter from the swimming pool followed.

"Sorry," Pete said. "My nerves are shot."

I told him, "We have an advantage. We know where they're keeping Wendy, and that's most likely where the kids are as well."

My phone vibrated, and Nick's Barry White ringtone sounded. "Crap, I don't need this now." I poised my finger over the decline call button but changed my mind. I answered, talking rapidly. "Nick, I am in the middle of something important and can't talk. I'll call you when I can, I promise." I moved the phone from my ear and started to hit End Call, but Nick shouted my name, followed by something that gave me chills. I put the phone back to my ear. "What did you say?"

"I've been abducted. They said they took me so that you'll have some skin in the game. Do you know what they mean?"

My heart beat hard as I answered, "Yes, I do."

"Listen carefully. I don't have long. Don't interrupt. These are your instructions. Everyone either lives or they die, depending on what you do, Lise. Police involvement means instant executions. At three o'clock this afternoon, I will call you and give directions to a specific location and an amount of time you have to get there. Meaning if you take too long, you will not receive any more calls, and everybody will die. We will proceed in this manner, over and over, until they are assured that you aren't being followed. At which point you will get the final location where you will take the painting and the briefcase." He paused. "Did you get all that?"

"Yes. Are you okay, Nick?"

"I love you so much, Lise."

"Nick?"

His voice dropped to a soft, heartfelt volume. "I mean it. I love you."

"Nick, I love—"

He interrupted me with urgent whispering. "We've seen their faces. The woman in charge is Edward's—" Over the phone, I heard a commotion. Nick yelled, "Hey! What'd you do that for?" A garbled response was followed by a smack. Someone had hit Nick. "I just told her I miss seeing her face." The phone call ended.

I sat there, sick to my stomach, staring out blankly.

Edward stood and rounded the table. He put his hands on my shoulders and leaned down. "Lise, what's wrong?"

"They've taken Nick."

Pete's face darkened.

"Who's Nick?" Mr. Teacher asked, and Pete told him.

"Nick was passing along their instructions. He said he was taken because they wanted to make sure I had skin in the game too." I swallowed hard as I thought over the conversation.

"There's something else, isn't there?" Mr. Teacher asked.

I nodded slowly and looked at Edward. "We were right about Eileen. Nick said he saw their faces."

"That's different." Edward said. "Why aren't they blindfolded, like the first two people who were kidnapped?"

"It's not just different, it's bad." I looked from Pete to Mr. Teacher to Edward. "They won't dare leave any witnesses alive."

The gravity of the situation caused a silence among us that seemed laden with weight.

"Fuckers are gonna kill them no matter what we do," Pete said, putting words to what we were all thinking.

Chapter 33

I'd thought about the situation from every angle, trying to come up with solutions, but each one sounded worse than the last. Finally, a new course of action came to me, one that I thought would give us the best chance. At the same time, I thought the idea bordered on insanity.

I found Elliot. "Can I talk to you a minute?" We went out back near the pool but far enough from everyone so as not to be overheard. "Mr. Teacher is Richard Charles, right?"

"Yeah. Why?"

I told him about how Nick had been taken and how the hostages had seen the abductors' faces, which most likely meant their deaths were imminent.

"So we're screwed, huh?" Elliot asked.

"Yeah." I paused. "Unless..."

"Unless what?"

"Unless Richard Charles can use those skills he had in Iraq and come up with a plan to free our friends."

"Hmm." Elliot grunted, thinking about it. He chuckled, and then his expression turned serious as he thought more. He raised his eyebrows. "Desperate times, huh?"

"Desperate as hell."

Elliot nodded. "Give me a few minutes. I'll find Mr. Teacher and meet you out front."

Ten minutes later, I exited the Thieves Kitchen bus and sat at the top of the steps leading to Edward's front door.

"Ah, Miss Norwood." Mr. Teacher and Elliot came out of the house. Mr. Teacher sat next to me. "Elliot said you wished to speak with me."

Elliot continued down the steps to the walkway and turned to look up at us.

"I'm not sure how to say this, so I'll just get to it," I said. "I understand that you have experience planning military operations, Mr. Teacher." I sounded like a cheesy 1940s movie private eye when I added, "Or, should I say, Mr. Charles?"

His anger came quickly, reflected in his eyes. He stood and stalked down the stairs to Elliot and grabbed him by his T-shirt. With no trace of an English accent, he said, "You told her?"

Elliot remained calm and kicked a pebble from the path. "You and me, we're brothers by battle. But, see, there's another battle coming, and we need your skills."

Looking from Elliot to me, Charles released Elliot. "Exactly what is it you want?"

I descended the stairs and faced him. He was angry, and I was wary he might resort to violence, but there was no time to be diplomatic. "During the war in Iraq, specifically the surge, you planned raids. In fact, you were famous for it."

Elliot placed a hand on Charles's shoulder. "Staff Sergeant, we need you to come up with a way to rescue the hostages."

"Bullshit!" Charles raged. He knocked Elliot's hand away and hurried to the bus. He yanked open the doors and ascended, dropping into the driver's seat. He reached toward the ignition, paused, then looked at us.

I held up the keys, which I'd taken before they arrived. I handed them to Elliot, who took them into the house. Charles glared at me then rose and disappeared into the bus.

I gave him a few minutes to calm down and then climbed on board. A typical old school bus, it was surprisingly clean considering how many kids had just been in it. Mr. Teacher—Richard Charles—was in a seat three-quarters of the way back. He gripped the seat back in front of him, and his head rested on his hands. He looked like he was praying in a church pew. Thinking that prayer wasn't a bad idea, I did a quick sign of the cross. I made my way back and took a seat across the aisle from him. I wasn't sure how to get a conversation started, but it didn't matter. He spoke first.

"I can't do that."

"From what Elliot told me, you're the only one who can," I said.

Charles raised his head and looked at me. In a defeated voice, with no trace of an English accent, he said, "Planning burglaries is one thing, but what you're asking..." He shook his head. "My plans failed. I am responsible for the deaths of every member of my squad. I can't bear the weight of any more."

"Before that, you had tremendous success during the surge."

Charles turned to look out the window next to him, not replying.

"The one failure was an ambush," I said. "You were set up. It wasn't your fault."

Charles slowly turned. The hatred in his eyes stunned me, and then I realized that loathing wasn't for me. It was for himself. "I was in charge, and it was my plan. Of course it was my fault."

"How many successful operations did you plan out and lead before the ambush?"

Charles sighed and leaned back, his gaze upward. "Dozens."

I gave him time to think about his successes versus his one failure.

Groaning, Charles got to his feet and paced up and down the aisle. "You must think I'm insane."

"I think..." I wanted to be honest and thought how to answer. "I think that you've suffered. I'm not sure why you've come up with this Faginesque persona, but I do believe you have the best of intentions in regard to the children."

He paced some more and then began speaking. "I was a musical theater minor in college. In my last semester, I was cast in our spring production, *Oliver!* And, as you have surmised, I played Fagin." Charles stopped walking when he was a couple of feet away. "I grew up a foster kid, and I know that most foster homes provide what the kids need. My last foster home was like that. But before that..." He paused. "Let's just say that I knew abuse. I took my history and wove it into Fagin's."

He was up and pacing again. "After two years of college, I enlisted. It turned out that I thrived in the military, had natural skills as a leader, and had a strategic mind when it came to combat and raids. But because of that last raid in Anbar, I was physically, emotionally, and mentally damaged, and I was discharged. I couldn't hold a job, and like many veterans, I took to living on the street. Several years ago, I came across a young homeless boy who I nicknamed Dodge. He lived in a car with his drug-addicted mother. In a rare state of sobriety and comprehension, she told me she knew she would die soon and asked me to look after him when she did. A self-fulfilling prophecy, I suppose, as she overdosed less than a week later. As it would happen, more and more children came my way. I took on the identity of Fagin or, as I called myself, Mr. Teacher.

"Like Fagin, I housed the children and trained them, mainly in theft. I already had some skill in burglary, shoplifting, and stealing from cars, from my foster care days. As a homeless man, I'd already resorted to those skills to survive on the street. Before fully immersing myself into this fantasy, I recognized I'd chosen this role because the last time I'd been truly happy was when I'd portrayed Fagin on stage."

We were silent, each in our own thoughts. Then I asked, "Had you known about the ambush, how would you have planned it differently?"

He sat down in one of the seats at the very back of the bus. "Short of calling it off or calling in an air strike? I suppose I would have worked on a way to distract the insurgents and then hit them from another direction."

I stood, walked toward the front of the bus, and turned. "Staff Sergeant, Richard, Mr. Teacher, whoever you are, my boyfriend and Pete's wife will die soon, as will three children you are supposed to protect." I sat back against the dashboard. Once again, Charles had his head down as if in prayer. "Their best chance at survival rests with you."

I stepped from the bus and left Charles with his tortured memories.

Chapter 34

Elliot was waiting by the door when I came back into the house. "Well?" he asked.

"We'll see. If not, I'll need your experience, Elliot."

"I'll help, but I'm not a genius at these things like Charles."

A little later, Edward stood at the sink, rinsing dishes and placing them in the dishwasher. The kids had eaten their fill of eggs and bacon, and some were sleeping in the living room. I had drawn a rudimentary map of the house and property, and Elliot, Pete, and I were seated at the kitchen table, studying the map.

"I don't know how we'd get from the gate all the way to the house without the kidnappers seeing us," Pete said.

Elliot pointed at the woods surrounding the house. "The woods would be best, but actually getting inside unnoticed will be tricky." He looked up at me. "Especially considering how many people you saw there."

"I asked Charles about that failed raid in Iraq and how he'd have planned it differently had he known about the ambush," I said. "He said he would have come up with a way to distract the insurgents and then struck from another direction."

"Exactly!" a voice boomed. We turned to see Charles standing in the doorway, eyes alight. He swept over, leaned on the table, and whispered in a cockney accent, "For the sake of my charges, until this plays itself out, I am Mr. Teacher."

Elliot, Pete, and Edward looked as stunned as I felt.

Mr. Teacher turned his attention to my poorly drawn diagram and started asking questions, wanting to know how far the house was from the road, in which window had we spied Wendy, and about the surrounding woods.

"How about roads that abut those woods?" Mr. Teacher asked.

"I don't know." I called to Edward, "Can I use your computer and printer?"

Edward pointed to the hallway with a dirty spatula. "My office is second door on the right. Password is s-m-capital P-small a and c."

I poured a fresh cup of coffee to take with me, and in ten minutes, I taped together numerous pages for a map of that part of the county. I brought it out to the kitchen table, and with a red pen, I drew a little square where the house was located and a circle to reflect the property.

Mr. Teacher bent over the map, and his index finger traveled over it while he muttered, "Excellent. No, no, that won't work. Perhaps."

I left him and went to the patio door, looking out into a bright, warm morning. I shivered as I realized that it may very well be my last—and the last for Nick, Wendy, and the kids. Gazing out at the ocean, I thought about these past couple years with Nick, about how he was not only my lover but my best friend, the best friend I'd ever had. I envisioned his face and then Wendy's. I thought about the three children and how frightened they must be.

"How are you faring, Miss Norwood?" Mr. Teacher asked. He, Elliot, and Edward stood behind me.

I gave them a small smile. "Stressed, Mr. Teacher."

"Take heart, Miss Norwood. A plan has come to fruition up here." He tapped his temple with a pen. "I'll now put it here." He held up a pad of yellow paper.

We reentered the kitchen, and Mr. Teacher said, "We're going to need assistance. People who've seen action and who can be relied upon under pressure. People with armaments."

"Is that necessary?" I asked.

Mr. Teacher looked at me gravely. "It's life and death, Miss Norwood. It's time we face the gravity of the situation and the lengths we are willing to go to save our loved ones."

I nodded, and he returned to his writing pad.

"A lot of my bros are vets like me. They'll be pissed when they learn what's happened to Wendy. They'll want justice." Pete pulled out his phone. "Let me see who I can pull together." He stepped out onto the patio.

As we waited for Mr. Teacher to solidify his strategy, I found a spot on a sofa in the living room and soon dozed off. I slept hard, and two and a half hours later, I woke with the little cowgirl's head in my lap. I heard unfamiliar voices coming from the kitchen.

Mr. Teacher called out, "Everybody, please come."

I paused as I got to the kitchen, little thieves streaming past on either side. While I'd slept, Mr. Teacher had taped more sheets of paper together, and they covered the table. On them, he had drawn a map that showed the house, property, surrounding woods, fence, and gate.

Edward walked up and handed me a cup of coffee. "He went on Google Earth and then drew it to scale."

Pete walked up with two bikers who'd arrived while I slept. "Lise, this is Stormy." He introduced a massive black man with a shaved head and a thick beard. He had on a pair of camo pants, a black T-shirt, and a worn leather vest that featured the patch of a well-known motorcycle club. He looked like he could bench press my car without breaking a sweat.

"Heard about you," he said in a deep, scratchy voice. We shook, his hand nearly swallowing mine.

"Thanks for your help."

"I'm here for Pete 'n' Wendy."

Pete indicated the other man. "This is Gray." Powerfully built but nowhere near as tall as Stormy, he was in black leather with tattoos visible on the backs of his hands and had a massive pistol mounted at his side like a gunslinger. His hair was a long tangle of gray, and he had serious lines on his face.

"Gray," I said in greeting.

Gray looked around the kitchen at all the kids, as well as Mr. Teacher, Elliot, and Edward. "Craziest army I've served with."

"Everyone, gather around," Mr. Teacher said, speaking with an easy confidence. "All my thieves, please stand to the back. Let the adults at the table." When everyone was situated, Mr. Teacher continued. "Thanks to Lise and Edward, we have good intel on where our friends and family are being held. However, we need more recon before we can move."

"I'm good for that," Elliot said.

I already respected Elliot for the work he'd done for me, but now I looked at him with new eyes.

"You let me borrow your car, Lise?" Elliot asked.

"Sure."

Mr. Teacher held up a hand. "Not her car. They're very aware of her car, so we don't want it seen out there."

"You can take the Tesla," Edward said.

Mr. Teacher said, "I want to thank Pete's friends for joining us. Can we expect more?"

Pete answered, "Expecting five for sure, possibly seven more."

"Weapons?" Mr. Teacher asked.

"Stormy and Gray brought an AK-47, .223 Remington, and HK SP5. Everyone will have sidearms."

"I hope your motorcycles are loud. The louder, the better," Mr. Teacher said.

Pete grinned. "We'll make a lot of noise. Other than my pickup and one other, the rest of the guys will be on bikes. Loud bikes."

"On the subject of weapons, do you have anything in the way of firepower, Miss Norwood?" Mr. Teacher asked.

"Ruger SR9 and a Glock 19."

"Excellent." Mr. Teacher stood and looked at me. "I've made two contingency plans. One is if they have you drop the ransoms somewhere other than the house. In that case, you can meet up with Pete and his friends after the drop and travel to the house with them. However, if they have you take the ransoms to the house, that does not bode well."

I nodded. "That most likely means they plan on killing me too."

"That's one way of looking at it," Mr. Teacher said.

"It's the only way to look at it," I mumbled.

"You're overlooking the benefit." Mr. Teacher smiled widely. "It gives us our third advantage." He held up his index finger. "The first advantage is that we know where they're keeping the hostages." His middle finger rose. "The second is that they don't know that we know." His ring finger joined the other two. "The third advantage, if Lise is taken, is that we will have an inside man... or in this case, an inside woman." He turned his attention fully to me. "They'll search you when you arrive, Miss Norwood. We'll want them to find one of your guns, so they'll think they disarmed you. Make it the Ruger. The Glock is lighter, and we'll hide that somewhere special." Mr. Teacher pointed a pencil at Edward. "You in?"

"Yes."

"Edward, don't do this because of me," I said.

"I'm not. I'm doing it because my security chief is behind all this." He gave a small shrug. "Not to mention, it's the right thing to do."

Mr. Teacher gave a nod, meaning that was settled. "Stage one, distraction. Everyone gets in place by two o'clock, an hour before Lise will receive instructions. Pete, you and your friends wait at this country tavern." He tapped a point on the map a little over a mile from the house. "Act like you're on a motorcycle run. Don't let anyone drink too much. I'll follow along with the Thieves Kitchen school bus and park behind the bar. If anyone asks, it's the party bus for your run."

Mr. Teacher used the pencil to draw an X on a road on the north-west side of the woods surrounding the house. "Edward and Elliot will be waiting here for stage two—extraction. You'll need something bigger than your Tesla, Edward."

"I have a Suburban I drive to the construction site," Edward said.

"Good. We may change the initial location after Elliot's recon, but for now, we'll say this is the spot."

"I assume that I'll be at home," I said.

"Right. In fact, you should leave soon. When this thing starts, they'll have eyes on you." He then detailed his plan, again highlighting a distraction that involved a faux brawl between good ol' boys and bikers. The extraction part, as he said, depended on the directions I got on where to leave the ransoms. He stood and smiled at the children. "The third stage is apprehension. We'll take care of that at Thieves Kitchen. What do you say, my dears?"

The kids all cheered like he'd just announced he was taking them to Disney World.

Chapter 35

Edward's house had been a cacophonous mix of noise and activity due to all the people there. My house was the opposite. The silence was unsettling. I paced my living room, and when I got tired of that, I sat, my knees bopping up and down in nervous anticipation as I waited for Nick's phone call to give me directions so I could deliver the ransoms. Ten minutes before three, I leaned against my kitchen island and watched the digital clock on the microwave as my fingernails tapped repetitively on the countertop. I stared as the minutes slowly passed, and when three o'clock showed, Nick's ringtone sounded on my phone.

I snatched up my phone. "Nick?"

"Hi, Lise."

"Are you okay?"

"Yeah."

"Can they hear me?"

"You're on speaker." There was a smack. "Ow! Fuck you."

"Nick?"

"Let's stick to the instructions, Lise. I'll get fewer bruises that way."

"Okay. Where do I go?"

After a brief pause, he said, "You have ten minutes to drive to the little convenience store on A1A near Publix." The call ended.

I was prepared for the three o'clock call, having dressed for comfort and mobility in running shoes, comfortable jeans, a dark T-shirt, and a sports coat to provide a pocket big enough for my Ruger. I ran out the door with a paper-wrapped painting tucked under my arm and the briefcase containing one million dollars in my hand. I rushed down to my car, put both items on the passenger seat, and got in. Ten minutes left me plenty of time. I got to the convenience store in six.

After I'd waited several minutes, "Can't Get Enough of Your Love, Babe" started. "Hi Nick."

"You have fifteen minutes to get to the statue in Ponce de Leon Park," he said and then disconnected.

Getting to Ponce de Leon Park in fifteen minutes was doable. Getting there and to the statue of Ponce de Leon in time was another matter. The thing I most feared was getting pulled over by the police for speeding, so I went no faster than ten miles per hour over the speed limit. I mentally debated which parking area would get me closest to the statue. I opted for the southern lot, parked, jumped out, and started sprinting while pointing the key fob over my shoulder to lock the doors. I would hate to get back and find that someone had helped themselves to a briefcase stuffed with cash and a painting worth into the six figures. I made it to the bronze conquistador with a minute to spare.

Nick called and told me to head to Walmart, and he gave me a whopping twelve minutes to get there. For the next hour and a half, I drove around San Marco, going where Nick directed me.

Finally, Nick called and gave me an address. "Enter the address in your phone, and it will take you to where you leave the briefcase and painting." I didn't need directions. Edward and I had been there last night.

I called Elliot. "It's a go. They gave me the address to the house."

"Then you've got a target on your back. Be careful," Elliot whispered. "Edward and I are in the woods. We have eyes on the house and will see you when you pull up. How much time inside do you want before the circus starts?"

"Ten minutes," I said, sounding nervous. "But if you hear gunfire, things have gone to hell."

"I have a good feeling about this, Lise. Distraction, extraction, and apprehension. We'll make it out the other side. You'll see." Elliot ended the call.

At least one of us felt good about it. I deleted the call to Elliot from the call log in case the kidnappers checked my phone and then thought about Elliot and Mr. Teacher in Iraq, taking risks like this day in and day out. The stress must have been monumental, the result obvious in both men, but right now, their combined experience left me with some hope as I drove toward the lions' den. Still, the closer I got, the more anxious I felt. As I approached the curve on the country road that led to the house, I pulled off to the side. Taking deep breaths, I calmed down a little and then realized I had to pee. If I died, I didn't want to go in wet pants. I grabbed an old napkin from the console, went around to the other side of my car, and did my business in some weeds.

I got back in the car, my stomach in knots. I put Minnie in drive, rounded the curve, and drove past the wall to the driveway. The gate was open, so I turned in, drove up to the house, and parked next to one of three SUVs. There was also a Ford sedan and a police car with a policeman behind the wheel, his eyes on me. Four very large men in dark slacks and white shirts waited for me at the bottom of steps leading up to the house. I grabbed the painting and the briefcase from the passenger seat and got out.

"I'll take those," a stubble-headed, pie-faced man said and reached out for what I carried. He fit the description of the man who had hit Dodge.

"No, you won't. I'm hanging on to them until I can hand them over to your boss."

"Hell you will."

"Fuck it, Walt. Let her carry 'em in," another man said. "See if she's clean."

Stubble forcibly spun me around and frisked me, quickly finding the Ruger. "You won't be needing this, sweetheart." He tucked it into his waistband and then found my phone. He dropped it to the ground and stomped on it. "She's clean now."

We started for the house, two men on either side of me. Now that the plan was underway, my anxiety was gone. No matter how this shook out, I would have a cool head.

Once we were inside, they directed me up a staircase, and we turned right into a hallway and walked to the door at the end that was secured with a padlock. Stubble removed a key ring from his pocket, went through the keys until he located the right one, and unlocked the door. I stepped into the room.

"Lise." Nick got up from a chair and started for me. He sported a split lip that was starting to swell, and the area around his left eye was puffy and red. Stubble stepped in, put a hand on Nick's chest, and shoved him to the floor.

"Don't mind him. He's got anger issues," Nick said and gave me a heartfelt smile. "Good to see you, Lise, even under these conditions."

"Oh, Nick. I'm so sorry you got involved."

"Hi, Lise." Wendy sat on a sofa, one eye swollen shut, her arm around a little girl.

"Hi, Wendy." I pointed at her eye. "What happened there?"

"I wasn't going to let these assholes take me without a fight."

"Atta girl. Pete sure is worried about you."

"I bet he's fit to be tied."

I nodded. "He's eager to bust some heads, that's for sure."

I looked around the room. The king-size bed and all the furnishings looked like they cost a pretty penny. French doors led to the balcony, and I understood why no one had tried to escape. A chain and padlock around the door handles secured them in place.

I looked at a muscular kid of about sixteen wearing only a loincloth. "I take it you're Tarzan?"

"Yeah."

I saw another boy, a bit younger. "Dag?"

"Yes, ma'am."

I knelt in front of the girl next to Wendy. "And you must be Olivia." Watching me with big eyes, she nodded.

"Mr. Teacher told me about you. He said you're very brave, and he wanted me to give you a message."

"What?" Olivia's voice was barely audible.

I whispered in her ear, "That you should do what I tell you, and you'll soon be back with him."

Olivia smiled then her eyes shifted, and she looked past me, frightened. She said, "Monster."

Chapter 36

Preparing to meet Eileen's stony gaze, I turned and blurted, "Trish?" Funny, bubbly, vivacious Trish the CFO was gone. The woman standing before me was steely-eyed, her expression stern. What demanded my attention most was the pistol she pointed at my chest.

"Is that my Ruger?" I asked.

"Ironic, isn't it?" Her lips rose slightly into a sinister half smile, nothing like her cheek-to-cheek grin when she was talking a mile a minute.

Three men stood behind Trish. The man I thought of as Stubble held a pistol as well.

"Put the briefcase down here," she said, indicating the bed.

I did as she instructed, and she stuffed my Ruger into the waistband of her pantsuit. She fiddled with the latches of the briefcase.

"They used a hammer to get past the locks," I said. "Might take a little finesse."

Trish finally opened it and looked down at the banded stacks of money.

"It's all there," I said.

She looked at me and then closed the lid. She held out a hand for *Cold Green Spring*.

I didn't want her to hold it, as she might notice that it was one pound, six ounces heavier than it should be. I slid my fingers into the seam of paper at the back of the painting where it was taped shut and ripped the brown paper, pulling it around to the front to show her the artwork.

"Let me have it," she said.

Since I needed to stall until the distraction began, I said, "Nope, not until I have some answers." I found myself facing the barrel of my own gun. Funny, but it looked a lot bigger from the receiving end. "I'd be careful if you shoot me. You just might put a bullet through the painting. *Cold Lead and Green Spring*, hmm. Sounds like a noir novel. And if you miss it and hit me, think of all that blood on the canvas. It'd be impossible to get that stain out."

She shook her head and gave me an unpleasant smile. Picking up the briefcase, she said, "Walt, unlock the doors."

Walt, aka Stubble, pulled the key ring from his pocket, fumbled through the keys with fat fingers, and selected a small one that opened the padlock. Trish, Stubble, and I stepped onto the balcony.

"A beautiful day," Trish said and breathed deep. "We should enjoy it. Sit." She pointed at a bistro set, a small table and two small chairs. Stubble stayed by the door as I sat in one and she the other. She placed the briefcase next to her chair while keeping the barrel of my pistol casually pointed my way. We sat quietly until she said, "You can't have answers unless you ask questions."

I decided to start with a hardball. "Did you kill that boy, Mackie?"

She seemed to think about how to reply. "They stole a briefcase. Not only did it contain a million dollars, but it was a million dollars that I was answerable for. If I lost it, I'd be as dead as that boy."

"You pushed him in front of a train," I said.

"I was impressing upon the other boy the lengths that I was willing to go."

"How did you find out where they were staying?"

"Because of our evening out with Detective Eve Martinez. What you two talked about, the band of little thieves. Or what did she call them? The juvenile magpies. That got us to focus our search on the streets, rousting junkies and bums, and we soon had their location. Really quite fascinating, aren't they? I mean the children. They're straight from a Charles Dickens novel."

"Is Eileen Warrick involved?" I asked.

Trish grinned, and it wasn't a pretty smile. "Is that what you thought? Edward believes that?"

I nodded. "She's disappeared. We thought she knew we were on to her and went into hiding. Edward and I found some financial paperwork in her suite with questionable entries."

"Construction expenditures?"

Now I was confused, but I rolled with it. "Yeah. Construction expenditures."

That earned a smile from Trish. "I've been with Edward for a little over five years. On a regular basis, I get briefcases filled with money, money that I insert into varied Burke Industries accounts, and then that same money is used to pay off shell corporations."

Come on, Pete. Where are you?

"You're laundering money through Edward's businesses."

"As an example, our Florida concrete supplier is Cates Concrete, but we also, on paper at least, purchase concrete from Alliance Concrete of Chicago. Alliance is one of those shell companies, a bogus business. The dirty money is laundered through Edward's accounts and then paid to Mainstay Concrete, ending up as clean as freshly fallen snow. We also use a nonexistent employment agency for fake payroll, a bogus company for heavy equipment rental, and a phony tool supplier. And that's just his construction business. Just about every division of Burke Industries helps me do my real job. That's what all this is about. That's why I killed that boy."

"Where's the dirty money come from?"

She didn't answer right away but eyed me as she decided how much to disclose. "I work with a Chicago group."

"You mean a crime syndicate," I said.

"Call it what you want. I'm not a member, though. I'm more of an outside financial consultant."

"And Edward never figured it out?"

"Edward has a good head for finance, especially when it comes to investments. But he leaves the vast amount of paperwork to me. For me, it's as simple as delving into a comic book. I thought I'd hidden the laundering well, so I was surprised Eileen found it. I'm not sure what alerted her or how she discovered it."

"So, what's with this?" I held up the painting and ripped off the rest of the paper wrapping. I held it so the painting faced her, while from the back, I could see my Glock 19 held in place by two clips behind the painting and secured to the thick picture frame.

"I never knew much about fine art. Working with Edward changed that. He was proud of his collection. As his CFO, I knew its worth. I immersed myself in learning about artworks as investments and decided I wanted to start my own collection. The funny thing about CFOs is that we are often frugal. We hate spending our own money. When I saw how much Edward's de Kooning painting was worth, I hatched a plan."

"You faked your own kidnapping," I said.

"Bingo. As I was the supposed victim, I didn't need anyone's help. I faked everything, from disappearing to contacting Edward after he gave up the painting. I even used real handcuffs to put bruises around my wrists. When we came down to San Marco for the arts center project, Chicago sent two men with me to make sure the laundering would go as planned. These men also answered to me. After meeting Marjorie Hamilton and seeing her David Hockney painting, I decided to add another piece to my collection. With the help of those two gentlemen, we kidnapped Marjorie's niece and followed the same procedures as when I'd faked my kidnapping."

"So, now it's *Cold Green Spring*," I said.

"Well, it's beautiful. When I asked Edward how he selected artworks to invest in, he said he usually just looked at a painting and knew he had to have it. That's how I felt about his de Kooning and Mrs. Kingman's Hockney. And now, thanks to you, *Cold Green Spring* is in the news, and its value has increased. I imagine the value will climb even more when it vanishes again."

Things were supposed to start ten minutes after I entered the house. My sense of time was all screwed up, but certainly, I'd been inside that long, if not longer. Struggling to come up with something to keep her talking, I said, "There's something Edward and I were curious about. Why did the briefcase handoff take place at the construction site?"

"A matter of convenience, really. We knew no one would be there at that time of night. Or, rather, we thought that would be the case. And if any cops happened by, being an employee of Burke Industries gave me a reason for being there, even though we already had a policeman there."

"You've grown from two men to a small army."

"Yes. Two men delivered the briefcase to us, which brought us to four. When the briefcase was stolen, Chicago sent four more men to help in its recovery."

"Not to mention a cop."

Trish shrugged. "It's a friend-of-a-friend-of-a-friend kind of thing. A crooked cop comes in handy."

"You kept Marjorie's niece blindfolded so she couldn't identify any-one. Yet, now..." I opened my eyes wide to make the point.

"Yes, that is a problem. Wendy did not go easily. She put up quite the fight, and she saw Walt's face." She indicated Stubble at the door.

"A gorilla with a crew cut," I said, quoting Dodge.

Stubble gave me the stink eye.

"The raid on the children's encampment did not go as smoothly as planned, and some of the kids got a good look at us. So what's the point?"

We stared at one another, knowing that Nick, Wendy, the kids, and I were under a death sentence.

"Why me?" I asked.

"Because you were already involved, helping out the biker and help-ing the police try to identify the boy. And frankly, because I knew you probably had the best chance of figuring everything out."

"Let's be straight with each other. You plan on murdering us."

The slightest smile played on her lips.

Yoo-hoo, Pete, where are you?

In an attempt to hold off the inevitable, I brought out a tired old saying. "You won't get away with it."

"To be honest, I thought I'd have to go on the run. Which is fine. Now that I have the briefcase back, the organization I work for would put my skills to use elsewhere and under a different identity. But you know what? The way things are going, I wonder if I can keep suspicion on Eileen. Maybe I'll be safe remaining as Edward's CFO. I'll have to go through the books and clean up everything for the time being."

"So what did happen to Eileen?"

"Her job was simple. Keep Edward safe. Instead, she went poking around where she shouldn't. She was looking over some invoices and found one from the bogus concrete company. She then came across the fake employment agency. She alerted me, not knowing that I was the one cooking the books. I told her we needed to go through the finances carefully but to keep it a secret until we knew for sure. I brought her out here, and she's now buried in the garden under a bed of elephant ear plants. They should grow quite large."

Finally, blessedly, I heard the approach of loud motorcycles. Trish seemed not to notice, but then motorcyclists probably rode a lot out on these country roads.

Pointing my Ruger directly at me, she gripped the briefcase with her other hand and stood. "Let's get back inside."

The roar of engines grew louder, and a second later, a monstrously large black pickup truck on humongous tires crashed through the gate, followed by Pete's pickup. Three men jumped out of the trucks as four men on motorcycles roared in and parked. The bikers started to fight the truckers right there on the property's front lawn. It was a bogus fight, the diversion that Mr. Teacher had cooked up, but it looked like they were really going at it.

Not wanting her to suspect this was part of a plan, I proclaimed, "What the hell?"

"Looks like the rednecks and the bikers don't get along," Stubble said. He looked at Trish and added, "We really don't want them drawing the cops out here."

Trish watched the fracas for a moment and then ordered, "Inside."

In the room, she told two of the men, "Come with me." She shoved the briefcase into Stubble's hands and pointed at me. "If she tries anything, break her neck."

Chapter 37

Stubble stuffed his pistol into a shoulder holster and set down the briefcase. He secured the chains and padlock around the French door handles and put the key ring in a side jacket pocket. According to Mr. Teacher's plan, Pete and his cronies would continue their faux fight. Pete would monitor the second-floor balcony off the room we were in, see us escape, and know when to pull back. If the Chicago thugs went out to chase them off, then the fight would turn on them and become real. That fear became reality at the sound of several gunshots.

"What the fuck?" Stubble grumbled and moved to the front-facing window.

A few seconds later, random shots turned to steady fire.

"Motherfuckers have guns," Stubble said.

While his back was turned, I reached to the picture frame and pulled my Glock from the clips. I'd already racked the slide, so it was ready to fire. I handed the painting to Tarzan and lifted the pistol. While holding it in the two-handed grip I'd been taught, I remembered something my instructor had said. *Don't point a gun at anyone unless you're prepared to use it.* I was ready.

"Hey," I called to Stubble. "I heard you like to hit kids."

He turned, and his eyes went wide for a split second before narrowing.

"Everyone behind me," I said. Once Wendy, Nick, and the three kids were in place, I instructed Stubble, "Take the chains off the door."

As the gunfire continued out front, he fixed me with a stare, and his hand moved to the inside of his jacket.

"One more inch, and you're dead," I told him.

"Just going for the keys," he said.

"No, you're not. You're going for your gun." I made a point to keep my Glock steady and aimed at the top of his simian nose and between his eyes. "Keys are in your side pocket."

Stubble sighed, moved his hand slowly, and pulled out the key ring. He riffled through the keys, eyes alternating between them and me, until he got to the key that opened the lock and removed the chain, gripping it like the formidable weapon it could be.

"Toss the chain toward the bed," I instructed, and he complied.

I let go of the gun with my left hand, pointed out the French doors, and addressed Wendy, Nick, and the children. "Go all the way across the balcony to the side of the house." Gunfire continued out front, so I added, "Pete and his buddies aren't going to shoot in our direction, but stay low just in case. Edward and Elliot are waiting for you on the ground and will help you get down." No one moved, so I shouted, "Go!"

Wendy and the kids started toward the balcony.

"I'll stick with you," Nick said, standing to my left.

I nodded, happy to have him stay. Once again using a two-handed grip, I took several steps to the right, keeping Stubble in my gunsight but also allowing me to see out onto the balcony.

Tarzan looked over the railing.

"Are Edward and Elliot there?" I called.

Tarzan gave me a grin and a thumbs-up. He leaned over the railing and dropped the painting. Next, he took one of Olivia's wrists, and Dag took the other.

"Count to three," Tarzan told her. She did, and on three, Tarzan and Dag lifted her over the railing and lowered her down to Edward and Elliot.

Tarzan and Dag helped Wendy over and down in the same manner. Tarzan said something to Dag, who then climbed over the railing and dropped to the ground. Running low, Tarzan crossed the balcony and back into the room.

"What are you doing?" I asked.

"This," Tarzan said and grabbed the briefcase from beside Stubble.

"You don't wanna take that," Stubble said.

"Actually, I do." Tarzan ran back across the balcony, dropped the briefcase over the side, and then climbed over and down.

"Now what?" Nick asked.

"Good question." I thought for a second. "Go get his gun, but don't get between him and me."

I took a step closer to Stubble as Nick approached him.

Nick stopped at Stubble's right side and reached across the man's broad chest and into his jacket. "Easy, big fella."

Striking as fast as one of Florida's Diamondback rattlesnakes, Stubble grabbed Nick and flung him into me. Our collision knocked me to the side but not down. Nick, on the other hand, found himself squarely on his ass. Stubble reached for his gun as he ran across the room. I got off a shot and missed just as he launched himself over the bed.

I grabbed Nick's arm, helped him up, and pushed him onto the balcony. "Hurry!"

Stubble fired a couple shots, and I aimed blindly behind me, giving him an answering shot, hoping he would stay crouched behind the bed until we were on the ground and running.

Nick got to the railing and turned. His eyes went wide, and he yelled, "Lise!"

I turned as Stubble charged through the balcony door and raised his handgun. I brought up my Glock, and we fired at the same time. My bullet struck him under his right cheekbone, and his body collapsed just as Nick grunted and flew back with enough force that he struck the railing and did a backflip off the balcony. I peered over and saw him on the ground, unmoving, his head bloody.

"No, no, no," I repeated. Quickly sticking the gun in my waistband, I climbed over the railing, jumped to the ground, and landed on my hands and knees.

Edward and Elliot knelt by Nick. Wendy stood nearby with the kids.

I crawled to Nick. "Hey! Hey, Nick, can you hear me?" He didn't acknowledge me. The left side of his head was bloody. I couldn't see where he'd been shot, but the flow of blood continued.

"Ah shit, did he get hit in the eye?" Elliot asked.

I couldn't see Nick's left eye for all the blood.

The gunfire out front was easing up, and Edward stood. "Lise, we have to go."

I gazed down upon Nick—my lover, my best friend. Was this it? Would I never speak with him again? Kiss him? Make love to him? Cold waves of pain fell onto me.

Edward put a hand on my shoulder. "I'm sorry, Lise, but we have to get the kids to safety."

"So you're just going to leave me? Edward, I really don't like you." The raspy voice came from Nick.

I gasped, my eyes filling with tears. "You're alive."

"I'll take your word for it." He struggled to sit up, and Elliot and I helped him.

He put a hand to his head. "Hurts like hell." He looked at the blood on his hand and then up at me with his right eye, his left still hidden by blood. "I can't see so good."

The sound of guns heated up again.

"Let's help him to the Suburban," I told Elliot, and we pulled Nick to his feet and got his arms over each of our shoulders.

Edward led the way, pushing through the limbs and foliage of the woods. Tarzan followed next, holding Olivia's hand, and then Dag. Elliot and I, Nick between us, brought up the rear. The gun battle seemed to be slowing again as we got to the Suburban. Elliot pulled open the door behind the passenger seat and had Nick sit on a middle seat, facing outward. I quickly took off my sport coat and threw it down. Next, I removed my T-shirt.

Nick, obviously hurting, managed to grin at me in my bra. "Now's not the time."

"Shut up," I murmured. Adrenaline helped give me the strength to tear a long strip of cloth out of my T-shirt. I passed it to Elliot, who tied it around Nick's head to serve as a bandage. I ripped apart a few more strips, and Elliot applied those as well until Nick's left eye and temple were well bound. Ignoring the spatters of blood on Nick's lips, I gave him a quick kiss and then helped him maneuver his legs into the vehicle. "You good?"

"So far. What happened with the big guy?"

"He won't be hurting anyone else."

Edward approached us. "You want my shirt?"

I looked down at my nearly bare torso. "Nah." I got in the front passenger seat and motioned Olivia over. "It's going to be a tight squeeze," I told her as I picked her up and placed her on my lap. Elliot moved a middle seat forward so Tarzan and Dag could slip into the back with the briefcase and painting. Wendy joined them back there. Edward got in the driver's seat in front of Nick, and Elliot sat in the seat behind me. We took off. For a big vehicle, the Suburban moved fast.

I turned to Nick. "Are you okay?"

"My head hurts, but other than that, I think I'm all right." He gave me a pained smile.

I grinned back and then turned my attention to the young girl in my lap. "Olivia, I didn't get a chance to introduce myself. My name is Lise."

She whispered back, "I know. Nick told us that you'd save us."

"He did?"

She nodded with great sincerity. "He said you're a private eye and a good guy. I wasn't so scared after that."

In the midst of this craziness, with my emotions so close to the surface, I felt a comforting warmth. My eyes teared up as I looked back at Nick, but he had turned his head to see out the back window.

I wiped the dampness from my eyes and told Edward, "It's not Eileen. Trish is behind this."

"Trish?"

"She's using your accounts to launder money for a Chicago syndicate."

"My Trish?" He thought a moment. "But what about Eileen?"

"Something alerted Eileen. We may never know what, but she started checking the paperwork. When she found anomalies, she didn't suspect Trish and took the paperwork to her to see what she thought. Trish killed her—or had her killed."

"This is a nightmare. Wait, what about the kidnappings?"

"She faked the first one then decided it was a good way to get her own private collection going."

"Holy sh—" Edward glanced at Olivia then finished with, "sheepdog."

He took a right at the first intersection we came to, and the property's stone wall was on our right. Pete's friends, on their bikes, came flying out of the driveway and turned to the right in front of us. Pete's truck, which sported countless bullet holes, followed. Once clear of the driveway, he braked. We stopped before the driveway and watched as Mr. Teacher drove his school bus in front of the gate and parked, blocking the entrance. He didn't leave enough room for a person to get through, much less a vehicle.

I lifted Olivia onto the console so that I could jump from the car. Elliot held his seat forward as Wendy climbed out from the rear seat. She stumbled, so I took her arm, and we rushed to Pete's truck.

I opened the door as an unintroduced biker slid toward Pete, who said, "They killed his truck."

"My condolences," I said to him. As I helped Wendy in, I told Pete, "Early Christmas present."

He took a moment to smile at his wife. "You okay, babe?"

"I am now," she said.

He looked past her to me, and his visage shifted. He was ready to stomp some serious ass. "See you at Thieves Kitchen."

"Thieves Kitchen," I said and closed the door.

As Pete took off, I ran to the bus. Mr. Teacher emerged, stuffing the bus keys into a pocket. I pulled out my Glock and shot out all the right-side tires, which would make the bus that much harder to push out of the way. Once we got back to the Suburban, Mr. Teacher jumped into the very back to sit between Tarzan and Dag.

Edward hit the accelerator.

Looking in the vanity mirror, I asked Tarzan and Dag, "Are you guys all right?"

"Woo-hoo!" Tarzan yelled. "That was great."

Dag gave me a thumbs-up and started a chant. "Lise, Lise, Lise." Tarzan quickly picked it up.

"Knock it off, you two," I said with a grin.

Nick started in at a quieter volume. "Lise, Lise, Lise."

Then Elliot and Mr. Teacher joined in. "Lise, Lise, Lise."

Laughing, Edward got into it as well.

Leaning her head against my chest, Olivia quietly chanted, "Lise, Lise, Lise."

My heart swelled.

"Nick said you were a badass," Tarzan said.

Edward grinned at me. "Such a badass."

"Your plan worked, Mr. Teacher," I said, looking at him in the rearview mirror.

"Like clockwork," Elliot said.

"There's one more stage," Mr. Teacher pointed out.

Edward, too, used the rearview mirror to look at him. "We could just leave that to the police."

"We all agreed to the three stages." Mr. Teacher counted off on his fingers. "Stage one, distraction. Stage two, extraction. Stage three, apprehension."

"They might not even come after us," Edward said.

"We still have the briefcase—thanks to Tarzan—and the painting," I said. "Trish might have written off the painting, but I don't think she can afford to say adios to the million."

Edward glanced in the rearview. "It's a moot point. They're behind us."

Chapter 38

"They couldn't have possibly moved my bus that quickly," Mr. Teacher said, twisting in his seat to get a view of their pursuers.

"On the north side of the property, there's a gap between the stone wall and the woods," Elliot said. "Could've been wide enough for them to drive out."

Edward glanced up at the mirror.

"You drive. I'll look," I said, pulling down the vanity mirror.

"Can you see how many there are?" Edward asked while accelerating.

"One SUV. Windows are too dark to tell how many people are in it."

While I watched, a second SUV roared up behind the first. "Number of SUVs just doubled. Trish told me she had eight men, plus the dirty cop. We can subtract Mr. Stubble from that number. Let me see your phone."

Edward dug around in a pocket with one hand while steering with the other and then handed his phone to me.

I called Pete, and he answered with, "Almost there."

"They got out somehow and are following us. Need to know how many there are. Did you guys take any out of play?"

"One guy for sure. He charged out the front door, blasting away, so we took him down. The cop took a couple shots and then hunkered down behind his car. Don't know if he was hit or not. The others stayed inside and shot at us out the windows."

"Okay. See you soon."

"We'll be ready."

"Could be as many as seven, plus Trish," I told them and then made my next call.

Detective Baker took a long time answering. "What's up, Norwood?"

"The dead boy's name was Phillip Reynolds, and he lived with an abusive uncle in Tampa."

"Whoa. Wait. Start over again," Baker said.

"No time. We're being chased by the guys responsible for the boy's murder, and we have five people they kidnapped with us."

"Kidnapped? And who's we? Lise, what the fuck—"

"If something happens to us, Patricia Meyers, CFO of Burke Industries, is responsible. She's the bad guy in all of this."

"Lise, what the hell—"

"There's a cop working with them."

"Dammit, Norwood, start over."

"See how fast you can rally the troops. We're heading to the old D.W. Roberts College, and we could really use your help."

"Lise—"

"We're counting on you, Baker," I said and ended the call.

I put Edward's phone on the console between us.

Nick leaned forward. "So, what's this about the old college?"

I explained Mr. Teacher's plan.

"It's never dull being your boyfriend," Nick said.

I yelled, "Everybody buckle up." Shifting over in my seat, I gave Olivia room between me and the console and fastened the seat belt and shoulder harness around us. Returning my attention to the mirror, I said, "They're keeping up."

Edward called to the back seat, "Mr. Teacher, if you would be so kind as to give me directions."

"My pleasure."

We traveled the country roads with the speedometer between eighty and ninety miles per hour, only slowing for turns.

"A left just ahead, Mr. Burke," Mr. Teacher said. "And then you'll have to do something to gather us some time."

"Oh?" Edward asked, sounding calm even though the Suburban was almost on two wheels as he made the turn.

"The driveway into Thieves Kitchen is about a half mile ahead on the right. We need a little time to prepare before they show up. A simple head start will do."

Edward looked into the rearview mirror and shouted, "*Hold on!*"

When I realized what he was going to do, I wrapped Olivia in my arms and pulled her tight against me. Edward slammed on the brakes, and the following car hit us hard. The second SUV's driver tried to miss the first SUV but glanced off it, which sent it careening off the road, where it sideswiped a tree.

Edward hit the accelerator, leaving both SUVs behind us. He made the turn into the old campus, and we sped down the bumpy road. He stopped when we got to where Pete and his friends had parked. They stood there with the rest of the children from Thieves Kitchen.

We got out, and Mr. Teacher clapped to get everyone's attention and announced, "Places, everyone."

I took Olivia's hand, directed Nick to pick up the little cowgirl, and we headed toward one of the buildings on the property that overlooked the swimming pool. Since Tarzan and Dag had been captive and not present when the plans were made, Mr. Teacher insisted they join us. We got to the second floor just as someone whistled, the signal that Trish and her men had arrived. The live oak leaves strewn across the floor of the old building crunched under our feet as we approached two windows that would give us the best view.

"We can watch," I said. "But stay low. If they start shooting, hit the floor."

Tarzan, Dag, and Annie Oakley positioned themselves around one window. Olivia nestled between Nick and me at the other. We looked down on a space surrounded by the old buildings. Some wild growth was close to the buildings, but in the center was what looked like a large patch of soil, leaves, twigs, and limbs.

"Where'd the swimming pool go?" Olivia asked.

"You'll see," I told her.

"What swimming pool?" Nick asked.

"You'll see," I repeated, smiling at him.

"I get it," Tarzan said.

All the kids from Thieves Kitchen lingered outside the farthest building to our left. Dodge and Geronimo were tossing the briefcase of money back and forth. They all acted as if nothing was going on, laughing and joking, a few running around playing tag.

The first of Trish's men came from the side of the building to our right, and then a couple more, as well as Trish, came from the other side. I counted five plus the cop and Trish, meaning Pete's friends had taken two out of play. The kids were still acting like they hadn't seen the intruders. Even from a distance, I could see Trish's face turn red when she saw Dodge and Geronimo playing catch with the million-dollar briefcase.

She shouted, "Stay where you are!"

All hell broke loose as the kids scattered. Dodge snatched the briefcase from the air and ran into the building behind him. Other kids dashed into buildings, some went around them, and a few of the kids ran between the trees into the woods.

"Get the briefcase!" Trish shrieked, and the men charged.

"Here it comes," I muttered.

One second, the men were charging across the grounds, and in the next, the ground was opening beneath them.

"What the hell?" Nick said.

Back at Edward's house, during the planning stage, Edward and Mr. Teacher had searched the supply shed by the swimming pool and discovered a pool cover large enough to cover the pool at the college. As part of preparation for the stage three apprehension, Mr. Teacher and the denizens of Thieves Kitchen stretched it over the nearly empty pool, securing it in place with bricks and heavy limbs and branches. They'd then thrown dirt, leaves, and debris over the pool cover, doing a masterful job of camouflaging it. Three of the men fell into the deep end. Three others, including the policeman, managed to stop before taking a tumble. Pete, Stormy, and Elliot charged from behind, slammed into the three men, and sent them tumbling into the hole. All six of the intruders found themselves tangled in the fabric of the pool cover. Pete's friends materialized with rifles and shotguns and ringed the pool.

The policeman, tangled in the cover from his neck down, shouted, "Put down your weapons. You're all under arrest!"

This caused everyone aboveground to break into laughter.

Mr. Teacher strolled to the pool edge. "Gentlemen, keep your hands where we can see them."

I was grinning when Olivia looked up at me. "Where'd the monster go?" she asked.

Trish was gone. Hands on the sill, I leaned out the window and looked to where she'd been. Then I looked the other way and spotted her. She'd gone around the back of our building and toward the one Dodge had disappeared into.

"She's going after the briefcase." I turned to Nick. "Stay with the kids."

Pulling out my Glock, I ran from the room, nearly tumbling down the debris-covered stairs. Regaining my balance, I got down to the first floor and flew out the nearest doorway.

Glancing at Edward, who stood with Mr. Teacher, I shouted, "Trish is going for the briefcase."

Edward started after me. We got to the building and went inside, through one room, down a hall, and into another room where Geronimo sat against the wall, his head bleeding.

"Are you all right?" Edward asked him.

"Yeah. That lady came in looking for the briefcase. I tried slowing her down, but she clubbed me with her gun."

"Which way?" I asked.

"Out back." He pointed at another door.

I ran out, rounded a copse of trees, and held out my hand to stop Edward. Twenty yards from us, Trish and Dodge were engaged in tug-of-war with the briefcase.

I wasn't a good enough shot from where I stood, especially with Dodge so close to Trish. The next best thing was to distract her. I aimed a few feet behind her and fired three rounds. Trish released Dodge, pulled my Ruger from her waist, turned toward me, and got off a couple shots. I ran to the nearest tree and ducked behind it. Looking for Edward, I saw him on his back, a hand held high between his neck and shoulder, failing to staunch the flow of blood.

"Fuck!" I called out to him, "Can you make it over here?"

"I think so."

"On three."

Edward nodded and then grimaced.

"One, two, three." I swung my pistol around the tree. Dodge was gone, and Trish was picking up the briefcase. I fired three shots and missed, but the gunfire sent Trish running for cover as Edward struggled to his feet and loped over to me.

He dropped beside me, and I asked, "How bad is it?"

"Hurts like hell. Plowed through just above the collarbone."

I got low to the ground and peered around the tree. The briefcase sat unattended. I knew Trish wasn't going to abandon it. A small hillock and a couple of big pines were nearby that she could be behind.

I pulled back. "We need to find out where she is."

"I got it."

I peeked my head around the tree again.

"Not cool shooting your boss, Trish," Edward yelled.

After a beat, Trish shouted back. "Take it up with human resources."

Edward laughed, winced, and then said, "We've got the briefcase covered, and the police are on their way."

I caught a flash of movement behind one of the trees. "I took two shots back at the house, three for the bus tires," I told Edward. "Another three while she was fighting with Dodge for the briefcase and three after she shot you."

"Eleven bullets. How many does that thing hold?" Edward asked.

"Fifteen-round magazine. Four left."

From across the clearing, Trish shouted, "Let me get the briefcase, Edward, and then you'll never see me again. I swear."

"Doesn't work that way, Trish."

"You're interfering in the business of some very dangerous people."

I glanced around the tree as Edward shouted, "I think those very dangerous people will take out their displeasure on you, not me."

Trish partially emerged from behind the tree. She hadn't seen me.

I whispered, "Keep talking. She's making her move."

Edward swallowed. "You were the one who was supposed to keep their money safe. Yeah, I know about the laundering, Trish. I don't think they're going to be happy about their men getting shot and arrested, either."

Trish ran for the briefcase.

I stood, stepped out from the tree, and brought up my pistol. "Stop!"

Trish kept coming, raised her pistol, and pulled the trigger. I returned fire. For a few seconds, we traded shots like cowboys at the O.K. Corral, and then my slide locked open after the final round. Trish got off another shot, emptying the Ruger.

Trish dropped the pistol and ran for the briefcase. I ran, too, but she was closer. As she stopped and bent to get the money, I threw my pistol. A Glock wasn't made from metal but a polymer. Still, it weighed over a pound and was as hard as steel. It spun as it flew, and when Trish stood, briefcase in hand, the pistol grip smacked her solidly in the forehead. She dropped the briefcase and staggered back, fighting to maintain balance.

I jumped at her, intending to make a flying tackle, but she stumbled to the side, and I only managed to snag her with a glancing blow, sending her to the ground. I rolled a couple of times and quickly got to my feet. I snatched up the briefcase and flung it as hard as I could in Edward's direction.

Trish swiped at blood pouring from where my gun had connected, and she growled, "You fucking bitch." She ran at me. Her shoulder struck me in the solar plexus, and I was suddenly on my back, unable to breathe. She stood over me, a stripe of blood down her face, and then she stepped from my vision.

As I got my first good lungful of air, Edward shouted, "Look out!"

I blinked up at Trish, who had a large tree branch held high in her hands. As she brought it down, I rolled to the right, and she hit the ground instead of me. My feet got tangled in her ankles, and she fell. We scrambled, each trying to get up and throw punches at the same time. It was not a graceful fight, but we each scored a time or two with our fists. Trish managed to struggle to a kneeling position and connected one punch to my face, followed quickly by another. I launched myself up, attempting to stand, but I stumbled back a few steps. Panting, I held my fist at my chest, arm at my side. When Trish stood, I charged at her and swung out my elbow, which caught her on the jaw. She flopped back on the ground and kicked out, her foot catching my shin. I fell but ended up straddling her chest. I punched her in the face, and my hand exploded with pain. I hit her a second time and heard an audible crunch as I smashed her nose cartilage. She didn't make a sound as I connected a third time and then a fourth.

I stopped when strong hands gripped my shoulder. "I don't think she's feeling anything right now, Norwood."

Breathing hard, I looked up. "About time you got here, Baker." I gazed down at my throbbing hand and then at Trish's bloody face. I punched her one final time.

Chapter 39

Monday

"**Y**ou look like shit, Norwood."

"That's what a woman wants to hear." It had been two days since I'd traded licks with Trish, and the left side of my face was swollen with purple bruises. I imagined Trish's face looked worse, judging by my hand, which was not only swollen but sporting a cast because of broken knuckles. "I still don't see why we have to talk about it here, like I'm a criminal or something."

I was in one of the interrogation rooms at the San Marco PD. Baker was seated across the table.

"That remains to be seen. I mean, you and your friends engaged in your own little war."

The distraction and extraction phase of Mr. Teacher's plan took place at the house outside the city limits, while the apprehension on the property of the old D.W. Roberts College was in the city limits. City PD and the county sheriff's department were working the case together.

"Let's list the fatalities, shall we?" Baker said. "First was that poor kid."

"Phillip Reynolds."

Baker gave me a nod. "Thank you for discovering the boy's identity. Phillip Reynolds, age eight. And then there was Burke Industries' head of security, Eileen Warrick, whose remains were found in a shallow grave behind the house that sheriff's deputies are now calling Waterloo Manor."

"That's kind of funny," I said.

He showed no humor.

I pointed out, "Patricia Meyers is responsible for both of those murders."

"I know that. But you're the one who killed Walter Anthony DeLucia, the guy you refer to as..." Baker flipped through sheets of paper.

"Stubble. And I'll take responsibility because it was self-defense. He shot Nick and would have shot me."

"And then your biker buddies from Daytona badly injured two others."

"Again, self-defense. They did not go there with the intent to hurt anyone but to create a distraction so we could free the hostages."

Baker shook his head for almost twenty seconds. "I can't believe you didn't come to me."

"I know. But I had my reasons, including that the police were helping them."

"Don't make it sound like the whole department was in on it," Baker said. "It was one crooked guy who I always thought was a piece of shit."

"Have you figured out how he got involved? Trish called it a friend-of-a-friend kind of thing."

"More of a family thing. Trask has a cousin who works with a certain Chicago syndicate. When they found out Burke Industries would be setting up shop down here for a while with their number-one money launderer, the cousin called Trask and let him know how to make a buttload of money helping out. Trask was game." Baker looked down at his paperwork. "About this guy who calls himself Mr. Teacher, I assume you haven't heard from him."

I shook my head. "Edward was the last to see him, while I was fighting Trish. As I'm sure Edward already told you, Mr. Teacher got the briefcase from where I'd thrown it and then checked out Edward's wound, telling him he'd be fine. Edward's attention was on the fight, and the next time he checked, Mr. Teacher was gone along with one million dollars."

"There are going to be more interviews. Not just with the PD but the sheriff's department. Some of you guys might be facing charges."

I shook my head.

"Damn it, Norwood, I'm serious. This Mr. Teacher guy is facing all kinds of trouble."

"I'll grant you that Mr. Teacher would face charges, but you don't know where he is. He just vanished—poof."

"And there are the bikers."

I leaned forward. "Are you recording this interview?"

"Yeah."

"Why don't you shut it off for a couple minutes."

Baker stared at me for a long moment then got up and left the room. He returned a minute later and sat. "Okay, shoot."

I didn't want to come across as smug. Baker didn't deserve that. Nor did he deserve having the rug pulled out from under him. As sincerely as I could, I said, "Look, I know some legalities may have been skirted."

"You think?"

"And I know you're doing your job. You're good at it. But while you're talking to me, Marjorie Katherine Hamilton is making calls to many of her influential friends, including the district attorney, state attorney, mayor, and governor. She is explaining what took place and why charges should not be brought against the bikers, Elliot, Edward, Nick, the kids, or me. If that doesn't work, Edward assured me that he'll provide use of his legal team, which he describes as fierce."

Baker sighed and shrugged. "All that is above my pay grade. My job is to look into the lives lost and find out who should face justice. You and those bikers can claim self-defense all you want, but you went there willingly. A crafty prosecutor could make a lot of hay with that."

"I know they could," I admitted. "But they won't."

Baker leaned on the table and put his hands to his face. For a full minute, he alternated between rubbing his eyes and massaging his temples, sighing a few times in the process. When he looked back at me, I saw that he'd shifted from Baker the cop to Baker the friend.

"It's a beautiful day," Baker said. "What say we take a walk in the sunshine?"

We strolled in silence along a sidewalk away from the police station. The few people we passed stared at my brutalized countenance, but we ignored them. Since the temperature was mild for a December day, Baker had left his jacket at his desk and had his sleeves rolled up and tie pulled down. I was in a Jason Isbell concert T-shirt, jeans, and sandals.

We got to a small park facing a tributary from the Intracoastal Waterway and sat on a bench facing the warm sun.

After several minutes, Baker took my uninjured hand in his. "You killed a man, Lise."

"Yes, I did."

"It's a big deal when you take a life, no matter the circumstances."

"Yeah, I get that."

Baker gave my hand a gentle squeeze. "Are you okay with it?"

I thought for a minute and then two. Shooting and killing that man might, at some point in the future, cause problems with my emotional well-being. But right then, basking in the Florida sun with Baker at my side, I could not work up one iota of sympathy for Walter Anthony DeLucia.

"I think I am."

Chapter 40

After an unseasonably warm few months, cold weather finally moved into northeast Florida. It was in the upper thirties when Olivia and I went to Marjorie's place a week and a half after the rescue. Kent informed us that she was across the property at the guest house. We left Minnie parked beside the main house and walked. When the forecast showed cold weather looming, I bought matching black wool coats and knit caps for Olivia and myself. I'd been feeling maternal the past few days and smiled at us in our matching winter wear. She looked like a cute little longshoreman. I supposed I looked like a grown, beat-up longshoreman. No longer swollen, my facial bruises had faded to yellows and browns, and I had to wear the cast on my hand for another week and a half.

A delivery truck was pulling away from the guest house. Marjorie stood on the porch, watching our arrival. "Hello, Olivia. Hello, Lise. How nice to see you."

"Hello, Mrs. Hamilton," Olivia called out happily.

We climbed three steps to join her and sat on a porch swing, Olivia between Marjorie and me.

Marjorie smiled at me over Olivia's head, her eyes sparkling. "They're coming today, Lise." She bent down to Olivia. "Are you excited to see your friends again?"

"Yes, ma'am."

"It's almost Christmas. What do you want Santa to bring you?" Marjorie asked.

"Me?" Olivia looked up at Marjorie and, in all sincerity, said, "I don't need anything."

Marjorie and I exchanged a glance, and I thought she felt the same little stab in her heart that I did.

"Everything ready?" I asked.

She pointed at the delivery truck as it passed through the gate. "They dropped off the last of the beds."

"I wasn't sure that you could pull it off, but you're a master at pulling strings."

"Like a crafty spider. Normally, something like this would take months, but I didn't want to leave the children in temporary shelters for too long. Luckily, heading up the Safe Homes for Children board and the organization's close relationship with the Florida Department of Children and Families cleared the biggest hurdles. As of now, this is a licensed foster-care facility."

"And, no doubt, you rode roughshod over anyone who tried to make you adhere to the bureaucracy that would normally have been involved."

"Did I ever."

I looked at the hand-painted sign over the door. It read Mackie's Home, appropriate as she was providing a home to the kids from Thieves Kitchen. It would undoubtedly be a loving environment until they became available for adoption. And I knew Marjorie would thoroughly screen would-be adopters before any papers were signed.

Marjorie leaned down to Olivia. "Why don't you go inside and explore?"

"Okay." She quickly disappeared into the house.

I reached into my oversize handbag, retrieved a file folder, and handed it to her.

"Any problems?" Marjorie asked.

"Not really."

Marjorie had hired me to track down Olivia's mother and get her to sign over her parental rights. It wasn't exactly legal that I'd given her a bribe from Marjorie for five thousand dollars, but what was one more instance of skirting the law in the grand scheme of things?

"How's Wendy?" Marjorie asked.

"She's doing better. The stress of it all accelerated her symptoms, but she's okay. Her doctor says with more rest, she'll be good to make the trip she planned for her and Pete."

"Is everything set for the painting?"

"Sotheby's has agreed to auction *Cold Green Spring*. Edward told them to put a reserve price of half a million on it. If it doesn't hit that, he'll buy it."

"He's a good man," Marjorie said.

"That he is."

"And Hugh Jackman handsome."

I laughed.

Marjorie and I talked a while more, and then Olivia came outside to join us. She seemed content to sit between us and write in her notebook with her gold pen.

"How do you like Mackie's Home?" Marjorie asked her.

"I like it a lot. I'm going to write a poem about it."

"We'll put it on a plaque and hang it by the door."

I said I had to go and told Olivia, "It was a pleasure having you stay with me."

She smiled. "Thank you for letting me."

Marjorie had found temporary homes for the other kids but had taken temporary custody of Olivia herself. I had been there the day Marjorie brought Olivia home. The next day, I joined Marjorie and Olivia for tea and ended up staying for dinner. The morning after that, I showed up to take Olivia to Cutler Park, which had a massive playground.

That was when Marjorie had taken me aside and asked, "Can you do me a favor, Lise?"

"Sure. What?"

"Can you take Olivia until the other children arrive? I've got so much to do until Mackie's Home officially opens and such little time to do it. You two have hit it off so well."

Marjorie made it sound as if I would be helping her out, but of course she was looking out for me. She knew that the only time I wasn't brooding from the emotional toll of recent events was when I was visiting Olivia. The little girl seemed to put my life into perspective.

"What if DCF finds out I'm keeping her?" I asked.

"I'm keeping her, Lise. She's just visiting you."

And so I had agreed.

"What's on your agenda today?" Marjorie asked.

I sighed. "I have some adulting to do. I've got to go see Edward and then have a heart-to-heart with Nick."

"It's not easy being a girl in demand."

Olivia ripped a page from her notebook, folded it twice, and handed it to me. "Here."

"What is it?"

"A poem. It's a Christmas present."

"Should I read it now?"

Olivia shook her head shyly.

"Then I'll wait. I'm sure it's lovely. Thank you very much." I stood, made my way down the porch steps, and then turned to take in Mackie's Home once more. "There's a special place in heaven for you, Marjorie."

She laughed at that. "I hope God doesn't take me too soon. There are a lot of young people I want to get to know." Marjorie's attention shifted past me, and when she looked back, there was definitely mischief in those brown eyes. "There's my new groundskeeper. I think he'll be a big help with the children. Why don't you go say hello?"

I said goodbye and walked toward the man in a red flannel shirt and khaki pants. He was placing blankets over colorful plants. Tall and thin, he was clean-shaven and sported a crew cut.

I approached him from behind. "Mr. Charles."

He jumped but smiled when he saw it was me. "Ms. Norwood. Please call me Richie." Not a hint of a British accent in his voice, but there was a touch of Southern.

"And you can call me Lise. How do you like your new job?"

He unfolded a square of fabric and put it over a hibiscus. "I like it, and I really like not being on the run. As a condition for my working here—hidden in plain sight, if you will—Mrs. Hamilton insists that I see a therapist twice a week. I think things are gonna be fine."

"I think so too."

"I'm especially eager to see the kids when they arrive."

"I know they'll love to see you." I looked at what he'd been doing. "What's with the little blankets?"

"Expecting a hard freeze tonight. Some of these plants won't survive without them." He started to cover a plant but stopped and looked at me. "I only had the best intentions for those children."

"I don't doubt that, and neither does Marjorie, which is why you're here. I hope you'll be happy."

"I am now."

"I'll leave you to it, then. I have to go see Edward and Nick."

"Tell Edward I said thanks again for the help."

"I will."

What only a handful of us knew was that Charles had given the briefcase with the million dollars to Edward, who was setting up a trust that would help cover college costs for the kids from Thieves Kitchen. Edward had several fundraisers planned to further that goal. Because of all the publicity that had come out about the children, the fundraisers would no doubt bring in the big bucks. Another reason for the fundraisers, however, was so that Edward could mix that million in with the legitimate donations. In other words, he was engaging in money laundering himself. We were all being loosey-goosey with the law these days.

I got in my car, unfolded the paper that Olivia had given me, and read.

I never knew what Christmas was,
When Monsters gave no peace,
Now I know what Christmas is,
It's having friends like Lise.
Merry Christmas!

I wiped my eyes and then started the car.

Chapter 41

There were words that struck fear in the hearts of men. What men didn't realize is that, as women, we don't want to say them. As I left Edward's beach house, his kiss still tingling on my cheek, I called Nick to say those dreadful words, "We need to talk."

"Sure, Lise. Come on over."

I was hit by an intense wave of mixed emotions, the foremost being the loneliness that came with missing my mother. "Hey, Mom, I know you're out there," I said as I drove, and it felt right. "I wish you'd still been around these past couple weeks because I could have used your advice. There was the crazy case that turned into two crazy cases. There was that poor boy who died so horribly. I've made my decision about my love life, and I've spent the past week with a sweet little girl named Olivia. She's had such a hard life, and Mom, she pulls at my heart. Look at me, getting all maternal." A thought occurred to me. It came out of the blue and struck me like a fist. The idea solidified, and just like that, I knew that was how things would be. I laughed. "All of a sudden, there's a new wrinkle. One last time, Mom. What's your advice?"

As loud and clear as if she'd been in the seat next to me, I heard her say, "Follow your heart."

I navigated Minnie to the side of the road through blurred vision. I'd been an emotional basket case since the rescue at Waterloo Manor, and when I was no longer a traffic menace, I allowed myself a good cry. I cried for my mother and for Mackie. I cried with happiness at the future of possibilities for the Thieves Kitchen kids. And I cried for myself, to shed all the negatives that had been building in my life. Thankfully, a bunch of unused napkins from Gordo's Food Truck were in my console. I wiped my eyes and blew my nose and then got back on the road.

Nick was on the wraparound covered porch of his old Florida cracker house. He sat in a rocking chair and greeted me with a smile.

I couldn't return it because of what I had come to tell him. "Nick, I have—"

"Wait. Can I have my say first?" Nick asked, almost pleading.

His bruises matched mine in color, and he still had a little scab on his lip. A bandage covered his left eye and the left side of his head, held in place by a gauze headband. The bullet had just missed his eye but had smashed through the zygomatic bone, one of the orbital bones around the eye. The bullet continued back, cutting a swath along the left side of his head, which required stitches. The doctor said that other than the fractured orbital bone, which would take some TLC, Nick's other injuries should heal up nicely, though he would have an impressive scar. I turned my attention to the surrounding trees. "Okay, you first."

"We've been on a plane, not the flying kind but the flat, level kind of plane. That describes our relationship pretty good. It's been comfortable and fun and great, but it's just..." He held his hand flat and moved it in a line from left to right. "Every now and then, one of us says we need to talk about where we're headed as a couple, but we never actually do talk about it. I think it's because we're so like-minded and both a little lazy." Nick faced me and took my hands. "Lise, I think we need to define what the next level is and then take it there."

"Nick, I should tell you—"

"And you'll get a chance, but hear me out. I want you to move in with me, into my home." My eyes widened, and before I could respond, he spoke rapidly. "I know how you feel about the house after what happened here last year, especially the room upstairs where the worst of it took place." He was excited as he pulled me into the house after him.

"Nick."

"Just wait."

We ended up in the kitchen. The table was covered with a scatter of wide sheets of paper.

"Blueprints?" I asked.

He had a gleam in his eyes as he explained, "Of the house. I've hired a contractor."

"You? You vowed to do all the remodeling yourself."

"This project is too big, and I want to make sure it's done right... for you."

"For me?"

"Come here. Look."

He pointed at the blueprints, but I couldn't make out what they were. "That's the room where the bad stuff happened. The contractor is going to take it from the house."

"I'm not following."

"The room is on the western wall at the end of the second-floor hallway. He's going to remove the room."

"You can't remove a room."

"Oh yes, you can. He's going to remove the ceiling and roof over the room and then take off the wall outside the room. Because it faces west from noon on, it will get a lot of sunshine. We're going to make it a second-floor garden." He laughed at my confused expression. "We have to leave one beam because it's load-bearing, but that's all right. We'll use it for our hanging plants. Maybe a swing. We'll have Adirondack chairs, and I'm going to put up a hammock. So, whenever you have a bad day—like, oh, I don't know, having to save a bunch of hostages—you can come home, to this house, and go up to your second-floor garden and sit among all your plants and flowers and vines and whatever else we grow."

"Whatever else we grow?" I muttered.

"That room will no longer be a part of my house—*our* house." He gently gripped my arms. "Look, I know Edward is a nice guy, and dammit, I wish he wasn't. I also know he's handsome, and I know he has more money than Midas. He didn't have to put himself out there and get shot, but he did. In fact, he did it for you." Nick paused. "Shit. I am not doing a good job of convincing you to choose me, am I?" He rubbed his temples. "What I'm trying to get at is that I can offer you a home—my home, *our* home—and a second-floor garden, and, well, me. I do want to take it to the next level."

I looked from Nick to the blueprints and back. Emotion struck again, and I wiped at my eyes while remembering the words *follow your heart*. "Nick, I'm sorry, but I don't want the next level."

After a long moment, he said, "Oh."

I was screwing this up. I took a deep breath and looked him in the eyes. "What I mean is, I don't want to *just* take it to the next level. I want to take it a couple of levels above that."

"Huh?"

"I want us to get married." I paused and then dropped the bombshell. "I want to adopt Olivia."

He couldn't have looked more shocked if he'd grabbed a live wire.

I quickly added, "When you were describing the second-floor garden, you said, 'whatever else we grow.' I want Olivia to grow up with us."

He turned away as he processed what I'd said.

We hadn't seen much of each other since the rescue. I'd told him I needed space to think. Before going to Nick's, I'd gone to see Edward and told him that yes, I was attracted to him, but what Nick and I had was indeed serious. I told Edward that I hoped we would maintain a client/private eye/friend relationship. He'd been wonderfully gracious.

In a weird way, I'd just proposed to Nick. I stared at his back. His response in the next few seconds would play a large part in my future.

Nick turned, and his smile lit up my heart.

About the Author

Andrew Nance is a writer, actor, and amateur historian. He spent over twenty years working in the radio industry up and down the east coast and still keeps his hand in as a volunteer at a local college radio station. He's had two young adult books published including *Daemon Hall* (Henry Holt Books for Young Readers), which was named an American Library Association Quick Pick for the Reluctant Reader, a New York Library Book for the Teen Age, and was nominated for an Edgar Award in YA, and for the ALA Teens Top 10 for 2008.

Andrew lives in St. Augustine, Florida with his family and can be heard playing jazz on Mondays from 5-7pm EST on WFCF, which is available on iHeartRadio online.

Read more at https://www.andrewnance.net/.

About the Publisher

Dear Reader,

We hope you enjoyed this book. Please consider leaving a review on your favorite book site.

Visit https://RedAdeptPublishing.com to see our entire catalogue.

Check out our app for short stories, articles, and interviews. You'll also be notified of future releases and special sales.

www.ingramcontent.com/pod-product-compliance
Lightning Source LLC
Chambersburg PA
CBHW020756190726
48285CB00006B/2058